7-2-86

Timor Mortis

Also by Will Harriss

The Bay Psalm Book Murder

Timor Mortis

Will Harriss

Will Harriss

Grounds for Murder

July 1986

Walker and Company
New York

Copyright © 1986 by Will Harriss

First published in the United States of America in 1986 by the Walker Publishing Company, Inc.

Published simultaneously in Canada by John Wiley & Sons Canada, Limited, Rexdale, Ontario.

Library of Congress Cataloging-in-Publication Data

Harriss, Will.
    Timor mortis.

    I. Title.
PS3558.A673T5   1986   813'.54   86-1332
ISBN 0-8027-5643-3

Printed in the United States of America

10 9 8 7 6 5 4 3 2 1

With love to Miriam,
my wife and friend

I that in heill wes and gladnes
Am trublit now with gret seiknes
And feblit with infirmite:
    Timor mortis conturbat me.

Our plesance here is all vane glory,
This fals warld is bot transitory,
The flesche is brukle, the Fend is sle:
    Timor mortis conturbat me.

The state of man dois change and vary,
Now sound, now seik, now blith, now sary,
Now dansand mery, now like to dee:
    Timor mortis conturbat me.

No stait in erd heir standis sickir;
As with the wynd wavis the wickir
Wavis this warldis vanite:
    Timor mortis conturbat me.

On to the ded gois all estatis,
Princis, prelotis, and potestatis,
Baith riche and pur of all degre:
    Timor mortis conturbat me.

He takis the knychtis in to feild,
Anarmit under helme and scheild;
Victour he is at all mellie:
    Timor mortis conturbat me.

—WILLIAM DUNBAR
d. 1520

Timor Mortis

1

SOMEHOW SHE HELD on until her Mexican housekeeper came home.

In spite of the slow trickle of blood from the wound in the back of her head, in spite of shock, and in spite of the weakness that always devastated her even on normal evenings because of her disease, she held on.

At 9:40 P.M. the housekeeper came home—by good luck, much earlier than usual on one of her evenings off. She did not panic. She had seen violence, blood, and death in Mexico. She took a pillow off the bed and put it under the old woman's head and knelt beside her in the shambles of the ransacked bedroom.

The old woman looked up and her lips trembled. At last she found her voice and spoke a few words in Spanish. As the housekeeper later told the police, "Señorita Atterbury, she say look in her pocket," and they did, turning out the pocket of the blue Chinese tribute-silk dressing gown she was wearing. They found a superb emerald-and-diamond ring, a hundred-thousand-dollar promissory note with the signature torn off, several Kleenex tissues, and a plastic vial full of pills called Mestinon. They thought all this mildly interesting, especially the note, but would far rather she had named her murderer instead of babbling trivia.

But the moving finger having writ, moved on; and the moving lips having spoken, lay still. Maria de Castillo Atterbury, spinster, seventy-three years of age, became an official murder victim at 9:45 P.M. on August 19.

The housekeeper put the phone back on its cradle and remained seated on a Queen Anne chair, waiting for the police to arrive from the West Los Angeles division. She gazed with deep regret and pity at the scene before her—regret for herself, because this quite likely meant the end of her job here and her return to San Miguel de Allende down in Guanajuato. But she was forgetting that the señorita wanted to leave her some money . . . no, no . . . Her pity was for Maria de Castillo Atterbury, rich, of a famous family, aristocratic, powerful, but lonely and unloved and maybe dying anyway from that strange disease nobody ever heard of. She spoke lovely Spanish for a *yanqui*, but, *Santa María madre de dios*, she was homely! And yet she wasn't at all backward about having her portrait painted by that pretty artist with the pretty name Alison. Maria Atterbury was as homely in the still-unfinished painting as she was in real life, but somehow the picture was eye-catching and colorful, with Maria's gray hair and red-velvet dress.

The portrait had been knocked off its easel at the far end of the bedroom, away from the mess, where the bay windows looked out from the heights over the Pacific and the crescent of lights around Santa Monica Bay. Fortunately, it hadn't fallen on its face on the carpet, for the oil paint was still wet. The canvas, cocked onto one of its corners, leaned against the window seat.

The housekeeper—her name was Socorro Contreras—glanced down again at Maria's body, supine on the floor. Maria's right hand rested on her bosom. A smudge of red paint, the same color as in the portrait, gleamed like blood on two fingertips. Maria had either been near the portrait when it fell, or perhaps she had touched it before the burglar struck her. Blood stained the pillow under her head.

Socorro assumed it was a burglar. The round door of the wall safe opposite the bed was open; the burglar had pulled all the books off their shelves and thrown them into a pile in the middle of the room; bureau drawers, end-table drawers, and drum-table drawers had been emptied on top of the books. Two Meissen teacups, both broken, and their saucers lay near the pillow. Knickknacks and small art objects lay on the pile. One of them, a white jade fish with crimson splotches, more than a foot long, came from the famous Atterbury store in Beverly Hills. The fish had sat on the mantelpiece over the fireplace where Maria could admire it, finning its way through the invisible waters of eternity.

There would be big headlines in the *Los Angeles Times* tomorrow. Not only was Maria a sixth-generation Californian, but she had controlled Atterbury's store, obligatory mecca of virtually every tourist who came to the Los Angeles area, since the death of her brother. Running the store under the provisions of a spendthrift trust, she had been regarded as a surprisingly effective president before her strange illness put her flat on her back and she was forced to surrender management to her middle nephew.

Socorro had been around the Atterbury family for more than a year, long enough to perceive that Maria not only would not be mourned, she would hardly even be missed, except perhaps by her youngest nephew—and of course by the portrait painter, Alison Dunbar Stephens. But that young lady's motives were mixed.

Well, so were her own, thought Socorro with a sigh.

She wondered who had done this terrible thing. She wondered where Maria Atterbury's registered nurse had disappeared to. She wondered how soon she would get her money—if it really was in the will.

The doorbell rang. She rose to let in the police.

2

CLIFF DUNBAR DID not wonder who had done this terrible thing. He had noticed a newspaper story about it, but he and Mona had been on their honeymoon—a fly-fishing honeymoon on the Deschutes River in Oregon, an enterprise that they regarded as combining the world's finest outdoor and indoor sports. Honeymooners are intent on celebrating life.

Back in Los Angeles, he had no premonition of what "running up to Malibu to see Alison" was going to lead to. If he had, he might well have taken Mona by the hand and fled back to Oregon. But Cliff was not clairvoyant, he and Mona loved his sister, and Alison urgently wanted him to come see her.

Mona hurried out of her hairdresser's shop on Westwood Boulevard near UCLA when Cliff pulled up in his orange Porsche convertible.

"Hop in, Mrs. Dunbar!"

She beamed at him as she slid into her bucket seat and gave him a kiss. "I love it when you call me that."

"And do I ever love you! What a prize you are, Mona! You're like a gold medal I've won for something."

"For the breaststroke, I would say."

"Darn you, Mona, I'm trying to be romantic!"

"I'm sorry, sweetheart. I really appreciate the compliment. I suppose it's the sort of flowery language I'm not used to yet—being married to an English professor."

"Ex-English professor."

"How does my hair look?"

"Great! Want me to put the top up?"

"On a beautiful September day like this? No. Besides, I'd like to see the wind that could mess up this Li'l Orphan Annie head of mine."

"Please do not insult my favorite hair. It looks like a dandelion."

"Not a hyacinth?"

"Dandelion."

"Not hyacinth hair? Classic face? Naiad airs?"

"Nope. Dandelion all the way. No more literary jazz."

"Oh, fiddle."

He drove south to Santa Monica Boulevard and got on the Santa Monica Freeway headed west toward the ocean.

"Did Alison say what her problem is?" asked Mona.

"Not exactly. She was pretty upset, and she hates to talk on the telephone in the first place. However, she was painting a portrait of Maria Atterbury before the woman was murdered, and now it seems they won't pay her."

"Who won't?"

"I don't know. The heirs, I suppose, or the executor."

"But why not? Surely they like the portrait!"

"I don't know. And just to complicate matters, she hasn't finished the portrait—and it's not in her possession."

"Where is it, then?"

"I don't know."

"What's the capital of North Dakota?"

"I don't know."

"Terrific. You're batting a thousand."

"What *is* the capital of North Dakota?"

"Bismarck, dummy. What does Alison expect you to do about her situation?"

"I don't know . . . uh, hold her hand? Give her advice?"

The orange Porsche zipped between the Rand Corporation think tank on the left side of the freeway and a Holiday Inn on the right, sped through the narrow, curving, dangerous McClure Tunnel, and burst out onto the Pacific Coast Highway, headed north for Malibu.

"Low tide," Cliff observed, glancing at the line of jumbled dark-brown rocks that form the breakwater in Santa Monica Bay out past the pier. Pelicans and gulls perched on the rocks, digesting their seafood cocktails. The water twinkled blue and silver in the September sun.

"There was a police car back in the tunnel," said Mona.

Cliff gave the brake pedal a quick tap and slowed to forty-five. The black-and-white debouched from the tunnel and sped up behind him. Cliff rested his left arm on the door and let the Porsche lug down to forty. The black-and-white paced him for ten seconds before the policeman at the wheel gave up and darted past him, scowling in disappointment.

"Thanks for the warning, Hawkeye."

"What's your rush anyway? Honestly! I think I'll buy you a thirty-six De Soto or a Studebaker! Just because you own a Porsche you feel obligated to rip around like Mister Toad of Toad Hall!"

Smiling, Cliff veered his car off the road and bounced it into the tiny parking lot behind the Ports of Los Angeles liquor store, where Santa Monica Canyon intersects the Coast Highway.

"Be right back."

He emerged in a couple of minutes carrying a bottle of Moët et Chandon champagne. A passerby with the reversed collar of a clergyman glanced at them with mild curiosity.

"What's that for?" asked Mona, eyeing the bottle.

He beamed at her. "To celebrate our first nag!" He folded her in his arms and kissed her freckled nose, her forehead, both cheeks, and her mouth.

"You silly bas—ket weaver," she said, noticing the clergyman just in time.

"By the way," said Cliff, pointing, "Maria Atterbury's house—or mini-mansion—is up there on that bluff. That's where she was murdered."

Mona looked up. On the other side of the street, the trunk of a lone Mexican fan palm poked high in the air like a gray finger before it burst out into green fronds. Behind it, the bluff—actually ancient ocean bed—rose steeply for a sheer two hundred feet.

"You mean that big house out near the edge?"

"No, that used to belong to Elsa Lanchester. I think another movie actress owns it now. The Atterbury place is farther along on the bluff, overlooking the ocean."

Mona peered upward. "You mean falling into the ocean, don't you? Look at that! Some of those garden fences and concrete sidewalks are actually sticking out over the edge!"

"I know. Every rainy season, part of the palisade peels off and mud-slides roar down onto the highway."

"Well, Maria Atterbury doesn't have to worry about it now."

"No, there's that."

"Who killed her?"

"They say a burglar. The place was ransacked."

Cliff drove out of the parking lot and back onto the highway. They followed the curve of Santa Monica Bay past the mouth of Temescal Canyon, the ocean end of Sunset Boulevard, and the J. Paul Getty Museum. The Porsche rounded the point at Topanga Canyon and headed into Malibu.

Cliff turned off the highway onto a short street leading toward a one-story shopping complex, but pulled into the parking lot of Alison's gallery, a separate white building with a red-tiled roof. Over the door appeared the name "Galería de la Playa" in black, Spanish-style lettering. Black wrought-iron bars covered the windows.

As Cliff and Mona approached the door, two teenage girls burst out into the sunshine, laughing, long blond hair swinging, the tips of their noses whitened with zinc oxide. Both wore bikinis—four isosceles triangles of cloth that left their backs and most of their tanned haunches bare.

"All right, Clifford," Mona said out of the side of her mouth, "put your eyeballs back in their sockets."

"It's a miracle," he said. "Where does Southern California get this endless supply of pretty blond beach girls? There must be a factory somewhere. And those bikinis! Of what, one wonders, will they consist next year?"

"Three Band-Aids, most likely. Let's see what your sister wants."

They entered Alison's gallery, elegant with its white walls and dark red Moorish-tile floor. The paintings on the walls were separated by generous spaces. A shelf along one wall displayed ceramic pieces, bronze sculptures, and milky glass, all cleverly lighted from various angles to create interesting shadows and moonglow. At the far end of the gallery Alison stood by her desk talking to a customer. She flashed a bright smile to Cliff and Mona, but turned her attention back to the customer, a square-built woman dressed in brown and black who was talking nonstop. Pheasant tail-feathers on her hat bobbed as she spoke. She was built so like a Victorian chiffonier that Cliff looked down at her shoes, half expecting to see ball-and-claw feet.

Alison was a colorful contrast. She wore crimson-velvet slacks and bolero jacket, and a ruffled white silk blouse. Together with her short, black hair, cropped in a boyish style, her petite figure, and her fair complexion, she bore a strong resemblance to Goya's portrait of the little boy Don Manuel Osorio Manrique de Zuñiga.

From a distance Alison looked vulnerable. Close up, her piercing blue eyes and forthright little nose notified the world that she wanted to be friendly but declined to be stepped on.

The customer left the gallery, tucking a small package into her purse. In the manner of the comic strips, Alison wiped her brow with a forefinger and exclaimed, "Whew!"

"Hello, Sis," said Cliff, giving her a kiss on the cheek.

"Hello to you, Big Bruvver! How are you two? Or need I ask? Mona, you look lovely!"

"How's business, Alison?" Mona asked.

"Paying the rent. It's an odd business, though. Did you happen to notice that teenager in the red-and-white bikini?"

"Cliff managed to draw my attention to her."

"And that dowager who just left? Guess which one bought a seven-hundred-dollar painting and which one a thirty-dollar ivory pillbox. Right the first time. One never knows, so I smile at 'em all. I wish I could quit this and paint full time."

"My offer still stands," said Cliff. "I'll grubstake you."

"Bless you. But no thanks."

"I've got the money."

"Which you earned. And that's the way I want to do it."

"Oh, pride, pride, pride! Why do decent people have to hamstring themselves with pride!"

"It isn't just pride. What if it takes me ten years to make it as an artist? You can't grubstake me forever. For one thing, you have a wife now; and there's Becky Litvak to consider. We're partners. I can't suddenly leave her in the lurch. We need each other. And she held the fort mornings while I painted Maria Atterbury's portrait."

"For which they left you holding the bag, I gather."

Alison's eyes snapped. "Yes! Let's have some coffee, and I'll tell you all about it."

From an alcove in the corner, Alison took a Silex from a hot plate and poured three coffees into Spode cups.

"If I can figure out where to begin," she said as they took seats around her desk. "My God, it's complex! Let's see if I can boil it down to the essentials. . . . Maria's brother was the one who really made Atterbury's the rich and triple-A store it is. When he died at seventy, Maria de Castillo Atterbury became president of Atterbury's for a while. Sort of by default. Her brother's will stipulated that Maria be in charge of everything while she decided which of his sons should take over the store. Be that as it may—"

"Which, by the way, is a beautiful example of the petrified subjunctive surviving in English," observed Cliff.

"That's more than you'll do if you keep butting in."

9

"Sorry."

"Anyway, it's been an Atterbury tradition for each president and vice president to have his—or her—portrait painted to hang in the store. Maria saw my work, liked it, and commissioned me to do hers. She was going to pay me five thousand dollars."

"Did you have a contract?"

"No, but she was an honest lady. She gave me a five-hundred-dollar advance and I gave her a receipt. Then her myasthenia gravis got a lot worse, and we had to postpone her sittings."

"Her what?"

"Myasthenia gravis. That can be—and in her case it was—a terrible, debilitating disease that hits you in the muscles and nerves and leaves you more and more exhausted as time passes. It may kill you and it may not. Well, the poor dear spent what little energy she could store up just getting out of bed and sitting for her portrait an hour or two in the mornings and talking to her relatives and her doctor and her lawyer. Then she'd have to collapse in bed for the rest of the day and night."

"That sounds awful!" said Mona.

"It was. I finished doing her head and arms and hands, and I had blocked in her dress, when she took a sudden turn for the worse and simply couldn't sit for me or even see me. She may well have been about to die—so it's pretty grotesque that a dumb burglar should come in and hit her over the head."

Alison filled them in on events as the police and Socorro Contreras had reconstructed them, including the puzzling request that they look in Maria's pocket.

"Anyhow," Alison continued, "I was left holding the bag, as you put it. There stood the portrait on an easel while the police investigation went on. And when they were through, Maria's executor froze all the assets of the estate, if that's the right verb, and refused to pay me the other forty-five hundred—'at least for the immediate present,' he says."

10

"Why not? There's no legal reason he can't pay you."

"I could never get a straight answer out of him. He just said there were legal complications that had to be cleared up."

"As long as you get paid eventually, though, does it really matter?" asked Mona.

"Yes, it does! Never mind that it's so unfair it stinks—I am now trapped in one hell of a predicament. I've scheduled a major exhibit of portraits by Southern California artists to be held here in the gallery in October, and I've mailed out hundreds of printed announcements, which, of course, mention my portrait of Maria. I've gotten a lot of publicity. You can imagine the damage to my reputation—and my embarrassment—if I don't show that portrait. And darn it! If I may toot my own kazoo, it's the best thing I've ever done, and I was counting on it to get me some more commissions."

"Couldn't you paint another one? A copy?" said Cliff.

"No. It wouldn't work. It'd be lifeless. That may sound irrational, but any good artist would know exactly what I mean."

"Couldn't they lend it to you temporarily so you could finish it?" said Cliff.

"Sure they could, but I'm not counting on it. I even offered to return the five hundred dollars and take the portrait back, but it was no soap."

"Okay," Cliff said. "I see my duty clear. I'll go reason with the guy. Who is he?"

"His name is Sidney P. Colfax the Third. His law offices used to be on Rodeo Drive in Beverly Hills, but now they're on San Vicente in Brentwood, and if you can stand talking to him for more than two minutes without retching, you've got the guts of a bear."

"He's that bad, is he?"

"Worse. None of your Vietnam rough stuff, Cliff. I only want the portrait. I don't want you in jail."

3

Mona stayed in Malibu while Cliff zipped back down the Coast Highway to Santa Monica Canyon and drove up the long slope to San Vicente Boulevard, where joggers run under rows of African coral trees aflame with red blossoms. As San Vicente angles closer to Wilshire Boulevard, it abandons sweatsuits and Adidas and gets down to business. The street features a mixture of one- and two-story buildings in the older, relaxed, Southern California style, and modern high-rise, black-glass office buildings.

Cliff was surprised to find that Sidney P. Colfax III occupied a modest reception room and office on the eighth floor of one of the black-glass boxes. Those roman numerals called for something better. So did, certainly, being executor of the Atterbury estate. Something was wrong here. Aside from a gray-haired legal secretary who looked as if her favorite drink was tarragon vinegar on the rocks with a twist, the outer room was home to a yellowing dracena and a sulky ficus benjamina that dropped dead leaves on the carpet.

"Did you have an appointment?"

"No, but if you'd tell him Doctor Clifford Dunbar needs to see him on urgent business . . ."

She flipped a switch on her intercom, as Cliff marveled at people's reaction to the magic word "doctor."

"Mr. Colfax will see you," she said and rose to open the door for him.

As he entered, he saw with a quick glance that the office was roomy enough to hold Colfax's desk, a leather couch, several armchairs, and a coffee table, but that three crowded walls had difficulty accommodating the man's law library.

Large plat maps on which Cliff glimpsed the name "Malibu" lay open on the desk. Colfax rolled them up and stepped from behind his desk to greet Cliff. The lawyer had obviously once been a rather handsome and lanky six-footer, but he had darkish bags under his eyes, his black hair was streaked with gray, and his midriff undulated above his belt buckle.

"If your business is urgent, Doctor," said Colfax, beaming, "that can mean only one thing: a malpractice suit. Am I right?"

"Uh, no. No rubber gloves left in the patient's nostrils, I'm afraid," said Cliff with a small smile. "I'm not a medical doctor . . ."

The sunshine in Colfax's eyes faded to smog.

"I have a Ph.D. in English literature."

Colfax struggled to remain genial. "And what is the nature of your urgent business?"

"I'm here on behalf of my sister, Alison Stephens."

Colfax frowned. "Oh, yes—the artist. I didn't realize—a different name."

"She's a widow. Her husband was a Navy pilot, knocked down by a SAM missile over Haiphong."

"That's too bad. However, if you don't mind my saying so, that is a very difficult young lady to reason with."

"She says the same thing about you."

"I'm not surprised."

"So I thought perhaps I could mediate between the two of you—as a cooler, neutral party."

"Neutral? You're her brother."

"Yes, but you can reason with me and I hope I can with you."

"Along what lines?"

"Well, let's start with the two obvious questions: Why won't you pay her the rest of her fee and, if you won't pay

13

her, why won't you give the portrait—and her paints—back to her?"

Colfax went back behind his desk, sat down, took off his glasses, held them by one bow in his left hand, and arched his left eyebrow. He looked sagacious and perspicacious, like an executive in a whiskey ad.

"Obvious questions with obvious answers. (A) As for the portrait, that appears to belong to the estate. And (B), since the police haven't finished their investigations, everything stays where it is."

"The portrait doesn't belong to the estate yet, surely."

"Oh, yes! Among Miss Atterbury's papers was a receipt for five hundred dollars signed by your sister."

"A down payment. She was supposed to get five thousand."

"We only have her word for that, don't we?"

"My sister's an honest woman and so was Miss Atterbury, she tells me."

Colfax merely lifted his hands in a helpless gesture.

"Besides which," Cliff added, "the portrait is obviously unfinished. If five hundred was to be the total commission, Miss Atterbury wouldn't have paid her the whole fee in advance. She'd have given Alison maybe one hundred—which, however, strikes me as a ridiculous figure."

"But possible—possible. Miss Atterbury was in a very bad state both physically and mentally there toward the end."

"What about my sister's offer to return the five hundred and take the portrait back and no hard feelings? She needs it for an exhibit in October, and that strikes me as a reasonable solution."

"I know all that, Doctor Dunbar, and I mentioned it to Grant Atterbury—he's the principal heir, you know. He was adamantly opposed, and I must say I agree with him."

"Why, for God's sake?"

"He doesn't want anyone to profit by exposing the distinguished Atterbury name to cheap sensationalism. Perhaps he'll arrange some sort of compromise at a later date."

14

"My sister wouldn't do that, Mr. Colfax. She's a serious artist, and this will be a respectable exhibit."

"Oh, come now, Doctor Dunbar! You know perfectly well that gaggles of thrill-seekers would flock around the portrait—and around your sister—and say things like 'My goodness, was she really that ugly?' and 'You mean you painted her right there in the room where she was murdered?' . . . No, thanks."

Secretly, Cliff had to admit that the man had a point, but he said aloud, "That's mere speculation, of course."

"Perhaps."

"And some moral issues are involved here."

"Quite so. But as executor of the estate, my concern is solely and properly with the legal issues."

"Reprehensible but true, I suppose. And if necessary, I suppose we could always take the Atterburys to court."

"Oh, yes."

"But that doesn't worry you? Or Grant Atterbury?"

"Not at all. You wouldn't get anywhere."

"You think not?"

"No. If this were a clear-cut case of nonpayment of a contract, and if you were very lucky, you might get a hearing in a month or two. You might even win something like a mechanic's lien. But there is no contract, is there?" Colfax put his double row of large, gleaming, square teeth on display.

"I'm talking about a full-blown civil suit in superior court," said Cliff.

Colfax got a good professional laugh out of that one. "You must be new in town," he said, swinging his glasses. "Are you aware of how long it takes to bring a civil suit to trial these days in Los Angeles County? An average of fifty-four months. That's four and a half years!"

Cliff was stunned. And Hamlet complained about the law's delay!

"In other words, you've got us by the short hairs."

"One might say that."

15

"What about ordinary human decency?"

"Don't blame me. Blame Grant Atterbury."

Cliff reflected on this conversation with growing puzzlement. "Mr. Colfax," he said finally, "when I pull back and take a bird's-eye view of this whole transaction, it strikes me as absurdly trivial. The Atterbury estate must be worth millions. For the life of me I can't understand why all of you are being so evasive about a nickel-and-dime painting—unless in some weird way it's connected to the murder."

"Evasive? I'm merely being conscientious in handling the Atterbury estate's assets. And how on earth could a painting have anything to do with murder?"

"Beats me. But something here calls for investigation."

Colfax slapped his desk. "Aha! I knew your name rang a bell! You're the one who solved that murder connected with the Bay Psalm Book forgery, aren't you? The one that knocked Perry Winthrop out of the governor's race! You're a private detective, aren't you?"

"No, I'm not."

"You act like one." He shot a piercing glance at Cliff. "Are you investigating the murder of Miss Atterbury?"

"Good God, no."

Colfax sat back in his chair. "I'm glad to hear it. The sooner this case is closed and the estate is settled, the better. A distinguished family like the Atterburys doesn't need this kind of publicity. I'd just forget it if I were you, Doctor Dunbar."

"Well, Sidney P. Colfax roman numeral three, I just don't think I will."

"You'd save yourself a great deal of trouble. The estate has the portrait, and possession is nine points of the law. In layman's terms, we have it, and the burden is on you to try to get it. And now you'll have to excuse me." In dismissal, Colfax made a show of fussing with some papers on his desk.

They exchanged chilly farewells.

4

BACK AT ALISON'S gallery, Cliff parked his car next to an aging black Cadillac with dents in all four fenders and, for a radio antenna, a coat-hanger bent into a diamond shape.

Inside the gallery, he found Alison and Mona and two strangers seated around Alison's desk, having coffee. One of the newcomers was a smartly dressed, black-haired woman in her thirties smoking a cigarette in a long ivory holder. She was rather too heavily made-up for daytime, and didn't need to be, for she was naturally beautiful. The other stranger was a man of about forty who, in spite of his well-tailored suit and Swiss Bally shoes, somehow managed to look scruffy. His disheveled black hair didn't help, nor did his sulky expression.

"How did it go?" asked Alison.

"He said no."

"You've been talking to Sid Colfax, I understand," said the strange man.

"Cliff, this is Lionel Atterbury and his sister, Consuelo Atterbury. My brother, Clifford Dunbar."

Cliff shook hands with Lionel and briefly held the extended damask hand of Consuelo Atterbury. "How do you do," she said with lofty dignity.

"Pull up a chair, dear," said Mona. "We're having a mutual commiseration session."

"Oh?"

"Yes," said Consuelo drily, "it appears that Lionel and I and your sister have all been diddled by destiny."

"Make room for a fourth," said Cliff, taking a seat.

"Membership is open to anybody that's been talking to

17

that jerk Colfax," said Lionel. "Did he talk to you like a legal brief? Every sentence broken down into As and Bs?"

"He only did that once."

"Pompous bastard. It's because of him I dropped in to see your sister on my way down from Santa Barbara."

"How so?"

"To apologize on behalf of the entire Atterbury family—with the exception of my brother Grant, who matches Colfax in jerkitude. I wanted to tell her I think the treatment she's gotten from both of them is shabby and disgusting and, if I can bring myself to talk to Grant, I'll try to do something about it."

"I gather you and your brother don't get along too well."

"Know what he said to me when I came down for Aunt Maria's funeral?—'Hello, when are you leaving?' "

"Some older siblings are like that."

"He isn't older. He's three years younger."

"But didn't Colfax tell me Grant is the principal heir?"

"That," said Lionel, "is how I was diddled."

"Were you cut out of the will?" Mona asked.

"Same thing as. Grant remains president of the store, controls ninety percent of the stock, and gets ninety percent of the profits. Connie and I get five percent each. Dad's the one that gave us the shaft. He was 'teaching me a lesson,' he said."

"Lie-oh-nell," observed Consuelo, "I hardly think it necessary to wash the family's dirty linen in public. But if you insist, for heaven's sake throw in your shirt and tie. I don't like being seen with you."

"Hah! Did you ever?"

"Not particularly. And if my car hadn't run out of amps or whatever in Santa Barbara, I wouldn't be here today."

"Connie, why in heaven can't you be more good-natured?"

She tapped her ash into an ashtray. "Only servants are good-natured in the morning."

"Don't knock servants. With your lifestyle you may have to moonlight as one yourself, on thirty-five thousand a year."

18

"And if you're going to continue with your exposé, I have got to have a d-r-i-n-k! Do you have anything stronger than coffee, Alison dear?"

"Only a bottle of sherry."

"What brand?"

"Harvey's Bristol Cream."

"Well, any old sherry in a storm."

Alison retrieved the bottle and a sherry glass from her cupboard and inquired, as she poured, "What about Rollie? Did his Aunt Maria leave him anything?"

"Not a bean. But of course he didn't want a bean."

"Who's Rollie?" Cliff asked.

"Our beloved baby brother, Rollie Freed," said Consuelo.

"Freed?"

"It's a long story," said Lionel. "Rollie was a late addition to the family. One of those embarrassing mistakes. He's only twenty-five. And for reasons I will forbear going into, he dropped completely out of the family—to the point of changing his name."

"What does he do?" Mona asked.

"He fishes for a living, at Paradise Cove," said Lionel. "At least he did the last I heard. I saw him in the crowd at the funeral, but I've only talked to him four or five times since Dad and Mother died."

"He's a throwback," said Consuelo. "Can you imagine an Atterbury up to his yang-yang in flounders and red snappers?"

Alison frowned. "I'm very surprised he wasn't mentioned in the will."

"Why?" said Lionel. "He didn't want to be mentioned."

"Because his Aunt Maria liked him so much. He dropped in on her for a short visit one day when I was painting her, and they had a grand time together. They got along really well."

"It's easy to get along with somebody who doesn't want anything," said Lionel bitterly.

"But it was more than that," said Alison. "After he left, I remarked to Maria on what a charming young guy he seemed to be, and she said, 'There are several injustices in this family that need to be corrected.'"

Lionel stiffened and his eyes went alert. "She said that? Did you think she might have been talking about her will?"

"That was my impression."

"And she said 'several injustices?'"

"Yes."

Lionel was excited. "Connie, don't you see what this means? I knew it all along! Sure, Aunt Maria went along with Dad's wishes for the time being, but neither one of them ever meant for that old vindictive horse manure to go on forever!"

"Lionel—"

"Dad himself told me he changed his will in favor of Grant just to use it temporarily as a club over me—'Until you straighten yourself out,' he said. Well, I did, didn't I?"

"Assuredly. After he dropped dead in his office and left dear Aunt Maria in control. Too bad for you she got conked on the coconut before she could change the will back again."

"That's a hell of a way to describe it."

"I cannot recall the coroner's terminology."

"Alison," said Lionel, "did Colfax ever come to consult Aunt Maria while you were doing her portrait?"

Consuelo heaved a sigh. "Lionel, really! A long-lost will would truly be romantic, but there isn't one, so forget it."

"How do you know there isn't? And how about letting Alison answer the question?"

"He came two or three times," said Alison, "but Maria always discreetly suggested that the nurse and I take a coffee break in the kitchen, so I don't know what they talked about."

"How did she behave afterward?"

Alison frowned, recalling. "Irritated. She complained once about how long it took him to do anything."

20

"See? See?" said Lionel. "I'll bet you she wanted to dictate new provisions to her will."

"Which she did," said Consuelo, "as you perfectly well know: She left five thousand dollars to Socorro Contreras, and Sid Colfax let Socorro have it in a preliminary distribution. *Y como tú sabes,* dear brother, *ella se fué a México entonces, sin decir nada más a nadie.*"

"Sure. Back to San Miguel de Allende, saying nothing to nobody, and more power to her. But when Colfax suddenly turns generous, I get suspicious."

"Whether you do or not, he's filed the will for probate, so it's no use crying over spilled crème de Chantilly. It does not appear, dear brother, that you will be resuming the presidential throne at Atterbury's."

"Nor will you, *hermana querida,* occupy once more your flat on the Avenue Foch."

"True, unless Grant has the good sense to sell the store. Then our little five percent would make us at least semimillionaires."

"Fat chance! That goofball will hang on till he bankrupts the place. Besides, both Grant and charming Gwyneth are too fond of having their asses kissed up and down Wilshire Boulevard. He'll never sell."

"Don't be vulgar."

"If it weren't for the gold mine, I'll bet Atterbury's would have gone broke before this."

"Do you mean a real gold mine?" Cliff asked, curious.

"The Eureka Mine up at Quartz Hill, not far from Edwards Air Force Base. The estate owns three-fourths of it. It shut down when production costs rose above thirty-five dollars an ounce, and opened up again when the government removed the ceiling. Took a while to get profitable again, though, because a worker got killed by fumes from the separation tanks. The court awarded three hundred thousand dollars to his family."

"You say you were president of the store once?" asked Mona.

"Oh, you betcha, yessir, sure—for six whole months, six years ago. Not long enough to qualify for an official portrait."

"Perhaps, Alison," said Consuelo, "it's just as well you haven't finished Maria's portrait. That mug hanging in the store would drive all the customers over to Saks."

"I agree she wasn't pretty," said Alison, "but she had a fascinating, complex character that came through in her face, and I worked like a dog to capture it. I like to think I did."

"I, on the other hand," said Consuelo, "if you will excuse the pun, thought she was a deadpan."

"Jesus, Connie!" Lionel exclaimed. "Show some respect! She was a tyrannical old bat, but damn it, she was an Atterbury! And I want to see the killer caught."

"I'll bet."

"What the hell do you mean by that? Of course I do! You may not, but I sure as hell do!"

"Oh? If you're so worked up about it, why don't you hire a private detective?"

"If I could afford it, I would! You think I have hidden wealth?"

"I believe you own a Suzanne Valadon drawing, or was it on the loan ledger?"

"What's the loan ledger?" Alison asked.

"The store lets family members borrow art objects from the stock," said Lionel. "At least it used to. On loan. Hence the loan ledger. Grant has called in everything that was on it, of course, the spiteful son of a bitch. But I *own* the Valadon. Dad gave it to me a long time ago. It's a pencil drawing of her mother—Maurice Utrillo's grandmother—whom she actually didn't like very much."

"Which you can either sell," said Consuelo, "or merely hand over to your detective, can't you? And I know just who that can be," she added with an arch smile.

"Who?"

22

"The famous Clifford Dunbar," she said, gesturing with her sherry glass, "who solved the notorious Bay Psalm Book murder."

Mona shot out of her chair, waving her arms, before Cliff could even clear his throat to reply. "Hold it, nix, no, and nothing doing! . . . No, Cliff, not a word till I've finished. See that crease of a scar running down the side of his face that he keeps rubbing when he's exasperated? Rub it for them, dear—that's right. That's from a Viet Cong bullet. He's got another one across the back of his head that's from a crazy printer who shot him for exposing the Bay Psalm Book as a forgery. He's got a small scar on his left wrist from two thugs who tried to knife him in a parking lot in Westwood. And two Mafia hoods machine-gunned our front door. Okay, one's a war wound, but all the rest came out of his one foray into amateur sleuthing, in which I could have been killed, too. And his new wife—that's me—says one is enough. No more."

"Holy smoke, Mona," said Cliff, rubbing his bullet scar, "regain your tranquillity! I had no intention of saying yes!"

"Good. Just so you know."

"What would be the danger in this case?" said Consuelo. "All you'd have to do is come up with the name of the killer and find the missing will in the hollow tree."

"Out of the question," said Mona. "I don't want a husband who looks like he's been through a Cuisinart."

"Lionel," said Consuelo, setting down her sherry glass, "we'd better be toddling before we bore these poor people stiff. And I have got to get to Dee-Dee's caterers, if that threshing machine you're driving will make it to Beverly Hills."

"Don't worry. I've got a fresh supply of amps."

"And look, you people: I'm giving a cocktail party Friday at my place in Beverly Hills. Why don't all of you come? You'll meet some charming freeloaders at the hors-d'oeuvre table. Strictly pro forma, I've even invited Grant and Gwyneth. I doubt if he'll come, but if he does, I'd love to see Alison beard the stuffed shirt. Yes, I'm aware that's a mixed metaphor."

"You wouldn't mind if I made a scene?"

"I'd fly into a snit if you didn't."

"Maybe I'll show up, then."

"And if you go, perhaps Mona and I will, too," said Cliff.

"Fab. Five o'clock. Here's my card with the address. It's handwritten because I'm only renting the house until I've chosen the fabrics for my new room at the poor farm."

"And at least consider the Valadon," said Lionel.

The two Atterburys took their leave, Consuelo saying a languid "Ciao!" as she went out the door. The muffler on the old Cadillac popped and roared, gravel grated under the tires, and in a whirlwind of amps they were gone.

"Well! What did you make of that?" said Alison.

"They're interesting," said Cliff, "I'll give them that."

"But everybody in that family seems to have a wire edge," said Mona. "Do they all hate each other?"

"Certainly there's a lot of animosity," said Alison, "and that seems to be the tie that binds—like cats that live next door to each other."

"I gather you've met them before, Ali," said Cliff.

"I have. Each of them came to see their Aunt Maria twice while she was sitting for me."

"What for? They didn't like her."

"She's where their monthly allowance came from."

"Oh."

"I remember Maria saying to me one day, in her dry way, 'The only Atterbury tradition that's faithfully observed is the children's annual return to pay their warmest respects and explain why their allowances have to be increased.'"

"Why should Lionel get an allowance? Doesn't he work?"

"Oh, yes. He manages a modest-sized art-and-gift store on De La Guerra Street in Santa Barbara, but he's on his third marriage, and he's paying alimony to his first two wives. That and inflation, he says, are killing him."

"Did they talk all that freely in front of you?"

"Up to a point, and then they often switched to Spanish. Darn, I wish I could speak Spanish like you! All I remember from school is *buenos dias* and *viva el revolución.*"

"*La revolución.*"

"Okay, *la.* Consuelo, on the other hand, has never done a day's work in her life. And Grant Atterbury once had the Mafia after him because he couldn't pay off his casino marker in Las Vegas and he didn't dare tell his father—but that was when he was in college, before he turned ultrarespectable."

"You seem to have learned a lot without the Spanish."

"How about the portrait?" said Mona. "Do you think Grant will let go of it if Lionel pressures him?"

"I doubt it, if only because it's Lionel."

"I have a better idea anyway," said Cliff. "I got it from Sidney Colfax."

"He gave you the idea?"

"Not on purpose. But he informed me that possession is nine points of the law."

"Meaning what?"

"Meaning that whoever has the painting in his—or her—hands is in the driver's seat. Anybody else who wants it has to take legal steps to get it."

Alison's blue eyes widened. "Are you thinking what I think you're thinking?"

"I think so, yes."

"I'm all for it! Let's hop to it?"

"Are you two talking about stealing it?" inquired Mona.

"Call it transferring proprietorship. Then Colfax can stew for four and a half years."

"Okay. When Becky comes back from lunch—ah, here she is now! Let's go!"

5

THE THREE OF them drove back down the Coast Highway to Chautauqua, hooked the car sharply to the left around the nose of the bluff that towered above the intersection, and climbed the hill in lower gear.

"Turn here," said Alison when they reached the top.

Cliff turned left onto a residential street, Corona Del Mar, that instantly said "wealth" to a visitor. A sign attached to a lamp post informed them that this was the "Entrance, Huntington Palisades." Another sign informed them that armed guards patrolled the district twenty-four hours a day.

At the moment, no gunfire disturbed the serenity of the street. Hummingbirds whirred among the flaming blossoms of red-flowering eucalyptus trees. Olive, liquidambar, banana trees drowsed in the sun. Two joggers, a man and woman in their thirties, ran past.

"Left again," said Alison.

Cliff turned into a cul-de-sac about a hundred feet long, nameless because it amounted to being Maria Atterbury's private street, and parked behind another car at the far end. They climbed out of the Porsche at the jagged western edge of North America. From this height, they looked out over the Pacific to the horizon some seventeen or eighteen miles away. Where the ocean met the sky, the blue bulk of Catalina Island crouched in the water, the dark silhouette of its mountains resembling a swaybacked horse.

The house was a white two-story, vaguely Spanish with its red-tiled roof and wrought-iron grillwork. A narrow semicircular driveway curved to the front steps and back to the street. A man in a khaki uniform sat on the steps, smoking a cigarette, but he stood up and flicked it into the bushes when the three visitors came up the drive.

"Howdy, folks. What can I do for you?"

He was a middle-aged man of medium height and medium build with pale red hair that would soon be graying, and pale blue eyes. A large blue-and-yellow shoulder patch identified him as a private security guard, and a nameplate over his breast pocket revealed that he was called Pinky Schiffleger.

After Cliff made introductions, Alison asked whether Schiffleger knew if the portrait was still in the house.

"Oh sure, it's still up-air in her bedroom—big as life and twice as ugly!" Taken by surprise by his own wit, he emitted a barking laugh.

"I'm the one that painted it."

"No kiddin'? Wull, all I've got to say is you're one hell of an artist, considerin' what you had to work with."

"Why, thank you!" Alison gave him so warm a smile— twinkling blue eyes, lovely teeth, and pert nose—that Pinky braced his shoulders a bit and hitched up his pistol belt.

"Could we go up and see it?"

The shoulders sagged again. "Heck, I'm sorry, I can't do that. Nobody gets in except police and family."

"Has anybody tried to get in?" Mona asked, curious.

"You mean beside police and family? Oh, sure. Teenagers, rubberneckers, souvenir-hunters, all like-at. You'd be surprised. Some people beg to get in so's they can take pictures. And some of 'em actually swipe little rocks, or take cuttings off them begonias and succulents. Crazy. They say it takes all kinds, but there's a few I could do without. Course, the main worry is real burglars."

"In the daytime?" said Cliff.

"You bet! If I wasn't here, they'd clean the place out. Course, it's the fella on the night shift has to stay on his toes."

"Well, we don't want any souvenirs or anything else. Alison just wants to have a look at the painting."

"I know, and if it was up to me I'd say sure, go ahead. But as it is, my name'd be mud down at the agency."

"Instead of Schiffleger," observed Cliff, peering at Pinky's badge. "Fascinating name!"

"Think so? Lots of folks kinda giggle at it. I come to California partly to get away from people calling me Shiftless."

"Lots of folks are illiterate. 'Schiffleger' means ship-layer or ship-builder, doesn't it?"

"Sure thing. Know your German, don't you? Yeah, I come from a long line of Krauts, but I only know a few words, myself. My grandfather come over from Schleswig-Holstein and settled in Akron, Aha. Never had anything to do with ships, though."

"Schleswig-Holstein is up north, next to Denmark. Your ancestors might well have been Vikings. You've got the right coloring."

"Hey!" exclaimed Mona. "Alison, that painting you were talking about doing. You know the one—Sigurd the Volsung?"

Alison's eyes widened. "Oh . . . that one! Uh, yes, I think I see what you mean." She made a picture frame with her fingers and thumbs. "It just might work. Mr. Schiffleger, would you mind taking your cap off for a minute and look out over the ocean? No, look serious now! That's it. Not bad. Not bad at all. You wouldn't have some blank paper?"

"Me? No."

"There's a good-sized scratch pad in the glove compartment," said Cliff, hurrying off.

When he came back, Alison produced a fragment of charcoal from her purse and began to sketch, occasionally using a finger to smudge a line for shading facial features, leaving highlights on the cheekbones and forehead.

"Great hair," Alison murmured to herself. "Wish I had color. No, don't smile. Hold still."

In a few minutes, she finished. "There! Just a quick sketch, of course, but what do you think?"

She handed the pad to Schiffleger. Surprise and delight lit up his face. "Well, dog my cats! That is really something!"

Alison had tightened a muscle in his jaw, suggested a sea breeze in his hair, created a slight frown, and put a dauntless glint in the narrowed eyes that could have belonged to a Norse raider about to sack his first of the season's English abbeys.

"You can keep it if you like," she said.

"Really? Won't you need it for that other painting?"

"No, now that I've done it once, I'll remember."

"Thanks a million, then! Hey, how about signing it?"

"With pleasure."

"If you get to be famous, it oughta be worth something."

"Maybe. It'll depend partly on how the critics and the public react to my portrait of Maria Atterbury."

"Oh."

"Listen, Pinky—you don't mind if I call you Pinky?—be a sport and let me visit my portrait."

Pinky scratched his head. "Wull, I don't know."

"You could go with us!" said Mona. "We'll promise not to touch a thing, and besides you've got a gun. We'll keep our hands to ourselves, look at the portrait, and leave. What do you say?"

"Oh, what the hell, sure. Come on."

He unlocked the front door and escorted them into the foyer, an oval space paved in large black and white squares of marble and onyx. Three hand-painted Japanese silk scrolls hung from ceiling to floor, depicting cranes, chrysanthemums, and lily pads. Schiffleger opened the door to their left and led them down a short hall, up three carpeted steps, and into Maria Atterbury's bedchamber.

It was forlorn now, cleaned and deserted. It was a long room, its rectangular lines softened by curving bay windows at the far end looking out over the ocean. Maria's king-sized bed was slightly inset into the wall on the right, facing a fireplace in the wall on the left.

The portrait still stood on an easel near the bay windows, and Alison's paintbox and palette rested on a low table next to it. The three visitors went straight to it—Cliff and Mona out of curiosity, but Alison with the air of a mother being reunited with a long-lost child. Tears came to her eyes as she stood, once more, face to face with Maria Atterbury.

"You really miss her, don't you?" said Mona.

"Miss her? It's more than that. It's just that she was so remarkable a woman and I . . . well, I hate to see her gone. I don't know how to explain myself."

"If she was as remarkable as you've shown her here," said Cliff, "I'm sorry I didn't get to meet her. Alison, this is terrific!"

The woman in the portrait had black hair streaked with gray, and wore a high-necked red-velvet dress with a suggestion of lace at the collar and at the breast. She regarded the viewer with an open, steady gaze that mingled bravery and self-esteem without arrogance. In the long and narrow face, one eyelid and the cheek below it drooped, adding a hint of cynicism, but Alison explained that this was one symptom of Maria's myasthenia gravis.

"She said, 'You don't have to make it a medical illustration, but do paint me just as you see me. And I'm sure you see me beginning to fall apart, which is part of life, so put it on record.' "

The mouth also drooped at one side—a further symptom— but curved slightly upward at the other, creating an impression of wry amusement, heightened somehow by a dab of blue shadow at the end of the curve.

"She had a sense of humor, too, didn't she?" said Mona.

"She did. Dark humor, but funny. At our last sitting she said, 'You'd better hurry, dear, or you'll find yourself painting a still-life.' " Alison's eyes teared again. "Oh, damn! You know what she was? She was a word you never hear any more. Damn it, she was gallant!"

30

"I can see that. . . . You really laid the paint on thick, didn't you?"

"Sure, to make the painting strong and rugged-looking, and she approved. She didn't want one of those slick pretty-pretty portraits like the other ones that hang in the store, so I slapped it on—sometimes with a palette knife. *Impasto,* you call that. She wasn't a bad artist herself, you know. That's one of her paintings there over the fireplace."

They turned to look at it. It was a landscape featuring an early California ranch house in the Spanish style, but given action and movement by the figure of a vaquero, whom Maria had captured just beginning to dismount from his horse, one leg swung back over the saddle.

"Not bad at all," said Cliff.

"That was the original De Castillo ranch house up in the Malibu," said Alison. "The family still owns about a square mile of that land, from the beach up to the first crest of the Santa Monica Mountains. It was granted to them somewhere around eighteen forty by Juan Alvarado, the Mexican governor of California. And ever since then, they've kept up the tradition of everybody in the family speaking Spanish, and everybody that marries into the family learning to speak it. It's a nice tradition—and it certainly didn't hurt business, either. They've always had a lot of wealthy Latin American customers."

"That Malibu land must be worth a fortune," said Cliff.

"Sure. J. Paul Getty owns a chunk of land next to it."

Alison undid the catches on her paintbox and raised the lid. "They made a heck of a mess in here," she said. "I always kept my tubes and brushes neatly arranged—and look at them! Somebody's taken them all out and just thrown them back in. The police, I suppose."

"Naw, it was prolly the burglar," said Schiffleger. "Way I heard it, he threw dern near everything in the room in a pile in the middle there—books, bedclothes, you name it. The pros'll do like-at when they're huntin' valuables. And then the police didn't know it was supposed to go back neat."

"Say, Mr. Schiffleger—" said Cliff.

"Heck, make it Pinky."

"Okay if I use the bathroom a minute, Pinky?"

"Uh, I guess so. It's over there in the corner."

Cliff disappeared through the door, closing it behind him. After a pause and the sound of flushing, he reappeared. "Well, Pinky," he said, "to quote Act One, Scene One of Hamlet, 'For this relief much thanks.'"

"I know just what you mean."

"And now we'd better clear out of here."

In the foyer, as Pinky lagged behind checking things, Alison turned to Cliff and said quietly, "Was that bathroom visit some sort of a trick or did you really need to go?"

"All I did, I must admit, was unlock the door leading to the outside, and I carelessly left it that way."

She squeezed his arm and Mona tittered.

In the foyer they thanked Pinky, he thanked Alison for the sketch, and they shook hands all around.

As they emerged from the house, with Pinky lagging behind locking up, a stout man in a dark blue suit came up the drive carrying an attaché case. He was balding on top but retained black hair at the sides like a monk's tonsure.

All three of them exclaimed simultaneously (after ad libbing, variously, "My God," "Good grief," and "Why, Cliff"), "It's Lieutenant Puterbaugh!"

Puterbaugh caught sight of them and halted in his tracks, slapped his thigh, and spun about to face the direction whence he had come, evidently wishing he could make reality go away and remold this sorry scheme of things nearer to his heart's desire. But when he turned again, they were still there.

"I don't believe this," he said. "I do not believe it! Fearless Fosdick and Tess Trueheart of Bay Psalm Book fame!"

"Hi, Lieutenant," said Cliff.

"Are you on this case, Lieutenant?" Mona asked.

"The important question is whether you are."

"No, we're not."

"Praise God from whom all blessings flow! And what the hell are you doing here, Mrs. Stephens? Do you know these people?"

"Cliff's my brother and Mona's my sister-in-law."

"Damn all. Why didn't you mention that before?"

"It never came up."

Lieutenant Puterbaugh rubbed his palm downward over his nose, mouth, and chin—that odd, universal gesture that people employ to register exasperation and give themselves strength. "Okay. And what are you three up to?"

"We came to check on the portrait," said Alison.

"You did, did you? And how is it?"

"Oh, fine. But when do you think I'll get it back?"

"Damned if I know. It isn't up to me."

Pinky Schiffleger cleared his throat. "Did you want to come in the house, Lieutenant?"

"No, I just dropped by to see if the cutworms are eating the petunias."

Pinky guffawed. "Tell me cops don't have a sense of humor?" He unlocked the front door again. "You still got your own key, though, don't you, Lieutenant?"

"I do. And listen, you people, as long as you're here, come back into Miss Atterbury's room with me."

"What for?" said Cliff.

"To see if Mrs. Stephens can recall any details she might not have mentioned before."

"Why don't you call me Alison? I don't mind."

He regarded her somberly. "I think we'd better keep it Mrs. Stephens for the time being."

Alison reddened again. Puterbaugh quickly said, "Ever notice that tile there, inset in the corner of the wall?"

They hadn't. It was a small square tile with a floral border surrounding the words, *"Dios bendiga cada rincón de esta casa."*

" 'God bless each corner of this house,' " Cliff translated.

"Didn't work, did it?" said Puterbaugh. "Let's go in."

They trooped back to the bedroom. "I realize the room's been put back in order," the lieutenant said, "but do you notice anything out of the ordinary, Mrs. Stephens? Anything out of place or missing that you recall from your sessions here?"

"Well, yes, several things. There was an original Utrillo on the wall near the fireplace. A street scene in Montmartre."

"That belonged to the store. She had it out on what they call the loan ledger and Grant Atterbury has taken it back. What else?"

"A very old ivory statue of the goddess Kwan Yin stood on that drum table. And there was a jade koi on the mantelpiece."

"Also on the loan ledger. Anything else?"

"Maria's medicine bottles are gone from her nightstand, and that porcelain lamp base is broken."

"The medicine's all accounted for. And the burglar—or killer—broke the lamp."

"What's a koi?" asked Mona.

"A carp," said Alison. "You know, one of those big colorful fish they have in ponds at a lot of Oriental restaurants. Maria's jade one was creamy white with red splotches here and there. The Chinese call it 'pigeon's-blood-on-snow.' "

"I want it!"

"Forty thousand dollars and it's all yours."

"Can you let me have two for seventy-five?"

Alison laughed. "Maria was crazy about that koi herself, so I was going to put it in her portrait. It would have helped the composition, too. I was going to put it about here," she said, indicating an oval on the canvas with her forefinger. "With the koi on the left, her hand showing on the right, and her face, the overall composition would be a triangle with a wide base. The impression that would give of balance and solidity was characteristic of her."

34

"Lieutenant," said Cliff, "a second ago you said 'the burglar or killer.' Didn't the burglar kill Maria Atterbury?"

Puterbaugh gave him a wry smile. "You picked up on that, did you? Very sharp, Fosdick! Okay, between you and me and the gatepost, I don't think there was a burglary here."

"No burglary?"

"One was faked. Oh, whoever did it tried to make it look like a burglary. The wall safe behind that landscape painting was open and we know four or five hundred dollars was taken; and the burglar supposedly got in by breaking a pane of glass in a kitchen window and undoing the latch."

"Why 'supposedly?' "

"Almost all the glass fell into a flower bed out in back. And there was no molasses or honey on the glass, so the burglar didn't pull the window out."

"He broke it from inside?"

"Or she. Yeah, you got it."

"So whoever it was probably came in through the front door. With a key."

"Most likely."

"But which way did he—or she—get out?"

"I think the killer heard Socorro Contreras coming through the front door and had to beat it fast. And all the doors and windows were locked or bolted or both when we got here, except one."

"And where was that?"

"Come here, I'll show you."

Puterbaugh stepped toward the bathroom. Cliff followed reluctantly.

"This door opens out on the garden," said the lieutenant. "It locks on the inside with a push button, and there's no knob on the outside. When we got here—"

Puterbaugh stopped in his tracks once more. His shoulders slumped, and he again massaged his face. When he turned again, his expression could have been that of Job in the Old Testament upon becoming aware of a new cluster of boils.

"All right, Dunbar, what the hell's the idea?"

"Beg pardon?"

"You were planning a little burglary yourself, weren't you, using your trusty Shell Oil card to slip the latch?"

"Why, I never heard of such a thing! Why would I do that?"

"The portrait, naturally. But it never would have worked."

"Why not?" said Mona.

"Aha!"

"Mona," said Cliff, "that was rather ill considered."

"Sorry."

"You will observe, Watson," said Puterbaugh, "that not only is the crack at the edge of the door too thin even for a credit card, but also"—he opened the door—"a strip of angle-iron covers it from top to bottom on the outside."

"Oh, drat!" said Alison.

"So I want you amateur criminals to knock it off."

"But that portrait is mine, darn it!"

"Maybe it is. But if it turns up missing from this house, I'll have to nail you for burglary, you realize that?"

"Oh, all right! But Consuelo and Lionel Atterbury think I ought to have it."

"How do you know they think that?"

"We were talking to them only this morning."

"All of you?"

"Yes. The two of them dropped in on me together. Consuelo even invited us to a cocktail party."

"What did they talk to you about?"

"Mostly their grievances against their Aunt Maria and Grant Atterbury and that lawyer Colfax. Lionel was sore because he thought Maria might have wanted to change her will."

"Sounds like they were talking pretty freely. You learned more about those people in a few minutes than I could get out of them in an hour's worth of third degree! I wish they'd invite me to their cocktail party. But that wouldn't be any use either. Every time I approach those people they clam up and go all wild-eyed like they just heard King Kong is in the city."

" 'A policeman's lot,' " said Cliff.

" 'Is not a happy one.' And for reasons I can guess at, the L.A. chief of police is dropping hints that maybe I should forget this case and track down the culprit whose dog has been leaving doodoo on the beach."

"What do you think his reasons are?"

"I see two of them, which overlap. The family seems satisfied with things as they are, on the whole. And that being the case, the aristocratic Atterburys would just as soon avoid all the publicity."

"Lionel Atterbury doesn't seem satisfied. He offered me a valuable drawing if I'd work on the case."

"And you didn't jump at the chance?"

Cliff laughed. "No. I'm not interested."

"That offer was probably window-dressing anyway."

"Maybe. We'll never know."

"Probably not. Rumor has it that if I don't close this case in two weeks, I can forget it."

"Lieutenant," said Mona, "your tone of voice tells me you suspect somebody in the family."

Puterbaugh reflected before he spoke. "Or somebody in their immediate circle. Look, this is not for publication, understood? As far as the public is concerned, a burglar did it. That's very handy—it covers our ass, if you'll pardon the technical police academy jargon. But can you imagine the stink I'd raise if I announced that I suspected the aristocratic Atterburys or their friends? With the chief thinking the way he does, he'd have me transferred out to Pearblossom tomorrow, running down overdue library books." Puterbaugh's face took on a dreamy look. "Christ . . . library books. Doesn't sound so bad at that."

They smiled in commiseration.

"Look, you people," Puterbaugh went on, "come have a

drink with me at the Golden Bull, down at the bottom of the hill."

"I thought you guys never drank on duty."

"We don't. I always take myself off duty when I order."

6

THEY SAT AROUND a low table at the Golden Bull, sipping Rob Roys, old-fashioneds, and margaritas, for which Puterbaugh paid.

"In case you're wondering why the sudden glad hand after our hassles on that Bay Psalm Book case," said Puterbaugh, looking at Cliff, "I've changed my mind about something. I've had an idea."

"No," said Mona.

"What do you mean, no?"

"He isn't going to do it."

"Why not?" He turned to Cliff. "You're going for your private investigator's license, aren't you?"

"No. I considered it, that's all."

"I had the impression you were hot on the idea, after the way you cracked that other case."

"For a while there, I was. I thought I was the new Sherlock Holmes. I even wrote to the Department of Consumer Affairs in Sacramento for a license application."

"That's the correct drill. And?"

"You know what the regulations require?"

"I haven't kept up. Tell me."

"First of all, I'd have to put in two years as an apprentice with a professional detective agency like Nick Harris or McKennish Karken or whoever, or—get this—have two years experience as a police detective!"

Puterbaugh was amused.

"And," Cliff went on, "each year is to consist of two thousand hours on the job. That means a total of four thousand hours hiding in bushes and peering over transoms. No, thanks. I'd rather go back to teaching medieval English literature."

"It isn't that bad. Besides, you'd have a hell of a time finding transoms in this day and age. The flophouses on Skid Row, maybe."

"Well, you get my point."

"Okay, then operate without a license. You can do that as long as you don't actually hang out your shingle or call yourself a private investigator. But I still think you ought to go for the license. Admit it: You'd really like to be a detective."

"Sure I would, except for those transoms."

"Cliff!"

"I know how you feel, Mona, but it's true."

"And if you worked on this case," Puterbaugh continued, "it seems to me you could kill two birds with one stone—make that three birds. You could help solve a despicable crime, earn a rare work of art for yourself, and probably get that portrait back for your sister."

"Mona, sweetheart," Cliff said, "in view of all these circumstances, shouldn't we give in and put on our deerstalkers?"

"Please, Mona?" Alison added. "For me?"

After looking from one to the other, Mona said, "Well . . . all right. But I want you to know I'm agreeing mostly because I want you to get that portrait. As for the murder, Clifford, I insist on one condition: If you—or we—are physically attacked by anybody at any time, you will instantly drop the case and leave it to the police. Agreed?"

"Agreed, if you'll permit a punch in the nose or two."

"If it's your nose."

"Thanks and welcome aboard," said Puterbaugh. "It's lucky you're independently wealthy. You can spare the time."

"I don't know about wealthy."

"Well-off, anyway. If you don't mind my asking, where the hell did your money come from? Your blackjack system? Surely not from teaching English literature."

40

"Our parents left some money to me and Alison, and I saved a lot of my army pay. But I really cashed in on a fluke: I wrote a workbook for freshman English, and by a freak of timing colleges all over the country adopted it. Next thing I knew, I owned my house on Sunset Boulevard outright. If I sold it today, I suppose some people would call me rich."

"Anyway, you'll fit right in with that Beverly Hills crowd. You've already met two of the Atterburys and Sidney Colfax, and your sister has met everybody, including Doctor Craig Rawlings—Maria's doctor—and Socorro Contreras. But for starters, let me give all of you a detective test."

He extracted a thick manila envelope from his attaché case and took out some glossy eight-by-ten photographs. "What's wrong with this picture?" he asked, holding it up. It depicted the scene of the murder, with Maria Atterbury lying in the chaos of her bedroom, surrounded by a jumble of books, the jade koi, the Kwan Yin, and loose papers.

They peered at it in puzzlement.

"Oh!" said Mona. "Things are backward!"

"Right on! They printed the negative backward down at the photo lab. I'm glad you'll be assisting Fosdick here. Okay, now take a look at this one." It was the same scene, printed correctly.

They squinted their eyes.

"No, no," said Puterbaugh. "This one's okay. I just want you to absorb the layout of the murder scene."

"But something is wrong!" said Alison.

"What?"

"I don't know. Something. I can't put my finger on it. At first, I thought this photo had been printed backward, too."

"Nope. Interesting, though. If anything occurs to you, let me know. . . . I have color photos here of Maria Atterbury's injury. Any of you feel a need to see it? No? Just as well."

"What kind of weapon was she killed with?" Cliff asked.

"We don't know. We never found it. But it was one of those good old blunt instruments beloved by thugs through the centuries. Maria received a pretty heavy blow at the base of the skull, and there was one oddity: Underneath all the lacerations and crushed tissue, the coroner found three puncture holes and a linear fracture down in the dent, laid out in a neat line like the Morse-code V for victory—you know—Beethoven's da da da dum."

"That rules out blackjacks and billy clubs."

"Could have been like a billy club, or maybe one of those miniature baseball bats for little tots, if you drove nails through it and inset a chisel blade. But there were no wood splinters and no bits of metal in the wound."

"I gather she was alone in the house at the time."

"No, she was never left entirely alone, but it was the same thing as. The registered nurse who took care of her was in bed in her own bedroom, drugged and completely out of it."

"Drugged? How did she get drugged?"

"Her evening tea."

"That makes it pretty conclusive that it wasn't just a random burglary, doesn't it? Could Maria have done that?"

"Conceivably, but it wouldn't make sense."

"Maybe the nurse drugged herself—to clear the way for the killer."

"Could be."

"What's the nurse's name?"

"I'll tell you on one condition: No wisecracks. . . . Her name is Stone. Rosetta Stone."

The corners of Cliff's mouth quivered. "Was she, uh, hard to decipher?"

"Watch it, Dunbar. The answer is yes. And I hope you can get more out of her than Sergeant Champollion did."

"Champollion, hey? Interesting name."

"French Canadian."

Puterbaugh watched him closely. Cliff remained sober. "Is Rosetta a hot suspect?"

"Not really. She had no plausible motive. And she just isn't the type to bump off her patient in cold blood and toddle off to beddy-bye."

"Who hired her? Maria?"

"Her doctor, Craig Rawlings."

"Is he a suspect?"

"Sure. Not only because he was her doctor, but I also heard rumors he was tied in somehow with Gwyneth Atterbury."

"Tied in in what way?"

"The way you'd expect. But they were both at the Shubert Theater in Century City at the time of the murder, seeing *Three by Albee,* so they have a good alibi."

"Doctors wear beepers. Couldn't he be called out, go kill her, and get back to the theater before the plays were over?"

"Maybe. But I doubt it. They were seen arriving, and here's a picture of them leaving."

Puterbaugh extracted a society photo clipped from the *Los Angeles Times,* showing Gwyneth Atterbury and Doctor Rawlings leaving the Shubert. They looked like Rhett Butler and Scarlett O'Hara coming out of Tara, except that Rawlings's tuxedo was more modern.

"Handsome couple," said Cliff. "Their relationship is pretty public?"

"I'm not absolutely certain there is one. He escorts her once, and the rumor mill starts grinding. Hell, I even heard rumors she was partly to blame for Colfax and his wife breaking up, and as far as I know they were never seen out on a date at all. Strictly legal business. But you'll find everything I know in this manila folder."

"I can keep it?"

"Sure. I have other copies, for whatever good they'll do me. Just let me know if you detect anything, Fosdick."

Alison, looking at her brother with great curiosity, suddenly slapped the table. "Hey! I just detected something."

"What?" said Puterbaugh.

"Cliff, your shirt pocket is flat! You aren't smoking!"

"Ah, at last you've noticed! Yes, after all these years, my Camels and I have parted company."

"Well, congratulations! But don't you miss them?"

"Sorely. Camels were my friends, and I owe a lot to them. I don't think I could have gotten through Vietnam without them. I loved the golden brown color—the palm trees, the pyramids, the sand. By the way, that's where Napoleon's troops found the Rosetta Stone, Puterbaugh."

"On a pack of Camels?"

"I even enjoyed the Surgeon General's warning; it was like having a father who was concerned for my health. So I quit because I wanted to live more years with Mona and enjoy more years of fly fishing."

"Ha!" said Mona. "Mind if I tell what really did it?"

"You mean that incident in the car? Darn it, Mona, that was just one tiny little added factor and you know it. You blow it out of all proportion because you know it makes a good story."

Alison was tickled. "Then I really want to hear it!"

"We had just left Klamath Falls after lunch," said Mona, "and Cliff was driving—and smoking. Well, somewhere on Highway Ninety-seven between Klamath Falls and Chiloquin, we thought we smelled cloth burning. We looked all over the place—ashtray, upholstery, carpet—nothing. But the smell got even stronger. Finally, Cliff felt something warm in his lap. You know how men's slacks bunch up when they sit down? Well, Cliff looked down and found he had burned the entire crotch out of his khaki pants."

They roared with laughter—all but Cliff, who could manage only a faint smile, like a gassy baby.

"It's a lucky thing those pants were cotton," Mona went on. "If they'd been polyester, our honeymoon could have been ruined."

"Not totally," said Cliff. "There was always the trout fishing."

"You fly fishermen are crazy," said Puterbaugh, rising. "And I have to run."

"Where are you off to?"

"Another murder case. Couple of evenings ago, some maniac clubbed a young couple to death with a two-by-four underneath the Santa Monica pier. I'm going to re-interview some of the locals who were around at the time."

"Before you go," said Cliff, "how about giving us a rundown on the Atterbury case as you see it."

"Okay, but only facts. It's a Thursday. It's Socorro Contreras's day off. She goes to a dance that night, a *baile* she calls it. She meets a handsome guy who finds out she has a good job working for a rich lady, and tries to borrow fifty bucks from her. She refuses. He's had a few and starts pushing her around. Another guy, who also would like to make time with Socorro, steps in and gets knifed in the chest. He gets patched up at UCLA Emergency Hospital and disappears. Guy named Hugo de Toronja. We're looking for him."

Cliff laughed delightedly. "You'll never find him."

"Why not?"

"*Hugo de Toronja* means 'grapefruit juice' in Spanish."

"Son of a bitch. Oh, well. Socorro decided to go home early. She got there at nine-forty, ran into the murder scene, and called the police. Rosetta Stone was in her bedroom, drugged."

"And now Socorro's back in Mexico."

"San Miguel de Allende. She's a hell of a nice young woman, by the way. We're still in touch."

"How about the rest of the gang? Where were they?"

"Except for Gwyneth Atterbury and Doctor Rawlings, who were at that play, they all have shaky alibis. Lionel Atterbury says he was at home reading in his house on West Valerio in Santa Barbara. Consuelo was at a big party at a movie star's home up on Summit Drive in Beverly Hills—one of those parties that are so gigantic that anybody at all could disappear for an hour or so and nobody would know the difference.

So nobody can guarantee that Consuelo was there all evening. Grant Atterbury tries to compose serious music, but he also plays clarinet in a schnickelfritz band with some other businessmen, you know, that oompah German stuff. They call themselves the Town Musicians of Bremen. They get together in Santa Monica every Thursday night at nine, play music, drink beer, maybe play cards. But that night, Grant showed up close to nine-thirty. After a lot of pumping, the other men conceded that he seemed distraught and that he got tighter than usual and acted sort of manic. Grant says he had business worries, and he has no idea why he was late. Sounds believable to me. A half hour here and there seldom means a thing. I don't think this case is going to be solved with a stop watch. Rollie Freed says he spent a quiet evening in his mobile home at Paradise Cove, snelling hooks and drinking Chianti."

"How about Colfax?"

"Oh, yes. Colfax visited his ex-wife in Brentwood that night with some legal papers concerning their property settlement. They had a violent argument, and Thelma, the wife, assures me she threw him out on his ear at eight forty-five. Brentwood is ten, maybe fifteen, minutes from Maria's house. So there's another one."

"You say Thelma blames Gwyneth for their troubles?" Mona asked.

"She had a strong suspicion, and she confronted Colfax with it. He denied it. But either way, after twenty years of marriage, she really took him to the cleaners, which is why he moved his office out of Beverly Hills and into a smaller one in Brentwood. And that's about all we know for certain. Not much, is it? So what do you think your first move will be?"

"Rattle Grant Atterbury's cage at the store," said Cliff. "Maybe he'll cough up the portrait. But he's more likely to give me the cold shoulder—or try to avoid seeing me at all."

7

"I don't agree with you," said Mona. "I think he'll put out the welcome mat."

"Woman's intuition?"

"Woman's intelligence."

Cliff made a left turn off Olympic Boulevard onto Roxbury Drive and guided his orange Porsche northward into the leafy, shady green residential district that extended all the way up to the parking lots behind the department stores of Wilshire Boulevard.

"But from what we've heard," said Cliff, "that sounds out of character."

"Maybe it is. But in or out, I think for the time being he'll want to demonstrate what an innocent, nice, and deserving guy he is. He can revert later."

They parked in one of the lots and strolled out to Wilshire, where crowds of smartly dressed people hurried between stores, and fleets of impatient drivers tried to honk each other eastward toward downtown Los Angeles or westward toward UCLA, Brentwood, and Santa Monica. The principal business district began on the other side of the street, but the Beverly Wilshire Hotel and the great department stores—Atterbury's, I. Magnin, Saks Fifth Avenue, Gump's, Bonwit Teller, and the rest—formed a single grand rank along the south side of Wilshire.

The facade of Atterbury's, the most prestigious of them all, gleamed with brass, plate glass, and squares of dark green serpentine resembling spinach jade. In one of the show windows a pretty young woman wearing an artist's smock was arranging an autumn display. She wore her short black hair in bangs, and a sheaf of black hair on each side of her face swung forward as she leaned to put a four-foot-long ebony dish on a marble coffee table. The dish was filled with English walnuts, against whose light-tan color the young woman had placed nine or ten ripe, red-orange California persimmons the size of a fist.

Cliff and Mona went inside to a brightly lit area where shoppers strolled about among Limoges and Lenox china, Baccarat and Steuben glass, Santan dolls, crystal ice buckets, and gift items and accessories such as heaps of ceramic fruits and vegetables, and geese cleverly carved from bundles of reeds.

"It's beautiful!" exclaimed Mona. "I want one of everything I see!"

"Avert your gaze . . . and don't even glance in there." They passed the entrance of a room that featured jade jewelry, silver from Denmark and Taxco, and Japanese pearls.

The executive offices were on the third floor. There were no escalators, only a small and crowded elevator, so they mounted a carpeted staircase. Turning at the landing halfway to the second floor, they came upon the portraits of the first two presidents of Atterbury's. The founder, Lewis De Castillo Atterbury, had had himself painted in the formal evening attire of his day. Fat and self-satisfied, seemingly as proud of his Gay Nineties mustache as of his accomplishments, he fastened his haughty gaze upward onto a sprinkler in the ceiling. Not so did Lewis Atterbury, Junior, the father of Lionel, Grant, Consuelo, and Rollie, who stared into the onlookers' eyes and informed them that he was their superior in business acumen, cleverness, aggressiveness, and money. His black hair was brushed straight back, revealing a high forehead and glittering brown eyes. Both portraits were rendered in the slick, flat style of portraitists who work from photographs.

"If Maria's portrait ever does get hung here," said Mona, "I wonder how it is going to look next to these two."

"It'll look odd," said Cliff. "Alison laid on the paint in that thick, rough impasto, but, worse than that, she's created a true work of art instead of a run-of-the-mill 'likeness.'"

"Betcha Grant never hangs it. At least, not right here."

The ambience of the second floor was so different from that of the ground floor as to be something of a shock. Instead of bright lights, noise, energetic people, and open displays on tables, shelves, and counters, the second floor was rather quiet, the ceiling lighting was subdued, and a handful of customers strolled about looking at pre-Columbian ceramic pieces in tasteful, but locked, glass showcases. There was a deity holding an ear of corn in each hand, pregnant-looking dogs, one with an ear of corn in its mouth, duck hunters, dancers, an acrobat so lithe that one foot rested on top of his head. Another case contained carved stone plaques looted from Mayan temples at Palenque and Tulum and depicting warriors and their captives, and a black onyx jaguar spotted with green malachite.

All of these articles bore price tags, but the prices were hidden from view. The only way to learn them was to ask a tall young man in horn-rimmed glasses and dark blue business suit, who sat at a little table at one dark end of the department, intent on entering figures into an account book under the light of a tiny desk lanp.

But if you presumed to tear this young man away from his duties and require him to unlock a case, the clear message was that you were a serious, committed buyer. Consequently, most shoppers gazed into the showcases with fascination, glanced at the young man, and moved on to the art gallery.

Cliff and Mona also moved on, up the stairs to the third floor, where a discreet sign informed them they would find the Oriental rug room, home furnishings, the Treasure Room, and the executive offices.

The president's office was tucked in a far corner, guarded by a very small woman behind a desk on which a nameplate identified her as Helen Turin, Executive Secretary. Her hair was iron-gray above a narrow heart-shaped face. She wore outsized bifocals in translucent blue rims, behind which gleamed a pair of highly intelligent and slightly mischievous eyes. She was keyboarding a business letter onto a video screen.

"I always feel like a praying mantis staring into that screen," she said, when Cliff and Mona stopped at her desk, "with my forearms poised like this, ready to pounce on a bug. Can I help you?"

Cliff said they were there to see Grant Atterbury.

"Oh, you're Mr. and Mrs. Dunbar," said Miss Turin, turning to her intercom. "Well—*chacun à son goût.* I'll see if he's free."

He was. Miss Turin rose to escort them, but Grant himself opened his office door and invited them in.

"Your secretary is something of a character," observed Cliff, smiling.

"Isn't she, though," said Grant drily. "She would have been fired a thousand times, but she's been at Atterbury's so long she could easily run the store herself, and she knows everybody from Beverly Hills to Cuernavaca. Indispensable and she knows it. Sit down. Would you like coffee or tea?"

Grant settled behind his desk. He wore a black wool suit with a vest, and a yellow necktie with black polka dots, thus managing to look modern and conservative at the same time. At six-feet-three he overtopped Cliff by an inch, but was beginning to turn flabby, losing the muscle tone of the Stanford basketball player he once had been.

"So what can I do for you?" he said, attempting a smile. "Or need I ask, since I've been in touch with Sidney Colfax?"

"You're aware, then," said Cliff, "that we have some questions about the portrait."

"To be specific," added Mona, "are you willing to let Alison have the portrait now?"

Grant burst out with a surprised laugh, but there was a glint of hostility in his eyes.

50

"You don't beat around the bush, do you? But what shall I say? If I instantly answer 'I don't know' and send you on your way, I'll deprive myself of the opportunity to get acquainted with a couple of interesting people—so why don't I just say, 'Let's talk about it?' "

His mouth stretched into a smile, and he laced his fingers together on his desk.

Cliff looked at him with interest. Smile or no smile, Grant's characteristic expression appeared to be an aristocratic sneer, which he achieved by tilting his head back, parting his lips slightly, and dilating one nostril.

"Terrific," said Cliff. "Why all the pussyfooting? Why wouldn't you return it to Alison or pay her to finish it?"

"Three reasons: The police locked everything up at first, not me. Second, legal advice. Third, I've had other things on my mind."

"You blame Colfax. Colfax blames you. Who's in charge?"

"I am. And frankly, I don't give a damn about the portrait. I have no intention of hanging it in the store—no reflection on your sister's talent—so certainly, your sister can have it back and welcome to it."

They were stunned. This was the war to which nobody came.

"When?" Cliff asked, after a pause.

Grant pursed his lips. "A week from Monday. I'll notify Colfax and the security agency. Is that satisfactory?"

"More than. On behalf of Alison, I sincerely thank you."

"You've rescued her from an awful jam!" said Mona.

He dismissed their thanks with a wave of the hand. "So I'm not an ogre. Anything else?"

"Yes—your aunt's murder. We've agreed to help investigate it."

"Sidney Colfax told me you emphatically denied doing just that."

"I did, but the situation has changed. We need to clear

Alison of all suspicion, Lieutenant Puterbaugh asked for my help, and your brother Lionel says he wants to hire me."

Grant shot up from his chair. "Lionel! Jee-zuss Key-rist! That nerd has absolutely no sense! I asked him to leave well enough alone!"

He wheeled about to face the wall, on which hung an autographed photo of Benny Goodman with his clarinet, and scratched his head. "What in hell can he hope to achieve?" he said, turning to them again.

"He'd like the murderer caught—"

"Sure . . ."

"He also likes to think a revised will could turn up," Cliff added with a small smile.

Both nostrils dilated. "Presumably making him president again? Wonderful! Then he could finish the demolition job he began here. Maybe you know what he did when he was president. Drunk half the time. Used to bring his floozies in here at one in the morning and give half the store away. Checked into the Eisenhower Medical Center in Palm Springs for the cure, and when he got out married a topless chorus girl out of a Las Vegas stage show! That last got him a fine write-up in *Newsweek* and Father bounced him out of the store. And you saw what he did to the ground floor."

"The ground floor?" said Mona, puzzled. "I thought it was dazzling. Isn't it—profitable?"

"Oh, yes, but it just isn't Atterbury's! Now it looks like every other gifty shoppy in Los Angeles. Atterbury's is supposed to be unique."

"You mean, more like the second floor, say?"

"Absolutely. Unlike Lionel, I respect tradition. I'd rather sell one rare item for five hundred dollars than sixteen common items at thirty dollars. Lionel actually put an ad in *New York Magazine:* jade earrings for thirty dollars. I tell you, our old Beverly Hills customers were shocked!"

"About the murder, though," said Cliff. "Mind if we ask a few questions?"

"I do mind. I've gone over everything I know with Lieutenant Puterbaugh at least four times. I've gotten to the point where I'd just as soon confess to the murder as plod through all those details again. Has he shown you his files?"

"Yes, he has."

"Then that's settled. Meanwhile, I suppose I should read the riot act to Lionel again, when and if I can find him."

"He'll be at Consuelo's cocktail party tomorrow."

"Oh, really? Then I think I'll show up myself, at the risk of giving dear Connie a heart attack. There's another one who'd like to find a new will hidden in the cuckoo clock. Did she invite you, too? She did? Not so you can play Sam Spade, I hope. You two really must drop that nonsense. You'll give it serious thought now, won't you?"

"We'll see."

"Good. In the meantime, if you two have never visited Atterbury's, I want to show you something. Come with me."

He escorted them out the door, taking Mona's arm. "Helen," he said to his secretary, "I'll be in the Treasure Room for about half an hour."

He led them down a corridor, leaving a surprised Helen Turin behind him, her eyebrows rising above her blue-framed bifocals.

Grant unlocked a solid oak door and accompanied them into an oval room in the center of which was a large oval table, made of dark walnut. Glass-fronted cabinets lined the walls except for three spaces in which hung an Utrillo, a Pissarro, and one of Monet's garden paintings from Giverny.

Grant unlocked several cabinets and brought out a succession of marvelous objets d'art. "Not priceless, though," he said with an acid smile. "We sell one or two occasionally. But I doubt that we'll sell this one."

He set before them a Chinese junk carved completely from a single block of jade—sails, rigging, crew, anchor, and anchor chain. "If you like ship models, you can take this home for thirty thousand dollars."

He followed this with a series of statuary heads: a bodhisattva from Angkor Wat, a Mayan Pacal, and a Hawaiian war god, Kokailimoku; then a three-legged Cho Dynasty jar, T'ang horses, gold ornaments from Monte Alban.

Grant made knowledgeable comments about each one, but Cliff was puzzled at the haphazard way he was bringing them out, and also at the rather searching looks that Grant directed at him and Mona. He seemed to be watching for their reactions, but it was difficult to divine what he hoped for or expected. Aesthetic oohs and ahs? Awe at his erudition? Pride over knowing *the* Grant Atterbury? Enlistment under his banner? Perception of his worthiness? Intimidating demonstration of how insignificant they were in comparison?

"And here," said Grant, "are a couple of things you may recognize." He placed an old ivory statue, a network of fine cracks enhancing its loveliness, on the table.

"A Kwan Yin," said Cliff.

"Exactly. And how about this?" He placed a carved jade fish on the table before Mona.

"Oh!" she exclaimed. "That's the jade koi!"

"Pigeon's-blood-on-snow."

"It's gorgeous! How lucky it didn't get broken that night!"

"Not likely. On the Mohs hardness scale, diamond is ten and jade is six and a half to six and three-quarters, depending on the variety—the same hardness as a steel file. You'd have a tough time breaking it—even those delicate-looking fins on its back and tail. This and the Kwan Yin both came from Aunt Maria's house. They were her favorites, along with that Utrillo."

He looked sharply from Mona to Cliff. This time, Cliff guessed that Grant was demonstrating how honest he was— how he refrained from looting the store's assets, and hence the estate's, for his own enrichment.

They walked back with him, thanking him warmly for his courtesy, shook hands, and Grant reentered his office.

54

Out on the sidewalk once more, Cliff turned to Mona. "Well, Schweetheart," he said, twitching his cheek like Bogart, "what do you think?"

"I'm utterly confused."

"So am I."

"What was all that about?" said Mona. "Not only did the welcome mat turn into a red plush carpet—but suddenly returning the portrait! That bowled me over!"

"Me, too. Especially because I had the notion, silly as it appears now, that it had something to do with the murder."

"Maybe it did. Maybe he was using it to buy us off."

"Plausible."

"Did it buy us off?"

"No. Just the opposite."

"I was afraid not."

"What did you think of Grant as a person?"

"I don't like him," she replied. "He looks like he's always smelling something bad."

"So of course he murdered his aunt."

"Right."

8

THE ORIGINATOR OF the "trickle-down" theory of economics may well have been inspired by the geography of Beverly Hills. The big money has always been up in the true hills of Beverly Hills north of Sunset, where Harold Lloyd, Mary Pickford, Ronald Colman, and Jack Benny once lived. The stream steadily dwindles as it trickles down on its way to Santa Monica Boulevard and the railroad tracks, where TV game show producers writhe in acute hypertension over whether their thirteen-week contracts will be renewed. The 500 block is the dividing line.

Consuelo Atterbury lived in a rented house at 601 North Acacia Drive, only a step up from 591 across the street. She seemed to be popular, though. Cliff had to park halfway up the block. Consuelo's house was painted Prussian blue with white trim. In a niche over the front doorway stood a white bust of someone unidentifiable. Julius Caesar? Millard Fillmore? S. Z. "Cuddles" Sakall?

A mumbling bumble of voices mixed with the tinkling of a piano emerged from the open front door. Cliff followed Mona and Alison into a dark living room painted midnight blue with white woodwork, already full of people. A few lamps glowed softly, softly enough to enable everyone to look his or her best, smoothing wrinkles in faces, wrinkles in trousers.

The guests formed the usual cocktail-party clusters. Some of them surrounded the baby grand and its pianist, a slim and smiling fellow with orange hair and plucked, burnt-sienna eyebrows. He was playing "Send In the Clowns" with professional skill. A conspiracy of pretty women sat on and around a blue-and-white-striped Empire divan, gleefully exchanging gossip. Other people leaned against the walls, drinking and chatting. A catered bar and table of canapés were set up in a small dining room to the right. Fitful traffic moved about, as people split off from one cluster and joined another, like atoms exchanging electrons from their outer rings. Lionel Atterbury, carrying an empty glass as he threaded his way through the crowd on his way to the bar, stopped in surprise when he saw the newcomers standing in the entry to the living room. "Why, hello! You actually came! . . . Uh, Connie'll be pleased."

"We hope you will be too," said Cliff. "We've decided to take you up on your offer."

"Offer?"

"The Valadon."

"Oh! Why, uh—yes, sure—of course."

"I should tell you, though, that we're working closely with Lieutenant Puterbaugh, so we won't be keeping any secrets from him. I've also told Grant. Is he here, by the way? We need to see him."

"You're in luck. The bastard's here, all right. So is Gwyneth."

"Brace yourself," said Cliff. "He's agreed to return the portrait to Alison."

"You don't tell me! Why? What does he have up his sleeve?"

"Maybe nothing. He doesn't want the portrait in the store."

"Listen—Grant is always one step ahead of everybody. Trust me. I even wonder why he and Gwyneth are here. They don't go slumming all that often."

"Slumming?"

"With Connie's crowd. I hope you get to meet the Rumanian. Let's go to the bar. I need a refill."

"I think we'd better pay our respects to Consuelo first," said Alison.

"She's out in the kitchen."

"The kitchen!" A thirtyish man with fiftyish bags under his eyes suddenly joined them. "Consuelo Atterbury in a kitchen? This I've got to see. Come on, I'll lead the way. We haven't met—I'm Kevin Flamm, ace talent agent."

They wedged their way through the crowd and down a short hall to a small kitchen, where Consuelo stood at the drainboard, drying a Baccarat glass with a Belfast linen napkin.

"My God, Connie!" exclaimed Flamm. "Are you washing your own cocktail glasses?"

Connie gave a languid wave with the napkin. "You know us—the nouveau poor."

"What happened to your Egyptian maid?"

"Nepta? She flew into a huffy over back wages and whatnot and flounced off to Giza or Khartoum, I suppose, where the baksheesh is lusher. Hello, dears. You know these people, Kevin? Alison Stephens, Mona Dunbar, and Doctor Clifford Dunbar."

"Doctor?"

"Of English literature," said Cliff.

"Well, aren't you getting la-de-da, Connie! Hey, wait a minute! I know who you are! You're the Dunbar that solved that Bay Psalm Book murder and knocked the California election ass over tincups! Listen, are you investigating Maria Atterbury's murder? When you solve it, I want an option on the story, okay? One of my clients is a director and the other one's a writer. I'll package and produce."

"And," added Connie, "I can star in it. Beginning next week, thanks to dear Father, dear Aunt Maria, and beloved brother Grant, I am desperately going to need a job."

"Baby, are you serious? Broke? An Atterbury?"

"My dear, I haven't a bean."

Flamm's eyebrows flew up and he snapped his fingers. "Connie, know what'd be great?—if you were the murderer and you played yourself in the movie! That would be a box office smash, an all-time first! Were you the murderer? Be a doll, tell me you were!"

"Sorry to disappoint you. Now, go. I'll be with you as soon as I've finished ruining my nails."

While Mona and Alison sought out the powder room, Cliff and Kevin made light conversation and surveyed the crowd. Grant Atterbury was leaning against the far wall chatting with an attractive young woman in a black cocktail dress who wore her black hair in bangs. She looked familiar to Cliff, but he couldn't place her.

At the far end of the room, the pianist had taken a break and was talking animatedly to a woman with wavy chestnut-brown hair, a sultry California tan, and full red lips. She wore a white dress with a low-cut square neckline. Judging from a quick glimpse, she appeared to be an extraordinary beauty. Cliff wondered if she was a film star he was unfamiliar with.

"Do you know that tan woman down there in the white dress?" he asked Kevin Flamm.

"That, my observant friend, is the famous Gwyneth, and I not only know her, I lust after her, like everybody else. Hell, I've walked past her five times this afternoon and therefore have had five . . . You're an English professor, what's the plural of hard-on? Is it hard-ons or hards-on?"

It was beginning to be difficult to like Kevin Flamm.

"I'd suggest you recast the sentence."

"Anyway, five of 'em."

"And how about the man over there next to the lamp—the one that looks like a combination of Clark Gable and Tom Selleck? He looks sort of familiar, but I know I've never met him."

"Aha! That is the equally famous Doctor Craig Rawlings, pill-pusher to the belles of Bel Air and Beverly Hills, and physician to Maria Atterbury. I suspect that he'd like to play doctor with Gwyneth, too. As wouldn't we all."

"I think I'll go introduce myself to him," said Cliff. "If you'll excuse me."

"To him? Not her? Christ, what ever happened to *cherchez la femme?*"

Cliff smiled and moved off through the crowd to where Dr. Rawlings stood, talking to a pleasant, round-faced woman of fifty who was merely plump this week, but would be fat by next week if she didn't lay off the chocolate mousse. As Cliff approached, the doctor shot him a quick glance, but instantly returned to the plump woman, gazing fixedly into her eyes. He was giving her his complete attention. Cliff began to see why the man was so popular a society doctor.

"Mind you, Audrey, I'm merely buttering you up, because I'm not at all sure you're going to like what I have to say." He smiled at her, revealing beautiful white teeth in a tan face, his close-clipped black mustache nicely matching his razor-cut black hair. From the look on Audrey's face, he could have told her he was starting her on alternate clysters and cold showers, like the Good Soldier Shweik in the lunatic asylum, and she would have replied, "Beg to report, sir, that sounds first-rate."

But she actually said, "I'll be brave. Give it to me straight."

"I know it's tough, but with exercise and a diet, just think what a knockout you're going to be! Now, I want you to start tomorrow with just a brisk walk around the block, and when you next come in we'll talk about a formal program, okay?"

He gave her a sideways pat against her right shoulder that both warmed her and dismissed her without her seeming to realize it. She walked off in what was obviously a rosy glow.

Cliff watched in admiration, the amateur observing a master at work. Doctor Rawlings saw him and evidently was annoyed at being caught "handling" a patient.

"Excuse me for eavesdropping," said Cliff. "I'm Cliff Dunbar, Doctor Rawlings. Former English teacher, now amateur sleuth. Lionel Atterbury has asked me to look into Maria Atterbury's murder."

"Oh?"

"I'm told you were her doctor."

"Right. So I could hardly be her murderer."

"I certainly wasn't suggesting you were. But just because you were her doctor doesn't rule you out. Look at Marcel Petiot, in Paris in the nineteen-forties. He killed twenty-seven people, took 'em apart, and then either burned the remains in a furnace or buried them in quicklime."

"Crude. If I had wanted to kill Maria, I simply would have injected an air bubble in her arm while giving her a shot. The bubble hits the brain and that's it. Undetectable. Far safer than bashing her head in, as some thug evidently did."

"But mightn't a murderous doctor do just that—maybe use a baseball bat—because it's so obviously undoctor-like?"

"Your Doctor Petiot might have. But the question's academic, isn't it?—seeing I was at the theater when she was killed and seeing she was going to die anyway."

"There could have been other motives for killing her besides just wanting to hurry her along."

Rawlings ignored that comment. His mind was elsewhere. "She certainly wasn't my favorite kind of patient. Myasthenia gravis is uncurable, but the general public doesn't know it. So it wouldn't have done much for my reputation, having a prominent society figure die on me."

"Then you might say the murderer did you a favor."

"If I knew who did it, I'd send 'em roses. I should never have taken over her case in the first place."

"Taken it over? You weren't her doctor from the start?"

"Christ, no. I took over from an old goat named Howard Gates who wanted to retire, and about time, too. He wasn't doing Maria any good, that's for sure. He was trained as a GP, and his medicine was so obsolete I'm surprised he wasn't treating her with ipecac and leeches."

"He asked you to take the case?"

"No. Not exactly."

"Who did?"

"Oh . . . the family."

"Who in the family?"

Rawlings flashed him one of his famous tan-face, white-teeth, Clark Gable smiles. "Excuse my French, but that's really none of your goddamn business, is it?"

The doctor's sudden belligerence took Cliff aback.

Cliff flashed Rawlings a winning smile.

"We detectives do pry, don't we? Tell you what: To keep things on the up-and-up, pro forma, and kosher, why don't I have Lieutenant Puterbaugh come ask you the question?"

Rawlings responded with a smile that would have frightened children. "Sure, why don't you do just that? At least I'll know I'm being pestered by a real detective."

"I'm real enough, Doctor. I actually report to Puterbaugh. I'm simply not licensed to peer over transoms."

Rawlings sneered, talking out of the corner of his mouth. "Are you licensed to pack a 'rod?'"

"Oh, I've got one of those, all right." He whipped out his wallet, extracted a slip of paper, and handed it to him.

"Department of Fish and Game? This entitles you to pack a rod?"

"Certainly. Mine's a nine-foot Scott PowR-Ply graphite for a number six fly line."

Rawlings pondered. "Dunbar, if you're planning on a career as a private eye, I recommend you see a proctologist. You show symptoms of becoming a first-class pain in the ass."

"Sorry. I got a little irritated with you, too."

Out of the corner of his eye, Cliff saw that Gwyneth Atterbury was now gazing directly at Craig Rawlings, or at Cliff, or perhaps at both of them. She left her position at the far wall and began to edge her way sinuously toward them through the throng.

Two men in the crowd held their drinks high in the air to avoid spilling as she came through, but Cliff noted with amusement that instead of pressing backward to make room for her, they saw to it that she had to rub against them. Narrowing her eyes, she gave each of them an arch smile.

"Are you also Gwyneth Atterbury's doctor?" asked Cliff.

"I am," replied Rawlings. Cliff could hardly blame him for being smug. No doubt about it: Gwyneth Atterbury's beauty was stunning.

She joined the two men, and Rawlings made introductions. Instead of a cordial smile and a handshake, Gwyneth presented a curiously watchful face to Cliff, who didn't quite know what to make of it. His first impression was that she felt guilty about something. (Murder?) But then the obvious occurred to him: This was a look he had experienced before—that of a gorgeous woman or handsome man who, meeting a new person, waits for the awed reaction that will be one more contribution to self-esteem.

She stood closer to Cliff than to Rawlings. Cliff found it disconcerting to look down at her five-feet-seven from his six-feet-two, partly because he was aware of being watched, partly because her beauty was so flamboyant, and partly because she was provocative. She wore a white Mexican cotton dress woven into a webby floral pattern that revealed hundreds of little patches of suntanned skin. The bodice was boldly square-cut, she wore no bra, and a patient man who was willing to risk being caught ogling her would occasionally have reaped the reward of a glimpse of pink nipple. Around her neck and suspended above the rising brown mounds of her breasts, she wore a Mexican silver necklace from Taxco, consisting of rows of slender silver rods and delicate rings.

Gwyneth turned to Rawlings and said, "Would you mind getting me a gin and tonic, Craig?"

As Rawlings moved off toward the bar, Cliff noted that Mona and Alison were back into action, mixing with people, talking, sipping drinks.

Meanwhile, a slight pucker crinkled Gwyneth's eyebrows, perhaps inspired by Cliff's not appearing sufficiently agog.

"When I was down at the end of the room chatting with Arnold, I wondered who that handsome man was talking to Doctor Rawlings. I think it's thrilling you're a detective. Do you find it thrilling?"

"Not really. For one thing, at a party like this I'd rather just socialize, not scrutinize people and hunt for suspects."

"Am I a suspect?"

"Of course. Everyone is. Although the only way you could have killed Maria would have been through a hired killer."

"I'm glad I don't know anything then, because, well, those eyes of yours! Two minutes of interrogation and I'd be in your power."

He laughed. "I don't want to play Svengali with you, but I do have a lot of questions I want to ask."

"Fab. But wouldn't a quiet place be better where nobody'll bother us and we can really let our hair down? Why don't you come up to the house and we'll have a drink and a good shmooze?"

One eyebrow arched and she laid a hand on his arm. The implication was that her quiet place would feature Fruit of the Loom and Beauty Rest.

Cliff looked into those liquescent eyes and felt a surge of pity for the human race, snatching at will-o'-the-wisp satisfactions that last about as long as snow on the desert's dusty face. Nonetheless, had this been 1972, with Cliff still a handsome young army officer, and had he been sent to Tokyo for R & R from the Vietnam battlefield, and had he met Gwyneth in his hotel bar there, he no doubt would have jumped at the chance to hop in the sack. But those days were long since over.

"Fine," said Cliff. "I'll phone you."

A faint smile of triumph flickered around her mouth. She dabbed at her nose with a Kleenex. "Do you have my number?"

"It's in the police files. Puterbaugh gave me a copy."

She appeared startled at the reminder that she was more than Die Lorelei—she was also a suspect in a murder case.

"But could I ask you two or three warm-up questions?"

"I suppose so," she replied.

"You were at the Shubert Theater with Doctor Rawlings the night Maria Atterbury was murdered. Did he get called out during the play?"

"No."

"His beeper never went off?"

"No."

"Were you and your husband satisfied with the medical care he gave Maria?"

"Of course. Craig is a wonderful doctor."

"How did Maria happen to find him?"

"She didn't. I found him. And Grant and I asked him to take over from old Doctor Gates, who wasn't doing her a bit of good."

She dabbed at her nose again.

"Did Maria like the idea?"

"Not much. I guess she had sort of a thing for old Doctor Gates, you know? But he wanted to retire, and if it looks like you're dying . . . well, like you'll try anything, you know? Especially if it's a doctor with up-to-date medical training."

"Maybe he can cure your cold."

"Yes, I suppose so."

"Too bad the murderer didn't give him a chance to show his stuff by curing Maria. Although from what he told me just now, there wasn't much hope of that."

"Well, as the Spanish say, *así es la vida.*"

"Yep, such is life. And death."

"Oh, you speak Spanish too?"

"I get along in it."

"Who do *you* think killed Maria?" she asked. "Who do you suspect the most?"

"Nobody. I just came on the case. How about you? Have you formed an opinion?"

"Not really. It could have been so many people. Maria never won any popularity contests. Naturally, you'd think it had to be somebody in the family, and yet it couldn't have been anybody in the family. The Atterburys think too much of their precious name to throw mud on it, even if that's what they want to do most."

"You surprise me. You're an Atterbury yourself."

"By marriage. Listen, Doctor Dunbar—Cliff. All I'll say is there's easier things in the world than being an Atterbury."

"The Spanish also say, '*Mira lo que haces antes que te cases.*' "

"Now, that I don't get, in spite of the Atterburys' required language course. *Qué quiere decir eso?*"

"It means, 'Look what you're doing before you marry.' "

"The Spanish are smarter than I thought. Where the hell is Craig with that drink?"

It dawned on Cliff that she must have hoisted three or four gin and tonics already. It would seem that booze loosened both her morals and her tongue. He pressed forward.

"If it had to be somebody in the family, who would it most likely be?"

"Me. Maria didn't approve of me, and I don't like bossy dikes. But I'm out of the running because there I was soaking up culture that evening with Craig—Doctor Rawlings. So that leaves Connie, because Maria cut her off at the pockets, and Lionel because she wouldn't change her will and put him back on the throne. But Connie's used to that—she always has been put down, as most women are."

"Ah, the Grand Duchess of Beverly Hills!" boomed a voice.

A beefy man in a black suit joined them, seized Gwyneth's hand, and bent down to kiss it.

"Hello, Bela," she said. "Somehow I knew you'd be here."

"Please!" he exclaimed, wagging two bushy black eyebrows at her. "When Consuelo Atterbury told me you might attend, I dropped everything. Do you think I would miss the chance to see you and your brilliant husband again? . . . And who is this distinguished gentleman? I don't believe we have met?"

Gwyneth introduced Cliff.

"Permit me," said Bela, with a little bow. He handed his card to Cliff, who looked at it with interest. "Bela Antonescu," it read. "Former Ambassador Extraordinary and Minister Plenipotentiary Without Portfolio from Rumania to Japan. Public Relations—Export-Import." An address and phone number followed. Cliff smiled, pocketing the card.

"Here you are, my dear. Hello, Bela." Doctor Rawlings had returned with Gwyneth's gin and tonic. "Sorry for the delay, but I got waylaid. People wanting free medical advice."

"I have not seen you," said Bela, "since the tragic event."

"What tragic event? Oh, you mean the murder?"

"Yes. To have expended your genius and your skill all in vain. At one blow—to lose not only a patient but a grand one of the legendary Atterburys. A monstrous tragedy."

"Quite a loss. Yes."

"Excuse me if I move along," said Cliff. "I'll phone you if any more questions occur to me, Mrs. Atterbury. And may I do the same with you, Doctor? I know I'll be wanting to talk to you some more."

"Fine, if you like whipping dead horses. Call my office for an appointment."

Cliff edged away from the trio with relief. He felt newly troubled, uncertain about his future. He liked the idea of detective work—the intellectual challenge of problem-solving in the cause of justice—but he didn't like talking to people like this last group. He would have to get over his aversion, however, if he became serious about continuing in this line of work, and develop emotional detachment. Once more, he felt a pang of misgiving over his resignation from the English Department at Los Angeles University. The fall semester would begin this month, and someone else would be taking over his Chaucer class. Far worse, he had removed himself from the company of people who read books and understood literary allusions. He had once referred to an error-prone shortstop for the Los Angeles Dodgers as the Ancient Mariner, because "he stoppeth one of three." It got a big laugh from librarian Link Schofield and other colleagues, but try that now, and most people would mark him down as an intellectual snob. They wouldn't understand it.

With a sigh, he looked about him and spotted Mona and Alison threading their way toward Grant Atterbury, who was still talking to the pretty young woman with the boyish haircut. She showed no sign of being put off by his aristocratic sneer; on the contrary, she seemed to be hanging onto his every word, with something like respect or admiration.

"Mr. Atterbury," said Alison, joining the pair, "could I have a word with you?"

"Take two."

"I want you to know how deeply grateful I am that you're returning Maria's portrait to me. It means a great deal to my career."

"You're quite welcome. But as I explained to your brother, I didn't intend to hang that thing in the store in the first place. No reflection on your talent, of course."

"Do you want me to return the five hundred dollars?"

"You earned it. Keep it."

"Well, thanks again. One more thing, though: It's crucial that I finish that portrait for showing in the exhibition at my gallery next month, and time is getting so short it's scary. Why do I have to wait another week for you to let me have it?"

Grant shrugged. "That's just the way it has to be."

"Forgive me for saying so, but that isn't an answer. I hate to be pushy, but a short handwritten note to that man Schiffleger and a phone call to Sidney Colfax—how long would it take? Ten minutes?"

"I don't have to explain my actions to you, Mrs. Stephens."

"But why?"

"I'll tell you why!" exclaimed the young woman Grant had been talking to. "The man's aunt has been murdered, he has her estate to settle, he's been busy with the police and a swarm of reporters, and he has a famous store to run. In

68

short, he has more important things on his mind than a half-baked picture of a prune-faced old maid! Or can you get that through your thick skull?"

"And just who the hell are you?" demanded Alison. "You're not his wife—or his girlfriend—are you? Butt out!"

With an enraged gasp, the young woman slapped Alison's face with her right hand and tried to grab a handful of hair with her left.

This was a mistake. Before one slaps someone's face and pulls her hair, it would be prudent to inquire whether one's opponent had been thoroughly grounded since early childhood in hand-to-hand combat by a father who was a World War II infantry officer. This young woman didn't ask.

Placing her thumb and index finger on the bare skin where the young woman's neck curved into her shoulder, Alison gathered up a skein of cervical nerves, pinched hard, and pushed down. The woman sank to her knees and Alison gently pushed her over onto her back. Action like that is a sure attention-getter at a Beverly Hills cocktail party, at least in the afternoon. Those who weren't already standing by hastened to squeeze up to ringside, including the pianist, Lionel Atterbury, and Consuelo.

"Wonnnn-derful!" exclaimed Consuelo. "I *adore* violence!"

Wild as a maenad, the young woman scrambled to her feet and started to fling herself unto the breach once more, but Grant caught her and said, "Molly, no. Please. Go to the powder room and tidy yourself up."

She hesitated, but at a quelling look from Grant, turned and flounced out. Grant said with something of a smile, "I didn't get a chance to introduce you properly, but that was Molly Teague, my window-dresser at Atterbury's."

"Would you mind calling her back to do that again?" said Consuelo. "I missed the main action, darn it!"

"We can always count on you to do the vulgar thing, can't we, Connie? You probably even mean that."

"Of course I do! That's why my parties are so memorable! But *revenons à nos moutons:* Why don't you stop acting like a tight-ass honky and give this girl her painting?"

"I fully intend to when it's convenient—and it will be convenient a week from Monday. And now, dear sister, toodle-oo and thank you for a wonderful afternoon. I hope to see you again in a year or two."

9

THE THREE OF them sat around the umbrella-table beside the swimming pool, its water turning a darker blue now, as the westering sun dropped behind the pine trees on the other side of the wall. The afternoon heat was almost gone.

They compared facts and impressions picked up at the cocktail party while sipping iced tea and nibbling dry-roasted peanuts. The tea was black-brown in the frosted glass pitcher. Yellow lemon slices floated over ice cubes on the surface.

"Who did you say taught you to make this?" said Alison.

Cliff smiled. "Goldina Fuller, the pride of Du Quoin, Illinois—my seventy-two-year-old second-best girlfriend."

"She's a sweetheart," said Mona. "The kind of midwestern grandma everybody should have."

"Well, that grandma is a genius. Teach me to make this stuff and I may never buy liquor again."

"Maybe I should teach Lionel Atterbury. It might help him stay on the wagon," said Cliff.

"Or Molly Teague. What do you suppose got into her? Two drinks and she wanted to fight?"

"If so, I must say she picked the wrong patsy."

Alison blushed. "I was so embarrassed I could have died."

"I compliment you on your restraint, though," said Cliff. "For not sending her flying across the piano in a hailstorm of Swedish meatballs."

"What set her off though?"

"I think it was your suggesting she was Grant's girlfriend," said Mona.

"Do you suppose she really is?"

"I'd say so. Either that or she wants to be. And did you see that pussycat smile on Grant's face? He loved being fought over."

"Which I find strange," said Cliff. "Can it be that Gwyneth isn't enough for him? They haven't been married all that long."

"Gwyneth wouldn't fight over him," said Mona. "I don't think she loves him. I don't think she loves anybody. And I'll bet she's lousy in bed. She's a goddess men are supposed to pay tribute to."

Cliff laughed. "And I'll bet she feels cheated, at that. Women as beautiful as that intimidate a man."

"How about Gwyneth and Doctor Rawlings?" said Mona. "Do you think some hanky-panky is really going on there, or is he just a convenient escort now and again? I know that may sound naive, but if you tried that convenient-escort stuff in Madras or Maupin, Oregon, they'd grab you by the collar and the seat of the pants and throw you back into California."

"You bet there's hanky-panky," said Alison. "Remember what Mom used to say, Cliff? 'That isn't love-light in his eye, honey, that's tail-light.'"

"I'm sure you're right, but the question for us is whether it means anything—anything besides sex play. We need to know two things about all these people: what they want, and what they'd be willing to do to get it."

"And then there's what people don't want," added Mona. "Like Consuelo, who seems resigned to not wanting anything, and Grant, who suddenly says he never did want the portrait so Alison can have it, but not for another week."

"Ali, think again," said Cliff. "Crazy as the idea sounds, can that portrait possibly be connected to the murder?"

"No. Unless we're failing to see the obvious. Why don't we whiz up to Maria's and have another look?"

"Schiffleger's been burned," said Mona. "He won't let us in."

"There's another way," said Cliff reaching for a white telephone plugged into the stone wall behind a ginger plant.

"Lieutenant Puterbaugh, please. Tell him it's Fosdick calling. Right—Fearless Fosdick. . . . Hello, Lieutenant. Listen, can you do me a big favor? . . . You guessed it. . . . Nine o'clock Monday morning? Thanks a million. Oh, one thing more. . . . Yes, just one. I read through the material in the file folder, and I saw your comment that nobody noticed anything unusual in the neighborhood the night of the murder. What I want to know is: Did anybody notice anything *usual*? . . . I don't agree it's a silly question. Do we even know what's usual? Anyway, I plan to park my car on the street over there next Thursday night and just observe for a while. So can you call that twenty-four-hour patrol in Huntington Palisades and clear me with them? Thanks another million. . . . No, we didn't learn a thing worth reporting—just some insights into character. See you Monday."

"I didn't quite follow that last part," said Mona. "Sitting around in your car."

"I'll tell you my strategy for the next few phases. I was thinking about something my friend Larry Archer—the librarian over at the Huntington—told me. He does a lot of sailboat racing, and he said a recurrent problem is what to do when other boats get well ahead of you. If you're more skilled than they are, you may not need to worry. But if they're just as skilled as you, there's no point in imitating every move they make because then you're guaranteed to lose. So you try the unorthodox—maybe do the opposite of your opponent—and pray for luck."

"So what unorthodox steps do you have in mind?"

"For the time being, I don't want to retrace Puterbaugh's footsteps and ask the same people the same questions. So I'm going to move on to three people who've been mostly overlooked: Rollie Freed, Doctor Howard Gates, and Socorro Contreras."

"Why Socorro?" asked Mona. "She was only the house-keeper, and she's clearly innocent."

"She was the last one to talk to Maria, and she sat there for quite a while looking around the room right after the killer left. But more important than that—sure, I can understand Puterbaugh allowing her to go back down to San Miguel, but Colfax? Since when did he get so generous, gladly arranging to give her that five thousand dollars in an advance distribution? Why? Just because she had a business opportunity? And did Grant give his okay? My guess is they might have been glad to get her out of the way and look like Good Samaritans doing it—which is why I think I'll go down and talk to her."

Mona's eyes lit up. "You mean we're going to Mexico? Two honeymoons in the same marriage? You're my kind of man, Clifford Dunbar!"

"I've got to be off," said Alison, rising. "Becky Litvak and I have a double date for dinner with a couple of artists."

"Anything serious?"

"Maybe for her, but certainly not for me. It's my last date with this cowboy. He thinks if he buys my dinner he's entitled to me for dessert."

"I've dated a few of those," said Mona.

"The last one got kind of nasty," said Alison. "When I wouldn't trade him nooky for gnocchi, he flew into a rage and tried to rape me. So I broke his nose and refunded his money. Well . . . got to trot."

They watched her walk pertly toward her car parked in Cliff's driveway.

"There goes one heck of a girl," said Mona. "Who would ever think somebody that sweet and petite could be such a stick of dynamite? She still looks like a schoolgirl. . . . And speaking of school, registration day at UCLA is coming up next week."

"I know."

"And instruction begins the week after that. I'm on the verge of my master's in physical therapy and kinesiology."

"Which I think is great. You'll keep us both in shape."

"But I have a devilish scheme you don't know about."

"Tell me."

Mona left her chair and sat on his lap, one arm around his neck. "Now that I have a rich husband in my toils, I have quietly raised my sights way up. Physical therapy is fine, but I've gotten interested in sports medicine; so I'm planning to apply for UCLA medical school next year. What do you think of that?"

Cliff smote his forehead with the palm of his hand.

"Pow! . . . You astound me, but I think it's marvelous!"

"Didn't know I married you for your money and connections, did you?"

He turned his head and kissed her in the shadowed groove between her freckled breasts. "Who cares? And since it's true confession time, let me tell you that all my sweet-talk was pure blatherskite. I was really after your body."

"Oh, goody! I thought you only wanted free proofreading. So, all we have to do now is solve the problem of what you're going to do with your life."

"Oh, I'll just try to keep the doctor happy."

"Attaboy . . . if you think you can keep up the pace you've set."

"Don't worry. I take powdered rhinoceros horn every morning in my orange juice."

He stood up and made for the house, carrying her in his arms.

"Oh," he said, stopping. "I forgot one thing."

"What?"

"It's true I'm crazy about your body, but is it okay if I'm wildly in love with you?"

"Why, bless your old-fashioned heart! I don't mind if you don't."

10

GOING UP THE Pacific Coast Highway toward Paradise Cove, Cliff briefly considered dropping in to say hello to Alison, but decided that his chances of finding Rollie Freed at home would be better the earlier he got there, so he sped on.

Along the highway as Cliff left Malibu behind, plants cultivated by man competed with plants that Mother Nature allowed to shift for themselves. He drove past a couple of nurseries, including one that specialized in African violets, but otherwise the highway was fringed with wild grasses, castor beans, miner's tobacco, fremontia bushes, and the tall stems and green-lace foliage of fennel.

Four or five miles north of Malibu, Cliff turned off onto the asphalt drive that drops sharply down into Paradise Cove.

Privately owned, the place strikes many visitors as a principality, like Monaco. The shoreline bends just enough to justify the word "cove." The community has a pier, a large parking lot, a fast-food window for beachgoers, and a good seafood restaurant. At the foot of the slope, a tan young man stood outside a tollbooth with a fistful of paper money, next to a sign that amply explained the fistful of money: "$5 beach parking, $5 pier fishing, $5 restaurant parking, $1 per person walk-in, $16 for over-sized vehicle."

Cliff gave the man a ten-dollar bill, and the man snapped out a five for him.

"You can park your car in the shade under that sycamore if you want to."

He did indeed; and he smiled at a poster tacked to the tree. "Last Hot Bikini of the Summer Contest," it read.

At the manager's office a pleasant woman of fifty or so directed him to Rollie Freed's mobile home on a quiet, sun-dappled lane. Rollie's place was six or seven units up the road, on the right. None of them looked in the least mobile. Rollie's featured a sloping overhang, covered with thick-butt shingles that projected from the roof on all sides and shaded the windows. The outer walls consisted of redwood siding. An American flag undulated in the light airs coming off the sea. A neat flower bed full of the pointillist red, pink, and white of begonias, impatiens, and geraniums bordered the pavement.

A Subaru Brat with a boat hitch was parked under the carport. A bumper sticker invited other motorists to "Honk If You Love Huitznahuatlecamalácotl."

Cliff was about to knock on the door, but stayed his hand when an arpeggio guitar chord resounded from inside and a man's voice burst into song:

"Ohhhhhh, I'd like to teach the world to give Itself an en-e-ma! . . . "

Delighted, Cliff leaned closer to hear more, but the music stopped and raucous laughter broke out instead.

Cliff knocked, then. He heard the creak of springs and the padding of bare feet, and the door opened.

"Good morning, sir!" said Rollie Freed in a cheerful voice. "What can I do for you?"

Cliff introduced himself and briefly explained his role in the murder investigation.

"Come on in."

Cliff stepped into a place that was clean and neat from one end to the other. The furniture was mostly what he expected to see: small varnished pine table and two chairs, cotton curtains in the windows, vinyl tile floor with a few throw rugs, a floor-to-ceiling bookcase full of neatly aligned books, among which Cliff recognized *McClane's New Standard Fishing Encyclopedia*. A navigation chart of Paradise Cove hung on one wall. On another, in the alcove containing Rollie's narrow bed, were some excellent watercolors of fish, sailboats, and the local scene showing the pier, the restaurant, children romping on the beach, and waves breaking against dark brown rocks at the northern cusp of the crescent shoreline.

Rollie pulled out one of the wooden chairs for Cliff and seated himself again on his bed, his guitar beside him.

Cliff's immediate impression of Rollie was solidity, of both physique and character. He was not big—five-nine or -ten— but broad-shouldered and muscular. His hair was a cap of tight curls, dark blond and clipped fairly short. He had a peeling red nose and blue eyes in a tan face. Salt air and sun had bleached his eyebrows to the color of straw, which made his eyes appear all the bluer. He wore blue jeans and a Mexican wedding shirt made of the rough off-white cotton the Mexicans call *manta,* embroidered with flowers and butterflies.

"I guess you heard me singing when you came up to the door," he said with a smile, more amused than embarrassed.

"Loved it. I was hoping to hear the rest."

"There isn't any rest. I only made up those two lines about five minutes ago."

"Shucks. Your bumper sticker cracked me up, too—honk if you love Huitz somebody or other."

"Huitznahuatlecamalácotl. A minor Aztec deity. I ran across the name in a book called *Leyendas Aztecas*—right behind your head there."

"You speak Spanish too, then."

"Like everybody else in the family. You do know, don't you—but hell, of course you do!—my name was Atterbury. And, uh, putting two and two together, I would guess that Lieutenant Puterbaugh has let you look at the dossier he compiled on me—and a juicy tome that must be!"

"True. It's what the critics call 'a good read.'"

"A page-turner."

"A sweeping saga of one of California's famous families."

"Soon to be a major motion picture. Like a beer? I've got Carta Blanca in the fridge."

"Great. Thanks. And listen, forget the dossier. My sister Alison claims you're the white sheep of the family."

"Hey! Alison Stephens is your sister? Now there is one terrific lady and a hell of an artist! Aunt Maria was crazy about her."

Rollie pried the caps off two Carta Blancas and gave one to Cliff with a glass. "Isn't it funny," he observed, "that Mexico makes the best beer in the world? They've got at least six brands that tie for Numero Uno."

Cliff agreed. They went silent for a space, enjoying the beer.

"How did you pick the name Freed? Was it symbolic?"

"Betcher ass it was. I never liked the name Atterbury anyway. Sounds kind of silly, like 'attaboy.' I've often wondered whether it actually means anything."

"It does. It means your English ancestors lived 'æt thære byrig'—in the fortified town. Your family's probably been merchants for five or six hundred years."

"Oh, yeah, I remember Alison saying her brother taught medieval English literature. As for Freed: Without overdoing the self-exposure, let me tell you how that came about. You know from the sweeping saga the hell I raised during my adolescent rebellion—stolen cars, shoplifting, burglarizing neighbors' houses in the nude. All perfectly normal, of course. Just trying to get my parents' attention," he added with a grin.

"Did it work?"

"In ways none of us expected. I knew I'd get punished, but I welcomed that: Punishment is attention, after all—not tender loving care, maybe, but attention."

"What was the punishment?"

Rollie pulled his bare feet up, crossed them under him, and picked at his toenails. He grinned in renewed wonderment at the memory.

"Psychoanalysis! Mind you, I'm sure they wanted to help

me solve my problems and thus help solve one of their problems, but I sensed a further secret message: 'Rollie, your behavior is so bad we're going to have your head examined. That'll teach you a lesson!' " He laughed delightedly.

Cliff laughed with him and said, "Sounds like Bre'r Rabbit being flung into the briar patch."

"Right on! And the Atterbury family was the tarbaby I was stuck to. Mind you, I resented being a captive patient at first. But it wasn't long before I made a sensational discovery: The process works! I started getting healthier and happier." He picked up his guitar. "Ever been in analysis?"

"No, I've never been unhappy enough to feel the need."

"Lucky you. Or maybe unlucky. Anyway, I learned many things both large and small. One of the small ones was why I used to think the funniest song I ever heard went like this."

Rollie strummed the guitar in two-four time and sang:

"Hurrah! Hurrah! My father's gonna be hung!
Hurrah! Hurrah! The dirty son of a gun!
 For he was very mean to me
 When I was very young.
Hurrah, hurrah, they're going to hang my fah-ther!"

"Lyrics by Oedipus," said Cliff. "What kind of man was your father—aside from neglectful?"

"Authoritarian and totally self-centered. He judged everything by reference to his ego and the store. Lionel was supposed to be heir to the throne. Grant was a backup in case anything happened to Lionel. Connie was a girl and therefore superfluous, but she was tolerated because she was beautiful and therefore was good PR for the store, so he turned her loose with an allowance to do as she pleased. And then, years later, along I came, unplanned, unneeded, and unwanted—one of those minor annoyances that will crop up now and again. They didn't know what the hell to do with me, so they supplied food, clothing, shelter, and an allowance, and otherwise ignored me."

"Where did you get the strength to rebel? Somebody in your family must have been a model of strength."

Rollie pondered this and his eyebrows went up in surprise. "Son of a gun! My father! Maybe I owe something to the old goat after all. Come to think of it, he gave the shaft to *his* father, and that's how the store began to develop into the institution it is today."

"What was it he did?"

"In the nineteen-twenties, when he was in his twenties, my grandfather sent him to France on a buying tour—you know: Limoges, Sèvres, Gobelin tapestries, all that stuff. He bought a lot of it, but he also got hooked on Utrillo's paintings and went all over Montmartre buying them up. Kind of an odd fascination, because my father was far from being an aesthete, regardless of what the 'View' section of the *L.A. Times* would have you believe. My theory is that all those bare walls in Utrillo's paintings, those sinister street lamps, those bleak streets with no people in them, that one closed window up on the sixth floor shutting in somebody's despair: all those matched my father's psyche. He also bought up a few drawings and paintings by Utrillo's mother, Suzanne Valadon."

"I know. Lionel offered me one if I solve your Aunt Maria's murder."

"Jesus Christ! Murder! And here I am shooting my mouth off about my father and Utrillo."

"Go ahead. It's fascinating."

"Yeah, but it isn't going to help your sleuthing any. In fact, I'd better warn you I've been out of touch with the family so long I can't possibly tell you anything useful."

"Except with your Aunt Maria, no? Finish about Utrillo."

"Okay. Utrillo was nutty as a pet coon, you know: dope addict, alcoholic, neurotic, psychotic. He used to trade his paintings for booze and food. Every bar and brasserie in Montmartre had his stuff. My father went around buying it up, and I mean cheap. The owners were tickled silly, of course. Dad also ran into Utrillo himself one day, painting on the Place du Tertre up by Sacré Coeur. A bunch of little French kids gathered around watching him and started begging him to let them paint too. So he let them take turns with a brush, and once in a while they'd put in touches he liked, and when they went away he left those touches in and painted out the rest. My father bought that painting too. He ended up with damn near an Utrillo monopoly. To keep the prices up, the store sold only one or two at a time. And it's one of Atterbury's best-kept secrets that there still must be a dozen or so in one of their temperature-and-humidity-controlled storerooms. Anyway, books about the store and about my father always mention his 'acquaintance' with Utrillo and how he was one of the first to sense the artist's talent. There's some truth to that, but part of his motivation was to irritate the hell out of his own father, who blew his top over how much money my father had spent. Say, listen, Doctor Dunbar—"

"Cliff."

"Cliff. I don't know what it is with me. Maybe it's the solitude, but I haven't been such a motor-mouth in weeks. *Sangre de Cristo!* I've got to have another beer to wash the cotton off my tongue. I'll get us both one."

Two more frosty Carta Blancas emerged from the refrigerator. He gave one to Cliff and said, "Put your feet up on the other chair and relax, and let's see if I can condense this. Father. Reputed to be art connoisseur. Bullshit. But great at sensing trends. Fads. New directions in public taste. Just a canny businessman. Grandfather dies. Father becomes Grand Mamamouchi of Beverly Hills. Chinese revolution. Mao comes in, rich jade merchants flee to Hong Kong to escape Communists. Need cash. Guess Who shows up and buys 'em out. A few years later, Guess Who suddenly gets sentimental about our Mexican heritage and buys up all the pre-Columbian artifacts he can get his hands on, just before the prices go

82

into orbit. Once more, like the Utrillos, the store quietly releases maybe eight pieces a year, usually to museums. . . . Hey, what the hell got me started on this?"

"I dunno, but I'm enjoying it."

"And wondering when we'll get around to Aunt Maria's murder. What exactly would you like to know?"

"Beats me. But it's possible you may have been throwing out clues without knowing it, so why don't you finish about your analysis?"

"That'll be easy. The big thing I learned was that I had to get completely out of that family or I was ruined. It was hard and it left scars, but I did it. I even changed my name so I wouldn't be tempted to fall back on the old ploy of just-a-minute-there-you-happen-to-be-talking-to-an-Atterbury so as to impress people or get out of a jam."

"How did your father take it when you did that?"

"You should have seen his face! An Oscar performance! Somehow the man registered outrage, insult, and relief all at the same time." Rollie glanced at his watch. "Listen, I have to go check my trot lines. Want to come along? We can talk in the boat."

"Sure. Sounds like fun."

Rollie put on socks, canvas shoes, a yachting cap and dark glasses, took two more Carta Blancas out of the refrigerator, and they went out.

They strolled down the lane and across the parking lot, through the shade of the sycamore and eucalyptus trees, and out into the bright sun at the foot of the pier. Rollie's boat was tied up at a floating platform along with a cluster of rental skiffs painted pumpkin yellow.

Rollie clamped his outboard motor onto the transom and they cast off. Rollie steered toward a bait boat anchored out toward the end of the pier.

"Take the cover off the live-bait tank, will you, Cliff?" The tank was a square wooden box aslosh with seawater in the middle of the boat. At the bait boat, a fisherman in black hip boots scooped half a dip-net of anchovies out of his own live-bait tank, swung it out, and emptied it into Rollie's.

"Thanks, Verne!"

Cliff replaced the tank cover and Rollie revved the motor.

"Okay," said Rollie. "Let's go see how many fish have committed suicide since yesterday afternoon."

"How far out are we going?"

"Close. Five hundred yards, maybe. Funny thing: Just down the coast at Santa Monica the water's no more than thirty feet deep for two miles out. Tom cod, mackerel, opal-eye, smelt, a few bonito—that's about it. But right below us, the bottom drops off to about three hundred feet, deep enough so we get real blue-water fish."

Sitting in the sun, rocked by the gentle swells, Cliff sank back into contentment so relaxing he almost lapsed into self-hypnosis.

"Rollie, that loan ledger at the Atterbury store."

"Yeah?"

"Does it really look like a ledger?"

"It actually is one—gray-green with red leather corners, double-column pages. Why?"

"People've mentioned it. Are your watercolors in it or has Grant called them in?"

"Ha!" Rollie grinned with delight. "Clifford, you just made yourself a lifelong friend. I painted those myself!"

"You did! Well, listen, I'm no art critic but they looked first-rate to me. Have you ever considered exhibiting?"

"Oh, hell no. There were certain things I wanted painted in a certain way, and to get 'em I had to paint 'em myself. But I don't want to be an artist. I'm too fond of eating. Besides, ever since I was a kid I wanted to be a fisherman—and voilà!"

Cliff looked at Rollie's beaming face, enjoying that rarity, a man who truly loves his work. Mona and Alison were like that, too. It gave Cliff a twinge to realize that he himself was still adrift, with no specific destination.

"But wouldn't it help to have a little more money?" He

84

gestured at the boat with his right hand. "You won't be content to stay permanently at this level, will you? Or do you have a chunk of Atterbury money in the bank?"

"Yes it would, and no I don't. Oh, I accepted a few thousand in what you might call severance pay to get me started down here, but otherwise it was a clean break."

"I was thinking of my sister. She owns a gallery, and I think she'd be interested in your paintings."

"Well, fine. That'd be great. I'll bring 'em by some time, and no hard feelings if she thinks they stink. . . . Here we are." He cut the motor and drifted toward a yellow marker buoy, the first of several to which his trot lines were attached. His initials were painted on it.

"Grab that, will you?"

Cliff caught hold of the buoy and held it for Rollie, who had slipped on a pair of gloves. Rollie took the line and began working it in hand over hand. Cliff peered into the deep water. After several minutes, something resembling a pink dumbbell shimmered below. When it reached the surface it proved to be a reddish-colored fish that seemed to have been chewing bubble gum, for it had blown a big pink bubble that protruded from its mouth.

"I haven't seen that before," said Cliff. "What is it?"

"Red snapper. When they come up from deep water, their air bladder pops right out of their mouths. Weird, huh?"

Rollie had eight hooks on his trot line and caught six fish: four red snapper, one sea bass, and one rock cod. He tossed them all in a chest, baited the hooks once more with anchovies, and lowered the line again.

"Not exactly rollicking sport, is it?" he said with a grin.

"Nope. I'm a fly fisherman for trout and bass. Two-pound-test tippet, and I release nearly all of them. Keep one or two for dinner once in a while."

"Sounds great. Well, I won't always be a meat-hunter like this." He fired up the outboard and they moved on to the next marker buoy. "My goal is to become a charter-boat skipper."

"Whereabouts?"

"Kailua-Kona—the Kona Coast on Hawaii, the Big Island."

"I fished it when I was a kid," said Cliff. "My dad was an infantry officer at Schofield Barracks on Oahu."

Red snapper were again in the majority at the next buoy. "Looks like red snapper will be my customers' catch of the day," said Rollie. "Whereas," he added, with great emphasis, "in July nineteen-seventy-nine a guy caught a record nine hundred fifty-four-pound Pacific blue marlin off the Kona Coast, on fifty-pound-test line."

Rollie's face went dreamy and wistful. "I damn near made it over there this month. So near and yet so far."

"What happened?"

"The murder. Aunt Maria. I've got a confession to make, but don't whip out your handcuffs just yet. She and I got along real well. I don't know that I loved her, but I liked her a lot and I dropped in to see her now and again—once while your sister was painting her portrait. Aunt Maria liked me, too, although I lost most of my significance to her when I abdicated from the family. Anyway, she wanted to help me buy a boat I had my eye on in Hawaii and still do. She was actually willing to give me—give me, mind you—a hundred thousand dollars."

"Did you take it?"

"Hell, no! She said the family owed that to me, at least; and I said one of the main reasons I opted out of the family was to get completely away from Atterbury money so I wouldn't be ruined. And she said, 'Okay, I'll loan it to you, then.' I didn't even want to accept that, but she kept insisting, and I saw it would make her happy, to say nothing of me, so I took it on condition she let me write her a promissory demand note so she could yank it back any time she wanted."

"Kind of risky, wasn't it? Did you consider the bind you'd be in if she died?"

"Sure, but she was killed before I could spend the money."

Suddenly, Cliff remembered, "Oh, hey!"

"Right," said Rollie. "The note was in the pocket of her dressing gown when she was murdered, and my signature was torn off. At first I thought she did it herself; it would be like her to try to force the money on me as a gift that way."

"But that doesn't quite make sense, does it?" said Cliff.

"No. She would have torn the whole thing up, or burned it or whatever. Which means that the murderer did it to throw suspicion on me."

"But that doesn't make much sense either, does it? If you had been the murderer, you, too, would have destroyed the whole note."

"Not only that," added Rollie, "there's the bank records: Aunt Maria's check to me with my endorsement on it, and the deposit in my account. No, that was clumsy. Whoever did it wasn't thinking any too clearly."

"You still have all the money?"

"Sure. It's in the bank drawing interest—which I will keep, but when Grant and Sidney Colfax catch up with me, of course I'll fork over the hundred thousand. I sure as hell don't want to get mixed up in an Atterbury lawsuit. I'm glad, now, I didn't jump on the Hatteras the minute I had Aunt Maria's check."

"What's a Hatteras?"

"The boat in Kailua. It's a forty-one-foot Sportfisherman with a full flying bridge. Sleeps eight. I know the guy selling it. He's asking a hundred forty thousand and I think I can get it for a hundred twenty, or I should say could have gotten it."

"Are you disappointed?"

"Oh . . . some. But, on the other hand, I'll be completely free of the Atterburys again and, what the hell, there's more than one way to skin a cat."

"You keep talking about being free of the Atterburys. What does that mean, specifically? Not depending on them for money?"

"That's half of it. It means I'm not willing to join the others in their endless round-robin, neurotic games in exchange for a little money."

"I don't get that."

"Let's see if I can put it in a nutshell, maybe a big nut-shell." Rollie cut the motor and laid the latest marker buoy by his feet. For a few moments his eyes followed an orange and black oil tanker headed up the coast toward San Francisco, its long, flat profile lying low on the horizon. A seagull glided down and hung suspended over their heads to see if Rollie planned to do any chumming with live bait; the answer being no, the bird flounced off with an angry screech.

"Atterburys are trained to hate each other, and at the same time glory in the name of Atterbury. I believe my grandfather at least disliked my father, partly because my father sneered at him and partly because he knew my father was twice the businessman he was. And then there's Lionel, Grant, Connie, and me. Like I said, Lionel was supposed to be heir to the throne. But Father was not only an authoritarian son of a bitch, he was a monumental egotist. From the time Lionel was a kid, Father told him he would replace him one day as head of the store, but could never equal him. He'd tell Lionel about his brilliant coups, buying the Utrillos and the jade and the pre-Columbian art, and then he'd say—I actually heard him say this several times, Cliff—'You'll never be the man I am, Lionel.' "

"That's a hell of a thing to say to a son," said Cliff.

"But the worst part of it was, Lionel not only believed him but went on adulating him and telling everybody what a great man his father was. Well, I should talk. I was sort of like that till I got into analysis. Meanwhile, Grant is being instilled with the idea that Father isn't all that sure of Lionel, and Grant better be prepared to take over in case Lionel louses up."

"Tweedledum and Tweedledee."

"Yeah—agreed to have a battle. Then Connie. Connie was completely out of it because she was a girl. Even so, if Father had just left her alone, she might have been perfectly contented with the social life of the idle rich—Monte Carlo, skiing in Switzerland, an occasional charity ball, that kind of shit. But, no. It had to be impressed on her that only lower-class women work, and only on jobs that don't require much brainpower. That meant she was far inferior to Lionel and Grant, whom she was encouraged to hate. And to finish her off, instead of being given means of her own, she had to depend on an allowance that she had to kiss ass to get and that Father cut down on whenever he disapproved of her behavior. And then there's me."

"Do you think one of them killed Aunt Maria?"

Rollie looked at him in surprise. "Now, that's a hell of a question. Do you really expect an answer?"

"That's up to you."

"It raises some nice moral questions. But let me point out that I don't hate my three sibs in the first place, and even if I did I don't know that I'd finger them for murder. How about you? What if you knew your sister Alison killed her? Would you turn her in?"

"No."

"Okay. With that out of the way, I'm willing to answer your question. No, I don't think one of them did. None of them hated her enough, and none of them would have gained anything. Grant got what he wanted; Connie was used to being short-changed; and Lionel's beef was with Father, not Maria. Sure, Lionel hoped she'd change her will, but killing her just doesn't fit his character."

"Do you even care who did it?" said Cliff.

"Not particularly. I think the murderer is somebody in one of the outer rings, but I'm not keen on vengeance. I'm sorry Aunt Maria's gone, but have you stopped to consider the ghastly punishment the guilty party is already suffering?"

"In what way?"

"Well, assuming you're not a sociopath with no feeling whatsoever, can you imagine a worse private hell than going

89

through life knowing you're a murderer? Straining to rationalize it somehow? Feeling like a hypocritical shit if someone claps you on the back and tells you what a fine fellow you are? No, the murderer has already paid, so on with the show. Mind you, I'm not talking about gangsters or killers who butcher innocent people for money."

"So you think I should just give up the sleuthing?"

"Up to you. I told you my sentiments, but most decent people would be disgusted with me, so if you go on with it, *vaya con Dios* and I wish you luck. I mean that."

"You've just made my job a little harder."

"How come?"

"As you spoke, I realized I largely agree with you, and I don't know that I want to."

Rollie grinned and reeled in his trot line. "Came out of the depths of your unconscious, did it—like the red snapper?"

"Yes. The cases aren't exactly the same, but I just thought of my own father. He was a fine infantry officer, good at his work, and he enjoyed the military life. But one day a few years back—I'm sure my mother's death had something to do with it—it dawned on him that although armies may be necessary, he wanted his life to consist of something more than being a trained killer. So Dad resigned his commission and went to work for the Nature Conservancy."

"Hurrah for him! *Your* father shouldn't be hung!"

As they moved off toward the next buoy, Rollie said, "You know who I really feel sorry for? Gwyneth."

Cliff felt the same way, but asked, "How come? Most people would say she's sitting on top of the world."

"Yeah, with the North Pole stuck up her ass. It's ironic: Just as I broke free of the Atterburys, she made the catch of the year and married Grant. Do you know her background?"

"No."

"She tells people her father's in government. Which he is in a way: He's a mosquito control officer in Orange County. That's useful work, of course, and something to be proud of, but not among the women in Atterbury social circles. If they found out about it they'd regard it as quaint, precious, dahling, and droll. They give her a pretty tough time as it is. 'Ahfter all, she hadn't a bean when Grant picked her out of the gutter, gawd knows where.' "

"At Consuelo's cocktail party yesterday, she commented that there are easier things in life than being an Atterbury."

"That's for damn sure. Bird in a gilded cage."

"Why doesn't she get out, then? In this day and age there's nothing to it. No-fault divorce, and there'd be a property settlement."

"She doesn't know what the hell to do. Were you able to sense that under all that sultry sexiness she's actually a confused and timid little girl?"

Cliff was now genuinely startled. "Uh—well, no, I can't say I did."

"She is, though. She doesn't know what she wants. She knows better, but she can't shake herself loose from the high school notion that the ideal goal for a girl is to snag a rich husband and live happily ever after. Okay, so she did it, and now she's puzzled because she isn't happy. I told her she'd be a lot better off controlling mosquitos."

"When did you tell her that?"

"I don't know. This summer. She actually came down to talk to me a couple of times—without telling Grant or anybody, naturally. She was feeling at loose ends. I took her fishing."

Cliff laughed. "Now, that is hard for me to picture! Gwyneth in a boat with her feet in bilge water! You don't mean this kind of fishing, do you?"

"Oh, hell no. We just trolled around out here for mackerel and bonito. Man, you should have heard her yell when a big bonito would strike and zing off toward Japan! She was beautiful! She was a different person—a warm and delightful human being. None of that Beverly Hills jazz. I wanted to shut her up in my place and save her soul."

"Through psychotherapy?"

"That's what it actually would take. I suggested it and then dropped the subject."

"How did she react?"

"Said she'd think it over. Meaning no. But I have hopes for her. She's basically a fine person. Hell, so are Lionel and Grant and Connie—and me, for that matter. We all started out as normal decent kids, and then our parents grabbed each one of us by the throat with one hand and the top of the head with the other and gave a good twist—a permanent kink. Then we all became barrels, the object being to fill us with bullshit and then nail down the lid. In the Atterbury family that's called child-raising."

"You're still pretty bitter about it."

"Betcher ass. That's why I want to be careful as hell when and if I ever get married. I don't want to turn my poor wife into the mommy and daddy I never had. I've got to be my own father. Okay, we can head back now."

"What about those two buoys over there?" Cliff asked, pointing to them. They were perhaps sixty or seventy yards away, over toward Point Dume, a rocky promontory marking the northern extremity of the bay.

"Nah. I've got lobster pots on those two, just in case any lobsters are left around here. Maybe I'll check 'em out tomorrow or the next day. Used to be a lot of 'em before scuba diving got to be a big fad here, but those guys cleaned 'em out. Some of 'em weighed twelve, fifteen pounds. Used to be a lot of ab, too, and now they're gone."

"Ab?"

"Abalone."

Rollie gunned the motor, and the boat wallowed toward shore leaving a heavy wake because of the added weight of Rollie's catch.

"Have you talked to Gwyneth lately?" said Cliff.

"Nope," Rollie replied, looking dead ahead. "She's too

busy, I guess, dealing with Grant and the police—and playing grownup Spin the Bottle with some of her admiring swains."

"Can I pump you for one last piece of information?"

"If I've got it."

"It's about your father's will and the trust and Aunt Maria's role. I never could grasp the legal details."

"It's not too complex. Originally, my father set up a spendthrift trust with Lionel in charge of things as head of the family and president of the store."

"What's a spendthrift trust?"

"Give me a chance! The idea is to force the beneficiaries to behave themselves—conform with its terms—and prevent them from squandering the assets of the trust. The will left a few shares in the store to various heirs, but most went into the trust. The heirs were to receive dividends, but not income directly from the store. Lionel was to be trustee, with total voting power of the stock, but he couldn't defraud the trust— by selling shares, say, or giving himself huge bonuses. He wouldn't need to, though, because he was to receive most of the income. Grant, Connie, and Aunt Maria were to get small percentages."

"What about you?"

Rollie smiled. "I was left two shares of Atterbury stock. I've kept 'em for souvenirs. So, my father built Lionel up and castrated him at the same time. He gave Lionel his own office at the store, but constantly undercut him and warned him— hounded him—not to drink, not to run around with loose women, not to give his floozies gifts from the store, not to cause scandal, not to get his name in the papers. Can you guess what Lionel did?"

"Just a shot in the dark," said Cliff, "but did he drink, whore, scatter largess, and get his name in the papers?"

"How shrewd you are, Dunbar. Once, he combined 'em all. He got drunk, took his sweet patootie down to the store at midnight, unlocked the front door, gave her a Chinese-silk cocktail dress worth five hundred dollars, socked a cop who was investigating the unlocked door, and ended up with his name and his picture on the front page of the *Beverly Hills Tageblatt*. Father thereupon made Grant the trustee and told Lionel if he didn't straighten up and fly right, that's the way it was going to stay—even though Grant didn't have much of a head for business, being more interested in music, plus black-jack and roulette in Las Vegas.

"Lionel, of course, went on proving his independence by means of cigarettes and whiskey and wild, wild women. Then he sort of leveled off, got most of it out of his system. The customers loved him, by the way. They even loved his being something of a scalawag. He was colorful. He was alive. He was genuinely interested in people. All kinds of struggling young artists wanted to work at the great Atterbury's, and he'd hire them and overpay them. He'd appraise people's an-tiques and art objects for nothing. That sort of thing. Then one day he was about to wrap up a ten-thousand-dollar sale to Mrs. Rosecrans—"

"Of the Rosecrans Boulevard Rosecranses?"

"None other. It was a complete silver service, plus Lenox dinnerware for eighteen, and all sorts of Baccarat glasses. Suddenly Father shows up and says, 'You run along now, Lionel, I'll take care of Mrs. Rosecrans.' Lionel trotted off like a good little eunuch. Mrs. Rosecrans was somewhat sur-prised, but then it pleased her to be waited on by the great Lewis Atterbury himself."

"Lionel didn't complain?"

"Nope. When I heard about it, I once more said to him, 'Lionel, can't you see that Father is not a great man but a prize prick? Don't you resent what he did?' Lionel just said, 'Oh, no—no,' and his eyes sort of wandered off somewhere, maybe to a spider on the ceiling."

"So what happened with the trust?"

"We all knew Father intended to restore Lionel as chief trustee, but before he could do it he dropped dead of a heart attack in his office. And then things got really interesting. It turned out that my father had not reworked the trust. He had made a will leaving everything to Aunt Maria, but putting her on her honor to draw up her own will to duplicate the original provisions of the spendthrift trust, with Grant as chief trustee—but only if Lionel failed to straighten himself out. Follow that?"

"Sure."

"So for a while there, Maria ran the store herself and did a hell of a good job, until she was hit with myasthenia gravis. Then she turned the presidency over to Grant. Meanwhile, she drew up her will, and since she and my father were close, and since she respected his wishes, she made Grant chief beneficiary while she watched Lionel's bumpy progress. You know the rest."

Rollie slowed the boat as they approached the landing. "Hop out and tie us up, will you?"

Picking up the bow line with both hands—left hand palm down over the line, right hand palm up under it—Cliff did a half twist counterclockwise with each hand, laid the right-hand bight over the left one, leaped nimbly onto the landing, and dropped the resulting knot over a bollard.

"Well, I'll be raked in a pile and burned!" Rollie exclaimed. "You know how to pick up a steamboat hitch!"

"Just showing off. I know three ways to tie a clove hitch, including that one."

Rollie hopped out and secured the stern line.

"Need any help with the fish?"

"No. I use the boat-launching hoist over there to lift the whole box out. Then I load it into the Brat and off I go. I'll drive the Brat down here first."

They walked back through the parking lot to the foot of Rollie's lane.

"I'll say good-bye to you here," said Cliff. "Thanks a hell of a lot for all the information."

"Have you deduced who the murderer is from what I've told you?" said Rollie with a mischievous grin.

"Nope. But I suspect you didn't do it."

"You're right, I didn't. And thanks for your help. It's nice to have company."

"My pleasure. It's nice to run into somebody who loves his work. I envy you. And listen: I'll mention your watercolors to my sister."

They shook hands and parted.

"Good luck!" Cliff called after him as Rollie strode up the lane. Rollie waved back without turning.

11

PINKY SCHIFFLEGER GREETED them at the front door the following Monday morning. "Hello, Lieutenant! Everything's under control. I got them cutworms buffaloed!" He laughed and clapped the lieutenant on the shoulder. Puterbaugh gave him a faint smile and said, "It's flea beetles in the dichondra got me worried now."

Pinky laughed all the harder. "Tell me the lieutenant isn't a card? What can I do for you folks?"

Alison explained what they were there for.

"Gosh, here we go again! Mr. Atterbury ordered me not to let anybody in without his okay—except police, of course."

"They're with me," said Puterbaugh, "and we're all here on police business."

"Okay, you're the boss, Lieutenant."

The portrait still stood on the easel in Maria's bedroom. Alison rummaged through her box of paints once more, and then scrutinized the portrait front and back. She frowned and scratched her head. "Lieutenant Puterbaugh, come look at this. . . . Careful, the paint's still wet."

Cliff and Mona also crowded in for a look.

"Somebody," said Alison, "has pried out every other staple I stretched this canvas with. Now why would anyone do that?"

"Looking for something," said the lieutenant.

"But what could they hide under a narrow strip of canvas?"

"Nothing very big, that's for sure. Something no more than an inch wide and two inches long. Gold coins? Microfilm? An important key? A message?"

"And who could have done the hiding?" said Alison.

"At this point, almost anybody. Maria herself, maybe. Rosetta Stone. Socorro. Anybody that's been through here."

"Next question," said Cliff. "Did they find what they were looking for?"

"Who knows, Fosdick? Why don't you feel around in there and see if they left a receipt?"

"Tell me you're not a card?"

Mona had been gazing off in the distance, a thoughtful look on her face. "Lieutenant, when your men from the crime lab went over the murder scene, did they vacuum the floor and the furniture and analyze all the stuff in the bag?"

"Sure."

"Did they find any staples?"

"Hey . . . good thinking. No, they didn't, which either means the killer carefully pocketed them, or else this was done after the murder. Not that that tells us anything. I suppose everybody on this case has visited the house at least once since then, or could have. Okay, we'll make a note of this for the record and hope it connects up with something."

On the way out, Puterbaugh told Pinky Schiffleger to start keeping a log of all visits and visitors, no matter who they were, family or nonfamily, although he felt sure he was locking the barn after the horse was stolen.

"How come you wanted me to go with you?" Mona asked. The orange Porsche had tooled up the slope of Santa Monica Canyon hooked sharply to the right and up a steeper grade to merge with Ocean Avenue.

"Because I love you, I enjoy your company, and I didn't want to leave you at home all by yourself."

"That's what I like to hear. Anything else?"

"Yes. In some areas, you're smarter than I am."

"You mean like southern California?"

"Duh, yeah. But I don't mean only geography. I mean certain subjects, too, like medicine. You know lingo that I don't. Also, I suspect you're a better judge of character."

He turned left off Ocean Avenue onto Georgina and went up a block and a half or so. Doctor Gates's house proved to be a white two-story colonial with four Corinthian columns. The door opened before they could ring.

"You're right on the dot," said the doctor. "I wish my patients had been as prompt. Come in, come in!"

The doctor's abundant gray hair rose up from his forehead and subsided on the back of his head like a breaker on the beach. His face was tanned to a dark mahogany, and his shirt sleeves were rolled up, revealing sinewy brown arms. The doctor was perhaps seventy, but would probably live to be a hundred.

He escorted them to a glassed-in sun porch, flooded with light and full of healthy green plants, and he seated them in comfortable wicker chairs with cushions covered in green and white flowered chintz. On a table beside the doctor's chair, a thick volume bound in dusty-rose cloth lay open, face down. Cliff noted with pleasure that it was *Martin Chuzzlewit*.

"Yes, I'm getting educated at last," said Doctor Gates. "My God, retirement is fun! Let me fix you two a gin and tonic. Some doctors think it expands the blood vessels. Good an excuse as any."

He produced three frosted glasses from a small refrigerator behind his wet bar and concocted a trio of drinks complete with limes.

"Okay," he said, settling in his chair. He gestured with his glass. "This is one of the things Maria Atterbury had to give up. Not the gin—the tonic. Anything with quinine in it worsens the symptoms of myasthenia gravis. She didn't find that a great sacrifice since she prefers wine anyway. Now, what else can I tell you within the bounds of ethics?"

"Were you Maria's doctor for a long time?" asked Cliff.

"You mean her 'primary care physician,' as they call it nowadays?" He snorted. "About fifteen years."

"Are you the one who diagnosed her myasthenia?"

"I regret to say I was."

"How bad a disease is it?"

"It's bad. It's incurable, so far, and it's expensive—although the cost didn't matter to her, of course. But myasthenia gravis isn't nearly as 'gravis' as it used to be. Up until nineteen thirty-four, a shocking eighty-five percent of patients died within two years after their symptoms appeared. Nowadays, it's seldom fatal, but it's still frightening and it's certainly bothersome. Myasthenics poop out fast. They wake up in the morning with a limited store of strength, and they have to be stingy about expending it during the day. Nonetheless, the common thing is to wind up pooped in the evening. It comes and goes, though. Some myasthenics can go for months at a time in perfectly normal health and then, socko!—a crisis floors them."

"You'd better back up a little," said Cliff. "I don't even know what the disease is."

"It sounds simple," said the doctor. "It's a lack of communication between the nerves and the muscles. Makes you weak as a cat. Maria Atterbury came to see me one day complaining it was getting so she had to take a nap in her office every afternoon, and lately the naps had been getting longer and longer. She was also seeing double part of the time and had trouble keeping her balance. Once she fell against a display table in the china department and caused a hell of a racket of broken dishes and a lot of embarrassment. By the time she got in to see me, she had the full set of symptoms."

"What are they?" asked Mona. "This sounds familiar."

Doctor Gates rattled his ice cubes. "Let's see, there are nine symptoms, five of 'em 'difficulties': difficulty walking, breathing, talking, chewing, and swallowing. Double vision. Loss of balance. High nasal voice. That's eight, isn't it? What the heck is the ninth?"

"Drooping eyelid?" suggested Mona.

"Right! How did you know that, young lady?"

100

"I've seen her portrait. And Alison Stephens told us that Maria wanted it in the painting."

"That's a charming and intelligent woman, that artist."

"She's my sister," said Cliff.

"Oho!" said the doctor. "Another one of those fortunate social escapes! Aren't I lucky that she is charming, and that I thought so! She's also talented, I hardly need say."

"You said myasthenia is incurable," said Cliff. "Does that mean Maria would have died soon?"

"I also said it's seldom fatal these days. It partly depends on who the doctor is. And of course any doctor named Gates is bound to be called Pearly Gates. You know the gag: The patient was at death's door, but I pulled her through? Ah, yes, to tell the truth, I was kind of relieved to pass her case on to somebody else. There isn't much satisfaction in just helping a patient to live with an affliction and tolerate some amount of pain. But that's what the doctor's function amounted to up with just about everything until the last forty or forty-five years. And then came the sulfas and antibiotics and Salk vaccine, and all the rest, and, lo and behold, we were actually able to cure some diseases!"

"May I ask you something?" said Mona. "What's your opinion of Craig Rawlings? Is he a good doctor?"

Doctor Gates smiled. "He's okay. He'd be even better if he could read."

Cliff and Mona raised their eyebrows.

"And I suspect he'd be better yet if he didn't have those movie-star looks, but that may be an envious old man talking. I'm sure he's adequate with most of his patients, especially when you consider that most people who come into a doctor's office are suffering from psychosomatic ailments. With Rawlings, they feel obliged to get better. They want his approval."

The doctor paused to give his lime an extra squeeze, and stirred his gin and tonic with an index finger.

"Trouble is, it's too easy for a doctor to get lazy. If patients flock to you because you're good-looking, ninety percent of them will get well regardless—or at least better. It's pretty easy to let your medical reading slide and just refer people to specialists if their cases get sticky."

"Are you referring to Doctor Rawlings now?" said Cliff with a smile.

"Now, where would you get an idea like that? We doctors don't like to bad-mouth each other, you know, especially in a courtroom. Consequently, before I expand on my remarks, let me remind you that I said Doctor Rawlings is competent and would be even better if he read more copiously. As would we all."

"Understood," said Cliff.

"And now, with that out of the way, let me describe how the son of a bitch handled Maria's myasthenia."

Cliff and Mona burst into surprised laughter.

"Tell us first how come he ever got brought into the case," said Mona. "I can't visualize Maria getting the hots for him."

"It was the family, mainly Grant and Gwyneth Atterbury. They persuaded Maria she should get a younger doctor with more up-to-date training. I can't blame her. Myasthenics have a lot to worry about, including the chance of sudden death, so they're willing to listen to anybody with new ideas. In this case, however, Grant and Gwyneth were the only ones with new ideas. I honestly don't believe Rawlings even knew what myasthenia gravis was until he was called in. As tactfully as I could, I tried to brief him on the disease and give him my opinion on the best way to manage Maria's case—her medication, an indicated thymectomy at UCLA Medical Center, things to avoid, and so on."

"And he listened with half an ear," said Mona.

"How did you ever guess? Yes, it was partly resistance to being lectured to by a superannuated old fart, and partly it was eagerness to strut his own stuff. To get any credit, he would obviously have to do things differently from what I did. For starters, he strongly opposed a thymectomy for Maria."

"Which is what?"

"Removal of the thymus gland, which often seems responsible for producing or triggering the body's production of antibodies that keep the receptors at the junction of nerves and muscles from functioning. About two-thirds of myasthenics benefit significantly from thymectomy. In fact, of all the forms of treatment we have, it seems to offer the greatest promise of lasting improvement or remission. This isn't just my opinion—it's the opinion of the local Myasthenia Gravis Foundation."

"Then why the heck would Rawlings oppose it?"

" 'Because,' he says, 'the risk is too high at her age.' "

"Could he be right?"

"If her physical condition had been lousy, he might have been, but it wasn't and her heart was good. Consequently, I concluded that Rawlings was unable to distinguish between the outlet of his digestive tract and a declivity in the soil."

Doctor Gates rose and took their glasses. "Let's have another one," he said. "My prescription on a warm day like this is gin and tonic, *dosim repetitur.*" He prepared another round with fresh limes and new ice.

"Now, on the question of medication he was on firmer ground, although I still didn't agree with him. The two chief drugs here are called Prostigmin, which is the older one, and Mestinon, which is probably the more popular and widely used one at present. The physician has to experiment to see what the right medication and the right dosage are for the particular patient. I thought Maria responded better to Prostigmin. Rawlings put her on Mestinon. Well, okay. Some patients need only two or three tablets a day. Others may down twenty to thirty of 'em, almost like popcorn. I had Maria on five Prostigmin; Rawlings put her on twenty Mestinon."

"Isn't that . . . suspicious?" said Mona.

"Oh, not necessarily. He had a right to experiment, too. But there's sort of a paradox here. Let's say you give the patient two tablets and the response is just swell; so you double the dose to four tablets, and to your surprise, instead of enjoying twice the benefit, the patient is worse off than before. The reason is that overmedication makes the symptoms worse. And by the way, so do other things, such as sedatives, tranquilizers, certain antibiotics, excessive fatigue, and emotional upset."

Cliff frowned. "I seem to recall the police report listing some rather strong sleeping pills among the medicines on her nightstand."

"I'm well aware of that," said the doctor acidly. "What she would need them for is beyond me, she was always so exhausted at the end of the day."

"Would you say, then, that Maria got a lot worse after Rawlings took over the case?"

"No doubt about it."

"Could it have been deliberate?"

"No comment."

"In what way was she worse?"

"Mainly, great fatigue started coming over her early in the day—to the point where she had to discontinue sitting for her portrait. And her hands got so weak it took an effort just to hold up a book and turn the pages."

"Did you drop in on Maria from time to time over the last couple of months?"

"Yes, I did, but only as a friendly gesture, not to butt in on her treatment. I also had an ulterior motive, though: I was waiting to see what Rawlings would do, with his hotshot expertise, if Maria went into myasthenic crisis, which I expected her to do at any time."

"Because of Rawlings's treatment?" asked Mona.

"Again, not necessarily. There are two kinds of crisis, and either one of them can kill the patient. That's why it's the myasthenic patient's worst bugaboo. One of them is the crisis of the disease itself. Rawlings couldn't be blamed for that. The other one is called cholinergic crisis, and it's the result of an overdose of an anti-myasthenia-gravis drug. That one would be Rawlings's fault."

"But wouldn't he be asking for it in that case?" said Cliff. "If not a murder charge, at least a malpractice suit for gross negligence?"

"Not at all. The two kinds of crisis are so much alike that even a specialist would have a tough time telling them apart. The catch is that the proper treatment for one crisis is the exact opposite of the treatment for the other. Pick the wrong crisis and the wrong treatment and the patient may well die. But if a specialist could make such a mistake, you couldn't blame Rawlings either."

Cliff frowned and lost himself in contemplation of the ceiling. He rubbed his bullet scar as he cogitated.

"Where'd you get the scar?" Dr. Gates asked.

"Vietnam."

"Considered plastic surgery?"

"No. I don't mind it except it's tough to shave down in the crease."

"Getting back to Maria," said Mona. "I've got several questions, mostly about the night of the murder. Number one: It appears that Maria was up and about that night, despite what you said about her extreme fatigue. How would you explain that?"

"Could be several things. With many patients, that fatigue comes and goes. She might have had a surge of energy that night just in the nature of things."

"Do you think that was likely in her case?"

"No. More likely, in spite of that registered nurse watching her like a hawk, she avoided taking a sleeping pill, and might even have been shrewd enough to lay off the Mestinon for a while to see what happened. If so, it's my hunch she returned to her former fatigue level, which at this point would almost convince her she'd had a remission."

"Why do you suppose she was so anxious to get up?"

"Your guess is as good as mine. Maybe she wanted to get

something out of that safe without being observed. The safe was found open, you know. Ordinarily, she wouldn't have been able to do that, but you'll recall that the nurse was out of it that night. Claimed she'd been drugged."

"And that," said Cliff, "brings up questions I wanted to ask. One of Nurse Stone's duties was to see that Maria took her medication, right? And that evening, not only did Maria not take her medication, but the nurse was sleeping like Rip Van Winkle. Claimed she was drugged. But if so, Maria's the only one who could have done it—her motive being her determination to get up. Fine, but how did she manage it?"

"You're forgetting the police report," said Mona. "They found tea things for two in all the shambles. Maria might have slipped her a mickey, so to speak, either with genuine chloral hydrate or maybe with sleeping pills she stashed away."

"Can I play detective, too?" Doctor Gates asked. "I earned my Dick Tracy gold badge when I was a kid in the early thirties. I fingerprinted every kid on my block back in Evanston."

"Go ahead," said Cliff. "I haven't turned pro yet."

"Rosetta Stone might have drugged herself to clear the way for the murderer, enjoy a perfect alibi, and blame it on Maria."

"Who hired Rosetta originally?" asked Mona. "You?"

"Gosh, no. She works out of an agency. Rawlings uses her all the time."

"Did Maria even need a nurse there full time?"

"It was a good idea, in case of emergency. The nurse was trained in CPR, of course. . . ." The doctor heaved a sigh. "Well, all this stuff we've been talking about: One blow on the head and it's knocked into a cocked hat. We'll never know how Rawlings would have behaved in a myasthenic crisis. The killer has saved his reputation. Ha! What if Rawlings killed her so she'd never have a crisis?"

"That's called preventive medicine," said Mona, to the delight of Doctor Gates.

"Is Gwyneth Atterbury a patient of Doctor Rawlings?" Cliff asked.

"Oh, yes. She was his patient even before Maria was."

"Was she ever your patient?"

Doctor Gates squirmed a bit. "Very, very briefly."

"Rumor has it that she and Rawlings might be lovers."

"Maybe. I have no proof one way or the other."

"But then they go to a play together the night of the murder and provide each other with airtight alibis."

"That sort of thing isn't too unusual in their crowd."

Cliff, recalling his chat with Gwyneth at the cocktail party, asked, "Is anything the matter with her nose? At the party she kept sniffing and snuffling. Does she have allergies?"

Doctor Gates peered into the depths of his gin and tonic. "Ethics," he replied, "forbids my discussing the details of her medical treatment. However, it's okay for me to chat about the mores of her social set and, as you're aware, the drug of choice among the smart set is nose candy."

"Cocaine," said Mona.

The doctor nodded. "I won't mention any names, but I once had a gorgeous female patient whose devotion to nose candy was so stubborn that she now has a hole in the septum of her nose almost the size of a dime. Ah, well, what are you going to do next?"

"Touch bases with Nurse Stone," said Cliff, "for whatever it's worth. You haven't told me what you think of her, by the way."

"Soundly trained, and she gives me the willies."

12

ALONG MONTANA AVENUE as it angles away southwestward from its junction with San Vicente Boulevard are several blocks of attractive apartment buildings in a neighborhood full of trees: redwoods, acacias, pines, and the medicinal-smelling eucalyptus. Across the street, on the other side of a chain-link fence, the rolling greenery of a country club overlaps Brentwood and the edge of Santa Monica.

All the apartments in Rosetta Stone's building faced on an interior courtyard full of plants suggesting the tropics: banana trees, ginger, bird of paradise, tree ferns. A fountain stood in the center, with statues of a lover and his lass under an umbrella, over which the same ten gallons of pump-driven water perpetually sprayed.

Rosetta had been expecting them in apartment 105, hard by the fountain. They heard a bouncing footstep, and the door flew open.

"Come in, come in, come in!" a pretty blond woman of twenty-five or -six exclaimed. "I'm just making tea to go with the sponge cake. Please seat yourselves!" She bounced into the kitchen.

Cliff and Mona sat down in chairs resembling the seats in an airplane: comfortable enough and upholstered in an easy-to-keep-clean fabric. Over the serving counter that half divided the living room from the kitchen, they could see the nurse as she poured boiling water into a blue-and-white Japanese teapot.

Cliff scrutinized the living room. It gave an overall impression of newness, but as Mona pointed out later, Rosetta kept the place so immaculately clean that everything merely appeared new. Autumn colors predominated: brown, beige, rust, yellow, white, a touch of red here and there.

"Sit on the couch—more comfortable!" Rosetta called out from the stove.

They moved onto the autumnal couch, in front of which was a coffee table covered in white-lacquered cork sheet. No ashtray. Cliff was glad he quit smoking. Smoking in here would be like smoking in a TB clinic. It would have been entertaining, though, to see how Rosetta would prevent smoking in her place and remain the charming hostess.

A small bookcase held a row of medical books on its upper shelf and a few record albums on the lower: a little each of Mozart, Vivaldi, and Ferde Grofé. Three photographs stood atop the bookcase, clearly depicting Rosetta's pleasant-looking mother and father, Rosetta graduating from nurse's training, and Doctor Craig Rawlings, who had signed his picture "Affectionately." A few prints hung on the walls: Escher's "Drowned Cathedral"; Monet's "Les Coquelicots," with its red poppies spilling down the slope; a Galerie Maeght poster.

Cliff and Mona looked at each other in quiet puzzlement. Cliff could not reconcile the jolly girl in the kitchen with the clean and attractive but impersonal room, which might have been the living room of "Model 4B" in a new tract, decorated for show. He rose and went out to the kitchen, hoping to see the refrigerator door aflutter with cartoons and memos held down by magnets shaped like pumpkins and watermelon slices. Nothing.

"Can I help you?" he asked, to cover up.

"No!" she exclaimed in mock shock. "You're a guest!"

He returned to the couch. Rosetta followed, carrying a laden tray. She poured tea and handed them dessert plates bearing forks and slices of sponge cake.

"Well, now! Isn't this fun?"

Rather an odd remark in the circumstances, but they hastened to agree.

"With the fountain out there splashing, any time I want to, I can imagine I'm having a cozy tea on a rainy night."

Cliff had to remind himself that by definition this girl could be no ordinary dope. She was a trained registered nurse, and you simply do not earn that badge by being vapid.

"I gather you're fond of tea," said Mona with a smile.

"I am! I love it all, from Earl Gray to lapsang soochong!"

"In fact, it's what did you in on the night in question."

"What night is that? Oh. . .that awful night at Miss Atterbury's!" She looked admiringly at Mona. "I wish I could be more like that."

"Like what?"

"You're so perceptive and forthright! You dive right in and get to the point! But, of course, I'm forgetting you two are detectives."

"Not really. Only a couple of interested amateurs."

"I'm just glad I haven't done anything wrong!" She emitted a peal of silvery laughter. "Or am I a suspect anyway?"

"Worse than that," said Cliff. "I ought to clap the cuffs on you right now. You look too suspiciously innocent. Every sleuth knows that a pretty blond woman who serves you sponge cake and tea and lives in a brightly lit apartment must be concealing a dread secret—especially if she's a registered nurse who knows all the medical tricks. Come on, Rosetta, tell us how you did it. That knock on the head was just a cover-up, wasn't it?"

"Oh, you!" she said, laughing. She gave him a little push on the arm that made him spill tea into his saucer.

"Goodness!" She jumped up. "I'm sorry! Let me take that . . . no, no—no trouble at all!" She hurried to the kitchen and returned with a clean saucer.

"Actually, of course," said Cliff, "Doctor Rawlings speaks very highly—"

"Isn't he wonderful? Absi-tively the perfect doctor! Isn't he the most impressive doctor you ever met?"

"In a way, yes. But I was going to ask you your opinion."

"He's perfect! Totally skilled, totally modern, totally caring for his patients, totally, uh, warm toward me"—quick glance at the photograph—"and a doll to work for."

"Would you say that's a universal opinion?"

"Oh, no. You'll never get a consensus on anything in the medical profession. Some people insist on having an older doctor because they're supposed to be more experienced. Other people want a young doctor because their training is more up to the minute. Some nurses, especially older RNs, think they know more than most doctors. And so it goes. I've even heard people knock Doctor Rawlings because he's handsome, which is the silliest thing I ever heard of. Do you think it's fair?"

"What do you think of his handling of Maria Atterbury's disease? Not everybody has your admiration of his skill."

Rosetta frowned. "I know, and you can't blame them, but you had to be there. Her prognosis was very negative, you know. She was going downhill every day, so no matter what Doctor Rawlings did, he was going to be criticized and he knew it and he gritted his teeth and went right ahead with what he thought was best. What was he supposed to do? If all he did was continue Doctor Gates's regimen, he'd just be marking time till the funeral."

"So what did he do?" asked Cliff.

"The first thing he did was have her take a break from sitting for her portrait in the morning, and stay in bed instead to store up some strength."

"Did it work?"

"For a while. But! Do you know anything about myasthenia?"

"We had a short seminar on it."

"Well!" Rosetta rolled her eyes heavenward, or at least second-storyward, heaved a little sigh, let her shoulders sag, and thrust both hands between her knees. "It turned out to be self-defeating. She got more energy, but used it to hound her nephews, especially Grant Atterbury, and hound Mr. Colfax, and hound Doctor Rawlings, and even hound me." She spread the fingers of her right hand on her chest and emitted another tinkling laugh, but the expression in her eyes was anxiety and watchfulness. Watchful for what, Cliff wasn't sure, but part of it had to be wanting reassurance that she was a marvelous person. "And as you may know, emotional upset is just as tiring for a myasthenic as running up and down stairs."

"Was that part of your duties—to prevent her from getting emotionally upset?"

"Supposedly, but I wasn't her mother! I couldn't tell a socialite lady how to run her life!"

"So what did you do?"

"I just reported everything to Doctor Rawlings so he could handle it."

"And what did he do?"

"Oh, a lot of things. He talked to Miss Atterbury like a Dutch uncle, and he gave her sleeping pills, and he told her not to try to conduct personal business or 'business' business for a while, and he changed her medication. She was a lot calmer and easier to handle after that."

"Is that the criterion for treatment—making the patient easy to handle?"

"It was certainly easier for me. But it isn't my place to question Doctor Rawlings's judgment. He's a doctor!"

"Does he call on your services often?"

"Yes, but not often enough to suit me!" Another silvery laugh. "I hope to work for him full time, eventually."

"By any chance do you sort of go for him?" asked Mona.

"Goodness!" Rosetta blushed and hitched in her seat and braided her fingers. "What a question!"

"You know me—" said Mona, "—forthright."

Rosetta took on a coy expression. "I'll tell you something if you'll promise to keep it among the three of us."

They promised.

"Well . . . from the start I fell for him like a ton of bricks."

"You'd have some pretty tough competition there, in Gwyneth Atterbury," Cliff observed.

"Oh, they're just casual friends."

"Uh huh."

"No. Craig told me so himself. Doctor Rawlings. Besides, she's married and she's got position and money, and she wouldn't give that up so easily."

"Maybe she wants too much. And given the way the world works, her beauty can probably get her anything she wants."

"Wouldn't you think she'd get tired of always being told how beautiful she is? I know I did." Seeing their questioning looks, she hastened to add, "Oh, yes! It was my mom and dad, mainly. When I was their little girl they thought I was the most beautiful thing that ever slid down the rainbow. They used to call me their 'beautiful doll' and their 'baby doll' and their 'darling little doll' and their 'kewpie doll,' and they dressed me up like a doll, and if I ever got angry at them they'd say, 'Now, now. Let's see you take that ugly frown off your pretty doll face!' And it was 'doll' this and 'doll' that, and doll, doll, doll all the time! Sometimes I actually got the feeling they were disappointed I wasn't a doll instead of an ordinary human, so they could just put me on permanent display up on the mantelpiece!"

Rosetta burst out with a cascade of laughter, but Cliff, seeing her eyes squeezed shut and her contorted face, thought of those pictures in psychology books whose captions ask the reader whether the people in the pictures are laughing or crying.

"I'm sort of joking, of course. I'm sure they expected some Prince Charming doll-collector to come along some day and collect me. It hasn't happened yet, and of course it was worse for them when I grew up and looked more like a department-store mannequin than a doll. Kind of ironic, too, that I'm a registered nurse, 'cause I had a registered nurse doll when I was little. . . . So I guess in a way I'm right back where I started!"

She burst into laughter again, but Cliff and Mona found it impossible to smile.

"Maybe we'd better get down to talking about the murder," said Mona.

"Oh, I'm no good at playing detective."

"If we can, you can. On the night of the murder you were out of it because somebody drugged you. Who do you think did it?"

"It would have to be Miss Atterbury. It was Socorro's day off, so we were the only ones there."

"Who prepared your tea?"

"Why, I did, of course."

"With tea bags or real tea leaves?"

"Real tea. Miss Atterbury hated tea bags."

"So you prepared it in the kitchen?"

"Yes."

"About what time was that?"

"Sevenish."

"Did you look inside the pot before you poured the water in."

"Why, no."

"So somebody could already have put the drug in the pot."

Cliff objected. "Wait a minute, Mona. If the whole pot had been drugged, Maria would have been drugged, too."

"So it had to be Miss Atterbury, right?" said Rosetta.

"Looks that way."

"Now it's your turn to wait a minute," said Mona.

"Yes, Myrna Loy?"

"Don't be sarcastic, Fearless. You've forgotten the other alternative." She looked at Rosetta. "You could have drugged yourself."

Rosetta looked astonished. "Why would I do a thing like that?"

"To put yourself out of the way and establish an alibi."

"I would never do such a thing!"

"Sure you would—if Doctor Rawlings asked you to."

114

Rosetta's blush spread clear back to her ears.

"But why would he want to do such a thing?"

"You tell me."

"He wouldn't have a reason in the world."

"That we know of. But if there were one, I guarantee it would have something to do with Gwyneth Atterbury."

"That's a terrible thing to say! You're implying he would want to—to—do something to Miss Atterbury—his own patient, that he's trying to save! A doctor!"

"And Rosetta here is a nurse, Mona. Let's not overdo it."

Rosetta gave Cliff a warm and thankful look.

"I wonder," said Cliff, "if you could give me some medical information and play detective at the same time."

"Certainly," said Rosetta, sitting up in her chair like a star pupil who has cooled her homework and knows it.

"I'm told that the typical myasthenic has pretty much run out of soup by the end of the day. And Maria supposedly was exhausted, totally pooped. Would you say that's true?"

Rosetta smiled. "Well, those aren't the exact words I'd use, but that's medically accurate."

"On that evening, did she have any trouble picking up and holding her teacup?"

Rosetta frowned and cogitated. "Come to think of it, no. No, she didn't. And some evenings, she couldn't even get her hand to lift the cup."

"But that evening, she not only managed her teacup, but she also supposedly drugged you, got out of bed, evidently walked to the far end of the room, and was able to open her safe for whatever reason. Where do you suppose she got all the energy?"

"She might have had a remission. It happens."

"But what a coincidental remission that was! On the same evening she has a remission, she drugs you . . . and gets killed!"

"I see. But I can't explain it. Can you?"

"All I can do is theorize. For instance, let's say she planned it all in advance and carried it off because she avoided taking any sleeping pills and, in fact, knocked off the Mestinon for a day. What do you think of that?"

"Oh, no, that's impossible. If she didn't take her medication, her muscles wouldn't have responded. She would have been the same as paralyzed."

"What if she had been taking far too much Mestinon?"

Rosetta lifted her hands in a helpless gesture. "I wouldn't know what 'too much' consists of. But I certainly wouldn't question Doctor Rawlings's regimen."

"Okay, then, regardless of the source of her energy, what on earth do you suppose she was up to?"

A strained frown marred the pretty, doll face. "She wanted to get something. Out of the safe, maybe."

"Could be. But only some money appeared to be missing."

Rosetta touched her index finger to her lower lip. "You said something a minute ago about Miss Atterbury walking to the far end of the room. How do you know she did that?"

"She had a couple of smudges of red paint on her fingers that undoubtedly came from her portrait."

"I wonder why she would do that."

"Ego. My sister tells me most people act narcissistic over their portraits. And they can't resist touching them to see if the paint's dry—which it almost never is, especially if there's poppyseed oil in the paint, which takes ages to dry. And anyway, it takes about a year for oil paint to dry completely."

"I guess Miss Atterbury didn't know that."

"She should have. Maria used to do paintings."

"Oh, that's right! Like that picture of the hacienda over the fireplace!"

"Exactly."

"I'm sorry I haven't been much help. Can I at least get you some more tea and sponge cake?"

"No, we'd better get going now."

"Thanks for your hospitality," said Mona. "And we'll keep our fingers crossed about that job with Doctor Rawlings."

116

Rosetta laughed and blushed again.

At the door, Cliff turned and said, "By the way, were you ever interviewed by a police sergeant named Champollion?"

Rosetta was bewildered. "Why, no. Lieutenant Puterbaugh is the only policeman I ever talked to."

"I thought so."

Cliff and Mona went out into the night.

"Tell me cops don't have a sense of humor?" said Cliff.

As long as they were in the Brentwood neighborhood, Cliff and Mona dropped by the house of Thelma Colfax, the lawyer's estranged wife, on the off chance that she might be in. Lights in the red-brick Georgian indicated that she was.

When she answered the door, however, they were treated to the shortest interview they ever had. Other than her being about five feet one and petite and having a full head of iron-gray hair, it was difficult to tell what Mrs. Colfax looked like. Although it was night, she wore dark glasses with large lenses, and a gauze bandage across her nose.

"The only thing I can tell you that has anything whatever to do with the case is that that son of a bitch of a husband of mine thinks he's in 'love' with that round-heeled, big-titted nympho of an Atterbury woman and is crazy enough to think he might get to marry her. Ha! Oh, boy, and do I ever hope he gets his wish! Well, I didn't see him for two weeks before the murder, and I've only seen him twice since then—once in my lawyer's office. I have now entered psychotherapy with a wonderful woman over in Encino to find out why I was originally attracted to the son of a bitch so I won't make the same mistake again, and I just had my face lifted to help me snag a good man when and if one comes along—or woman, for that matter. Come to think of it, a warm, feeling woman sounds damn good and I'm going to give it serious consideration. As for Sidney: Screw him. He's out of my life and I don't want to talk about him. Everything I know is in the police files anyway. So, no offense, but good night and good luck." She closed the door.

"Well, that was a show-stopper, wasn't it?" said Mona as they went back down Thelma's sidewalk between the rose-bushes.

"Yes, indeed. Colfax is back in it up to his neck, and I'm with Thelma. I'd rather not talk to him at all."

13

AMONG THE UPS and downs in his feelings about detective work, Cliff's experience that Thursday evening was a downer. He had parked his Porsche under one of the red-flowering eucalyptus trees at the intersection of Altata Drive and Corona del Mar, and sat back to watch.

Five minutes, and he was squirming with boredom. He couldn't read. For thirty or forty seconds he listened to KFAC with the volume turned low, but the *1812 Overture* was ludicrous played pianissimo—especially if he intended to wait for the volleys of cannon-fire at the end. After twenty minutes, peering over transoms sounded exciting.

An occasional car came up the street and rolled into a driveway. A patrol car of the security agency prowled past. A squirrel scampered down a tree trunk and seized a fragment of a Ding Dong dropped by some hapless school child.

It grew darker and cooler. The glimmering landscape faded on the sight, and all the earth a solemn stillness held.

Cliff thought of "stake-outs," and how stultifying it must be to sit like this for two or three days. Vietnam was like this sometimes, but the Cong could usually be counted on to liven up the party.

Eight o'clock came and went. Eight-fifteen. The patrol car passed again. At eight-fifty Cliff heard running footsteps behind him on Corona del Mar. He got out of his car and waited for the two joggers coming down the sidewalk.

"Please excuse me!" he said, holding up his hands.

The couple wore navy-blue sweatshirts, sweatpants tied at the waist with a white cord, and running shoes.

Cliff explained what he was doing and asked, "By any chance did you jog past here on the night of the murder?"

"Yes, we did," said the young man, panting. Both he and his partner continued to run in place. "But listen, we can't stop and talk now. We have to keep our pulse rate up. Why don't you meet us back at our house in about ten or eleven minutes? We're going to turn left on Toyopa and circle around for about a mile." He gave Cliff the house number on Corona del Mar. Cliff thanked him and drove over to the one-story house, whose red-tile roof was surrounded by ginger plants, jasmine, and the long, folded fronds of banana trees.

The young couple returned, glowing with health, and escorted Cliff into their kitchen, where they downed glasses of bottled water and turned the fire on under a coffeepot. When it was hot, the three of them sat down with their cups in a breakfast nook. They were husband and wife, and their names were Dennis and Misty.

"Okay, fire away," said Dennis.

"First, did you notice anything unusual that evening?"

"No, or we would have reported it to the police."

"We've talked it over a lot," said Misty, "and darn it, there just wasn't anything. The neighborhood looked like it always did."

"We actually felt cheated," said Dennis with a laugh.

"Yes!" Misty agreed. "A gen-u-wine murder right on our street, but without the newspapers would we ever have known about it? Heck no."

"Too bad," said Cliff. "Judging from clock-times in the police reports, it seems likely the murderer was still in there when you two passed by. . . . That is, if you passed by at the same time as you did tonight."

"Oh, we did," said Misty without hesitation.

"Then I gather you always jog at the same time of evening."

"No, it all depends. Sometimes we don't jog at all."

120

"Right," Dennis agreed. "If you jog every day, it gets to be a bore. Nor is it good for you."

"Then how come you're so sure you jogged that particular night at that particular time?"

"Mainly from reading about the murder in the evening newspapers the next day and recalling where we were at the time."

"Also," added Misty laughing, "we remembered getting into an argument over the correct spelling of a word."

Many times, over the following days and weeks, Cliff was shaken to realize that he was on the verge of passing over that remark; but the curiosity of an English teacher saved the day.

"What was the word?"

"Caduceus," said Misty.

The detective half of Cliff's brain sent up antennae.

"You know—" Misty went on in her sprightly way, "that staff with the wings and snakes? The doctors' insignia? Dennis thought there were two d's."

"I guess I was thinking of 'caddie,' " said he.

"How did you come to pick on that word?" asked Cliff.

"We saw a caduceus when we jogged that night. It was on a car in front of Maria Atterbury's house."

"What kind of car was it?"

"I've never paid any attention to it, have you, honey?" Dennis shook his head. "Some kind of black car is all."

"You didn't mention it to the police?"

"Oh, no. Actually, we'd seen the caduceus so many times before, we never gave it a thought."

"But, sweetheart," said Dennis. "Don't you realize what Mr. Dunbar is saying? We have been stupid as hell, you know that? We should have reported everything we saw, unusual or not!"

Misty's mouth dropped open. "Omigod! The doctor!"

They became excited. "Who was her doctor?"

"I'd rather not name names," said Cliff. "She had two of them at different times."

"Are you going to tell the police about this?"

"Absolutely. So I think you'll be hearing from a Lieutenant Puterbaugh from the West L.A. Division. In the meantime, rack your brains and see if you can remember any more details about that car and the timing and anything else you saw."

"Migosh, we sure will!"

Cliff left feeling more sure of himself, having met two people who undoubtedly would have made worse detectives than he was.

14

CLIFF, MONA, AND Alison met for lunch at the Sandpiper, on the Coast Highway at the mouth of Sunset Boulevard. Because of its location, the place attracted all sorts of people: idlers from Pacific Palisades, office workers from Santa Monica, beach bums, Hell's Angels, Japanese tourists just back from the Getty Museum.

Alison was fascinated with Cliff's discovery. "Which doctor do you think was lying, then?"

"I'd say Rawlings, of course. I can't feature ol' Doc Gates on a rampage."

Mona frowned. "There's another possibility. That could have been anybody's car. Heck, you can buy a caduceus symbol for your license plate at the carwash, and it does inspire people's trust. They see a caduceus and lay all suspicion aside. It's as good as a clergyman's collar."

"You may be right. I'd better tread softly when I quiz Rawlings about it, which I'll have to put off till next week, it looks like. He's in San Francisco for a medical convention."

"But you'll be in Mexico anyway, won't you?" said Alison.

"Yes. It'll be like a second honeymoon for me and Mona before she has to go back to school."

"And what will you be doing after she goes back?"

"Let's not go into that. Instead," said Cliff, opening the portfolio he had brought with him, "take another look at that photo of Maria's bedroom and see if you can figure out what bothered you about it the first time."

He extracted the large glossy print and gave it to Alison.

She peered at it, but before she could think too long, Cliff said, "Quick! What was your instant reaction?"

"Again," she said, looking up, "that there's something wrong here, but I am still totally flummoxed. I simply cannot figure out what it is. Everything in this piled-up mess, and everything else in the room, is familiar to me and looks . . . 'correct.' But something still bothers me anyway."

She handed the photo back to him with a sigh. "Maybe we should forget it, though. Could be I'm just too eager. And maybe it's just the fact that a mess is 'wrong' by definition, or that any room where there's been a murder looks 'wrong.' "

"Could be. Okay. We'll try it again later."

As Cliff took the photo and tucked it back into the portfolio, someone passing by bumped his elbow.

"Hey, watch what the fuck you're doing!"

They looked up to see a burly biker holding a glass of beer, some of which had slopped out foaming onto his hand. The man's small and angry eyes burned in a face surrounded by a scraggly blond fringe beard. His beer belly bulged over a heavy chrome-plated chain that served as a belt and most likely as a handy weapon.

"And you ought to watch your language," said Cliff.

"Listen, smartass, you did that on purpose."

"Make you spill your beer? Not guilty."

"I say you did. I know your type. You're one of those bozos don't like bikers."

"God knows that's true. But you had to go out of your way to bump my arm."

The biker's face turned red and his head shot forward. "Why, you shithead. You tellin' me it's my fault? Come on, let's step outside."

"To fight? No, that'd be a serious mistake."

"For you, maybe."

"Look . . . I do not want to fight, and neither should you. You're out of shape and it may sound as if I'm boasting, but I assure you I'm sort of an expert in the martial arts. So why don't we—"

124

"Outside!" The biker jerked his thumb toward a side door.

"Tell you what," said Cliff. "I'll even apologize."

"Out!"

"Let's drop this. I'm sorry I made you spill your beer. I'll even buy you a fresh one."

"Outside, shithead!" said the biker. And then he uttered the unpardonable: "Don't think I'm going to let you off just because you're sittin' with a coupla floozies."

Wearily, Cliff rose to his feet. "Okay, let's go."

"Cliff!" Mona exclaimed.

He lifted a hand. "Don't worry, it's all right."

"After you, Alphonse!" said the biker, with a little bow and a vicious grin.

Cliff walked along a row of empty booths in a less-used ell of the restaurant, with the biker treading close behind him. Pivoting on the ball of his left foot, Cliff suddenly whirled and speared the bunched thumb and fingertips of his right hand into the man's solar plexus, just below the sternum. The biker doubled over in agony and gasped for breath. Cliff took him by the shoulders and wafted him gently, as o'er a perfumed sea, into one of the empty booths and slid into the seat opposite him.

"I don't know who sent you," said Cliff. "I suppose whoever it was told you that one blast of violence and I'd quit the case, but I also suppose you're tough enough to refuse to tell me who it was. I don't blame you. You want your pay."

The biker said nothing. He stared at Cliff with bulging eyes like a bulldog swallowing a beefsteak.

"But look here," Cliff went on amicably, "I wasn't kidding about the martial arts. I was a combat infantry officer in Vietnam. I'm a peaceable type now. However, if you absolutely insist on fighting me after you recover, well, okay. But if we do, I'm sorry but I *will* have to mark you up a good deal so you'll think twice about bothering me again. By that I mean once you're down, I'll have to do some serious work on your face with my shoe. I'd prefer not to do that, but you decide, okay?"

Cliff put his hands together on the table, interlaced his fingers, and rubbed his thumbs together, smiling pleasantly.

The biker's forehead, meanwhile, had turned a greenish white, which made the little beads of sweat along his hairline look cold. After a further minute's rest, having recovered his breath, the biker stood up and, averting his eyes from Cliff, lurched down the aisle and out the door.

Cliff returned to his own booth and slid onto the bench next to Mona. "He changed his mind," said Cliff.

"My God, what a thug!" said Alison.

"I don't know. He turned out to be pretty reasonable once he calmed down."

Mona looked at him suspiciously. "Clifford . . . Was there more to that brute than met the eye?"

"Yes. He had a fat behind, too."

"You know what I mean. Was he hired to rough you up?"

"I don't know; I didn't ask." Cliff felt his eyes widen slightly at the realization that he was telling Mona the first lie of their marriage. "Besides, how would anybody know about our agreement?"

"I believe I let it slip at the cocktail party."

"Who to? Or to whom, as I used to say in English 1A?"

"I can't remember. But I suppose word could have gotten around."

"I suppose so, but regardless this was just a half-tight thug looking for a fight. Also, don't forget: If I quit the case, you wouldn't get to go to Mexico with me."

"Okay, but I'm still holding you to your promise."

"Give my love to Socorro, will you?" said Alison. "I think you're going to like her. However, you're going to a hell of a lot of trouble just to verify that Socorro came home at nine-twenty or whatever, and Maria said look in her pocket."

"Maybe there'll be something more. And it was nine-forty."

15

CLIFF AND MONA flew to Mexico City, rented a VW, and drove north on Highway 57 to Queretaro. There they turned off and motored the remaining forty-one miles to San Miguel de Allende. They covered the hundred and eighty miles in a little over three hours, thanks to the mostly traffic-free four-lane toll road to Queretaro.

Mona made the trip seem even shorter by reading aloud about the area in a guidebook written by a man named Bloomgarden—probably not a Mexican name, though lovely, she speculated. San Miguel, founded in 1540, was declared a national colonial monument by the Mexican government. The book confirmed that one couldn't construct a new building, raze an old one, or tear up a cobblestone street in the town without a permit, and permits are hard to get.

The VW came over a low crest and began a long descent down the side of a hill, from which they had an aerial view of the whole town. Instead of the usual white church with red-tiled domes and round arches, the salient landmark was a cluster of pink spires in the French-Gothic mode.

Cliff parked the car on the edge of the Parque Principal. The park contained rows of ficus trees pruned into the shape of gumdrops, and a bandstand. A few contented-looking old men and women sat on benches under the trees. A campesino in blue jeans and blue shirt drove a donkey down the street, almost hidden under an eight-foot-high bundle of corn stalks.

The pink Gothic church stood on one side of the square. On the other three sides were inns, cafes, the police station, and two buildings with arcades containing both sidewalk booths and indoor shops selling silver, pottery, shoes, and tinware.

"I love this town!" exclaimed Mona, looking around her. "No wonder Socorro Contreras was in a hurry to get back here!"

"It's also the cleanest town I've seen in Mexico," said Cliff.

"*Serapes y rebozos, señor? Señora*? The best in Mexico. Very cheap."

The vendor who approached them looked like a cowboy with his straw sombrero and a hand-rolled cigarette between his lips. A pile of brilliantly colored wool articles lay on his shoulder.

"*Quizás más tarde*," Cliff began. "But you speak English!"

The man smiled. "Enough for sell serapes and rebozos."

"We're looking for the shop of Socorro Contreras."

"*Está allí—a la vuelta de la esquina en la Calle Canal.*"

"Around this corner?"

"*Sí, señor.*"

Socorro's shop was an exploding rainbow of red, green, blue, solferino pink, and white serapes, rebozos, ponchos, bedspreads, and sweaters.

The young sales clerk in the shop spoke good English. She informed them that Señorita Contreras was at home supervising a stonecutter.

"Would you like for me to call her on the telephone? They installed her telephone only yesterday."

"Please. We'd much appreciate it."

The girl took pride in putting the call through. She spoke rapid Spanish, too rapid and too colloquial for Cliff to follow.

"She says she will be happy to speak with you. Go to her house, at Number Forty-two Calle Hospicio." The girl gave them directions, and they set out on foot.

"Isn't she a charmer, though!" said Mona.

"Aside from making the best beer in the world, composing the best popular music, producing the best popular singers, and speaking the finest and clearest Spanish, Mexicans may well be the best-mannered people in the world."

128

"Sounds as if we should all be Mexicans."

"One could do worse."

Socorro's house was small but elegant. She met them at the wrought-iron gate and led them into the patio, where water cascaded into the stacked scallop shells of a cantera-stone fountain.

"Pardon me a moment," she said in English. "I must give instructions to Pifa—Epifanio," she added with a smile.

Pifa the stonecutter knelt in the grass with mallet and chisels, listened carefully, and nodded his head. It was a sight Cliff and Mona had never seen: a craftsman cutting stone to order, to fit around window openings that had been knocked into the walls of the old house.

Socorro then escorted them into a pleasant white adobe room bright with green cactus, brown pottery urns, and black decorative ceramics from Oaxaca, and served them margaritas made with freshly squeezed lime juice.

"And what are these questions you have?" she inquired. "I hope I can answer, but please to remember that I still talk English only a—only a small."

"And I speak only classroom Spanish," said Cliff, "and Mona speaks only French, but we should be able to understand each other. Mainly, I should like to know—*quisiera saber*—exactly what were those last words that Maria Atterbury said to you when she was dying."

"I told the police. She say look in her pocket."

"Yes, but what were her exact words?"

"She talked in Spanish. She say, '*Dile que mire en la bolsa.*'"

Cliff was puzzled, "All in the third person singular."

"*Mande?*"

"In English it means she said, 'Tell him or her to look in the pocket.' Are you sure she didn't say, '*Diles que miren en mi bolsa?*' 'Tell them'—plural—'that they should look in my pocket?'"

Socorro frowned. "No, she say, '*Dile que mire.*'"

"Also," said Cliff, "would *'la bolsa'* and *'mi bolsa'* mean the same thing in Spanish? Always?"

"No, not always. Usually, you say 'la bolsa.' But if you want to give *énfasis*—emphasis—to this pocket—" Socorro patted her thigh, "—you would say *'mi bolsa.'* However, Señorita Atterbury, she talk very good Spanish but not perfect. Also, her Spanish was . . . *anticuado?*"

"Old-fashioned?"

"*Sí, eso es.*"

"How was it that Gwyneth Atterbury discovered you here? It was Gwyneth, wasn't it?"

"Yes. I work as a maid at the Academia Hispano Americana. Two summers ago. Señora Atterbury was a student, learning Spanish. Six weeks. She hire me to come to Los Angeles for cook and be maid for Maria Atterbury. And help the nurse." Socorro laughed, in a mixture of pleasure and embarrassment. "The pay was . . . *estupendo!* I live in the house, and I receive three hundred fifty dollars a week! Believe me, that is many, many pesos! I save almost all the money; the Señorita leaves me five thousand more; and quick I buy the *tienda* in the Calle Canal. Now I am a rich woman in San Miguel Allende, and the men want to marry me. Even Pifa wants to marry me!"

"Were you happy with your work there?"

"*Cómo no?* I like Maria Atterbury very much. *Muy simpática, la señorita,* and she talk—speak—Spanish."

"And Gwyneth Atterbury?"

Socorro hesitated. "I don't like to sound . . . *ingrata,* but soon I did not like her. She arrive to be so, so, in Spanish we say *'pedigüeña.'* "

"Sort of pushy and demanding? She strikes a lot of people that way."

Cliff and Socorro fell silent, remembering her, but Mona spoke to the point: "The question is, demanding about what? What did she want? I'll bet she wanted you to be a spy for her."

"What is 'spy?'"

"*Espía,*" said Cliff.

"Exactly," said Socorro. "Always she wants to know what passes in the house of Maria. Everything Maria does. The people she sees. What she says. Anything she writes."

"Writes? Like letters?"

"Yes. And one or two times Maria writes things she wants Señor Colfax to put in her *testamento.* You understand '*testamento?*'"

"Yes, it's the same in English."

"Did Colfax do the things she wanted?" Mona asked.

"She want to leave five thousand dollars for me, and she tells me so I know she appreciates my help. And he did put. But she writes more than that, I think. I do not know. I never saw, of course; but one or two times she get angry with Señor Colfax because he take so long to do little things."

"How about you?" said Mona. "Did you like Colfax?"

"A strange man. He pay very small attention to me, but of course I was only a servant, and I do not believe he likes Mexicans. Yet, when Señorita Atterbury dies and I hear about her *testamento,* I ask Señor Colfax if it is possible to receive the money *pronto* because I have the opportunity to buy the *tienda* in San Miguel. Suddenly he is very generous. He makes a special favor to me. He gives me the money, and he regulates things with the police so I can go to Mexico."

"But let's get back to Gwyneth," said Mona.

Socorro lowered her eyes. "I don't like to talk bad about a person who has been a benefactor." She put the accent on the "tor," the word being the same in Spanish. "But she want too much. She get angry with me because I do not . . . *fisgonear, curiosear* . . . enough. *Comprende usted?*"

"Is that sort of like spying again—*espiar?*" said Cliff.

"Yes. But you have a good word in English. It is like that funny black-and-white dog in your comic papers."

"Snoopy?" exclaimed Mona. "You didn't snoop around enough to satisfy her."

"*Eso sí que es*. But that nurse snoops and tells the doctor and I think the doctor tells Mrs. Gwyneth Atterbury. I do not like the doctor either. He does not really want to be a doctor, I think. Most of all, I think, he wants to be a member of . . . *la gente copetuda*. I do not know the English."

"High society?"

"Something similar, yes."

"Who do you think killed Maria Atterbury?"

She shrugged. "I can have no idea."

"Can you think of anyone who was angry enough to kill her?"

"No. Consuelo Atterbury and her brother Lionel are angry with her because she would not give them more money, but not that angry. Besides, if they kill her, they get nothing."

"Well, are you willing to say who you think is the most likely suspect—*el sospechoso el más probable*?" said Cliff.

Socorro emitted another laugh more liquescent and charming than the water in the fountain. "I am!" she exclaimed. "Because I want to buy that *tienda* before it is too late!"

"I am glad," said Cliff, "that it was impossible for you to do it. I would hate to put so charming a lady in prison although it would make prison a pleasure for the other prisoners."

"I thank you for your *piropo*. But why is it impossible for me to be the killer?"

"Because you didn't have enough time. We know at what time you had your argument with Grapefruit Juice—*Hugo de Toronja*—that you arrived home at nine-forty, and that you called the police at once. You didn't have time to kill Maria and tear up her room."

Socorro sighed. "That is the mere truth. Permit me to give you another margarita."

"Permission granted. *Viva México*."

She poured their drinks in a fresh set of glasses with margarita salt sparkling like frost around the rim.

"Your Pifa could make a fortune around Beverly Hills."

"Please don't tell him until he finish here. I was fortunate to get him. He wants to become famous like Ceferino Gutiér-rez."

"Who's he?"

"Oh, he's the Indian who carved the parish church."

"He carved . . . the church?"

"Yes. All by himself, by looking at postcards of French cathedrals."

"Fantastic. He did a beautiful job, too."

"Socorro," said Mona, "can you recommend a good place for us to stay?"

"There are many good ones now," said Socorro, "but if you would like to spend a day or two in paradise, go behind the church down the Calle Aldama to Number Fifty-three, the Villa Jacaranda."

They took their leave of Socorro, found the Villa Jaca-randa, made reservations with Gloria, and hurried off to the Academia Hispano Americana on the Calle Insurgentes, two blocks from the park.

Señora Samaniego, in the office of administration, looked as if she should have been the president of a computer soft-ware firm in Beverly Hills. She was slim in her tailored gray suit. Her black hair was pulled back and tied behind, allowing large bright blue eyes to dominate her face. Cliff and Mona were not surprised to learn that she was half Mexican and half *yanqui* and both her Spanish and English were not only flawless but idiomatic.

"Oh, yes," said Señora Samaniego, "I remember Gwyneth Atterbury quite well." She smiled mischievously. "Who wouldn't? A knockout like that doesn't come down the pike every day."

"No comment," said Cliff.

"Attaboy," said Mona.

"So! I take it you're familiar with the fever and fret she can create. Not that it's all her fault, but the skill-level of our men students took a sharp drop that summer."

"How was she as a student?"

"We've had better and we've had worse. Some people come here with the best of intentions but get caught up in socializing and don't study at all. Gwyneth Atterbury was very good at combining the two, I must say. At the end of her six weeks I would say she spoke pretty good tourist Spanish—enough to haggle over the price of serapes in the Parque Principal."

"We wanted to use candid snapshots of her with other students, in our brochures, but she wouldn't give her permission. There was one shot in particular that showed her with another student who was a doctor, and he was as handsome as she was beautiful. He looked like a combination of Ricardo Montalban and Clark Gable. What a box-office draw that would have been! Disgracefully misleading advertising, of course," she said with a laugh.

Mona and Cliff gaped at each other. Was it possible?

"What's the matter?" said Señora Samaniego. "Have I said something—indiscreet?"

"No, no, no," said Cliff. "But by any chance do you still have those photos?"

"Oh, yes." She dragged a cardboard box from under a table and extracted a handful of glossy photographs. She riffled through them and handed two photos to Cliff. They showed a conversation group of students sitting in a circle of beehive chairs. One photo showed the profile of the group teacher on the left, and Gwyneth and Doctor Rawlings three-quarters-face on the right. They were looking at the teacher, not at each other. They looked studious. They looked innocent. They looked beautiful.

"That's the doctor," said Señora Samaniego, pointing. "His name is Rawlings."

"We've met him," said Cliff. "May I keep this?"

"If you like, but what for?"

"They may be totally innocent of any wrongdoing, but these two at least figure in the murder of Maria Atterbury. Have you heard about that?"

"Oh, yes, from Socorro Contreras."

"I wonder why Socorro never mentioned the doctor to us in connection with Gwyneth Atterbury," said Mona.

"Perhaps she never assumed there was a . . . liaison . . . between them. I didn't myself. After all, Mrs. Atterbury first met Socorro here; it would be natural for Socorro to assume that she also first met the doctor here."

"I suppose so. But it still seems odd. By the way, Socorro thinks the doctor really wants to be a member of something she called '*la gente copetuda.*' What does that mean?"

"That's the Mexican equivalent of 'the jet set.' And I think Socorro's right!"

Cliff and Mona talked over the day's discoveries while soaking in a Jacuzzi under a spreading tree that overarched a patio at the Villa Jacaranda. In the intimate little dining room they had enjoyed a salad of basil, tomato, and mozzarella with a light, rice-wine vinegar dressing, followed by chicken breast veronica with seedless green grapes, glazed baby carrots, and a dessert of flan, the Mexican custard. Now they lay in the water with glasses of a chilled French Chardonnay close to hand.

"This is Mexico?" said Mona, paddling her feet. "I must say, this trip would have been worth it, even if we hadn't found out anything useful."

"I have plans for that photo. I think I can stir up trouble showing it to the principals."

"To what end?"

"I don't know. Shake 'em up. I just have a feeling it will knock somebody off base."

"I'd say Grant Atterbury. He pretends to be so cool and blasé and modern, but you mean to tell me he doesn't care if his wife plays doctor down here for six weeks? Please!"

"What if he doesn't love her anymore?"

"Makes no difference. His ego and the Atterbury image

135

would still be at stake. And I doubt if he ever did love her, really. I can't visualize him truly loving anybody."

"What about Socorro and that 'tell him or her to look in the pocket?'" said Cliff. "I couldn't make heads or tails of that."

"Neither could I." Mona sipped her Chardonnay. "However, Charlie Chan, I'm surprised you haven't even mentioned the most important bit of information Socorro passed on to us."

"Viz.?"

"About Maria's every move being watched and reported on. Even if Socorro began balking at the idea, I'll bet Nurse Rosetta reported everything to Doctor Rawlings, who reported to Gwyneth, who reported to Grant, who probably reported to Colfax, who probably knew it all in the first place."

"That's a lot of reporting. Did you know your legs are beautiful under bubbling fizzy water?"

"Oh, oh, the wine is getting to you. Try to keep your mind on business."

"I am. Your business."

"This could be important. Try not to be a smartass."

"Okay. Continue."

"Those notes Maria wrote for Colfax, that nothing ever came of, apparently. I'll bet if you got into his files you'd find a bundle of them that he just filed and forgot."

"I'll bet I wouldn't. If he was up to skulduggery, he'd burn them. Are you joining Lionel in thinking she wanted to change her will?"

"Sure. Don't you remember Alison saying that she remembers Maria saying she remembered . . . now you've got me doing it!"

"The wine's getting to you. Was your mother frightened by French wine before you were born? Your hair is exactly the same color as that Chardonnay."

"And yours is burnt toast! Will you let me finish?"

"Sorry. You may proceed, counselor."

"Maria said something like, 'There are a lot of injustices around here that need to be corrected.' Sure, she wanted Socorro remembered in her will, and she was, but Colfax may have been prompt about that because it didn't involve much money or trouble. But what if she wanted to leave Rollie a couple of hundred thousand to buy his boat? Or what if she wanted to strike a blow for oppressed second-class women and leave half a million to Consuelo so she wouldn't have to beg from men anymore? Or make Grant go fifty-fifty with Lionel? I'll bet Colfax would drag his heels like Jacob Marley's ghost. He wasn't on Maria's side."

"I'm sure you're right. We'll know more when we get back to Los Angeles."

"Let's not hurry." Mona lifted her glass and looked at the full moon shimmering in the golden wine. "I have a feeling that the moonlight, and that nightingale, and this tropical night, are trying to tell us they're the most important things in the world right now."

"They're almost right."

"Almost?"

"Yes. My dear, what would you say to an obligatory bedroom scene?"

"Obligatory, my foot! I volunteer!"

They rose from the water and strolled down the narrow path toward the French doors of their ground-floor room, their arms around each other and Mona's Chardonnay-colored hair on Cliff's shoulder. Moonlight and birdsong followed them all the way.

16

Colfax, behind his desk, smiled at Cliff with amusement. "Well, *Doctor* Dunbar, I assume you've hit on some clever legal gambit you'd like to try out on me, so proceed. I'm all ears."

"No, I merely want you to look at a couple of photographs." Cliff removed the eight-by-ten glossies from a manila envelope. "These are two students who spent six weeks together studying Spanish down in San Miguel de Allende."

Like a good courtroom lawyer, Colfax assumed an attitude of casual indifference toward the piffling exhibits being offered by opposing counsel. He glanced at the photos. The glance became a closer look. The look became a stare. For fully half a minute, Colfax bent forward staring at the faces in the pictures.

Cliff was totally unprepared for what then happened. Colfax clapped his hands to his face, burst into convulsive sobs, and doubled over onto the desk, his shoulders heaving.

"What is it, Mr. Colfax?"

After several racking sobs, the lawyer managed to gasp, "Gwyneth!" He heaved himself to his feet and turned to the window, his back to Cliff, his hands still over his face, sobbing, tears seeping through his fingers. Cliff came over and tried to put an arm around the man's shoulders. Absorbed in his misery, Colfax was unable to notice. He leaned on the windowsill, his head bowed.

"She lied to me! She used me! Oh, yes! Keep the will as is! That's all I had to do! She loved me! She'd get the Malibu

138

property. We'd develop it together. We'd be millionaires and lovers! Lovers! She has always lied to me!"

Colfax struggled for control, but managed only to subside into spasmodic chokes and steady weeping.

"What a fool! Talk of blind fools! Love me? Me instead of Rawlings? He's just her physician? How could I not . . . so . . . Fooled myself! Why? I have a mirror! I could have looked in it! I could have seen the gut and the wrinkles and the gray hair! What in God's name did I think I was seeing? Dunbar, want to see what the biggest goddamn fool in the world looks like? Well, take a look!"

He dropped his arms and presented his red and ruined face.

"You're not the biggest," said Cliff, softly. "And you're certainly not the first man to get himself bewitched by a siren."

Colfax twisted in pain and broke into fresh sobs. "Thelma! Oh, my God, Thelma! What have I done to you! How could I have done this! You've been so good! You didn't deserve this!"

Colfax bolted for the door. "I've got to go to her! Now!"

Cliff hurried after him. "I'll drive you. You're in no condition."

The two of them sped through the outer office without even a glance at the astonished secretary.

The trip in the Porsche took a mere four or five minutes in which neither man spoke a word. They went up the front walk together, and Colfax rang the bell. Cliff stepped back a few paces.

The door opened to reveal Thelma with a dark scowl on her face; but the scowl altered into wonderment as she gazed into the anguish—the devastation—in her husband's face.

Colfax could do no more than stand there. He could not speak. He could not apologize. He could not plead. More tears welled in his eyes as they looked at each other.

Finally, Colfax lifted one trembling hand. Thelma looked

at it, looked into his face, and rushed into his arms. They both burst into tears and, swaying awkwardly, lurched into the house, and closed the door.

Cliff turned and went back down the walk to his car, unable to decide whether he was a Good Samaritan or a sadistic bastard.

17

MATTERS WENT MUCH differently at Doctor Rawlings's office, in a medical building at Wilshire and Linden. First of all, Cliff had to cool his heels for half an hour, but at least the waiting room was pleasant.

Two lithographs by Chagall hung on the raw-silk-covered walls, and the coffee table offered copies of *Vogue, Fortune, The Economist, Architectural Forum,* and *Paris Match.*

The door to the inner complex opened, and Rosetta Stone appeared in her registered nurse costume—a life-size Barbie doll.

"Doctor Dunbar! When I heard you were here, I could hardly wait to break away and hurry out to seize the opportunity to say hello." She paused for exactly the right beat, tilted her head to one side, and said, "Hello." Just like in the movies.

"Hello, Rosetta. Am I to surmise that your dreams have come true?"

She giggled. "Yes, I'm here full time now, and everything—and I mean everything—is working out fabulously!"

"What does everything include?"

She merely smiled and rolled her eyes. "The doctor will see you now. How is Mona? I thought she was really neat."

He assured her Mona was still well groomed, and followed her down a carpeted hallway to Rawlings's glass-and-mahogany office. The doctor motioned to an upholstered black-leather chair and said, "Have a seat." He looked terrific. He wore an unusual white tunic with two rows of white buttons like those on a chauffeur's uniform. It was short-sleeved, so it revealed his muscular brown arms and a Rolex Oyster wristwatch inset with diamonds that must have cost thousands. Below the Clark Gable mustache, the doctor's lips were compressed and the expression in his blue eyes was cold. He pressed a button under his desk and the door closed.

"How was the medical convention?" said Cliff.

"Routine."

"I just got back from San Miguel de Allende. Mona and I went down there to interview Socorro Contreras."

"It's just San Miguel Allende."

"You can say it either way," said Cliff cheerfully, "according to Mrs. Samaniego over at the Academia. We checked in there, too." He watched for Rawlings's reaction. There was none. "You and Gwyneth Atterbury were there together."

"We were there at the same time. Not together. What are you trying to make out of it?"

"Nothing, yet. Merely filling in background."

"I don't have much time to spare for background-filling. What's on your mind?"

"Two joggers recently told me that, on the night of the murder, they saw a car with a caduceus on the license-plate frame, in front of Maria Atterbury's house."

"Oh . . . well!" Rawlings held out his wrists. "Put on the cuffs! Shall I call my lawyer?"

"Who do you think that car could have belonged to?"

"What kind of car was it?"

"They didn't notice."

"Have you asked old Doctor Gates?"

"Not yet."

"Well, ask him. It couldn't have been me."

"Of course. You were at the Shubert Theater that night. What play was it you saw?"

"Three plays, if you want to get technical. *Three by Albee*, it was called."

"What were they?"

"*Zoo Story, Walking,* and *Finding the Sun.*"

142

"I didn't get to see them. How were they?"

"Now, listen, Dunbar—"

"I know. You're busy. But I'm looking into a murder, and I should think you'd be interested, seeing she was your patient."

Rawlings's eyes flashed. "Yes, she was, but what the hell does the quality of a stage play have to do with it? If it was lousy, are you planning to accuse Edward Albee?"

Cliff shrugged his shoulders.

Rawlings drummed his fingers on his desk. "Okay, they were very good. Considered classics. What more do you want to know?"

"I don't know. How was the quality of the production in *Zoo Story*? Did they give it the full treatment with live animals on stage the way they used to, or did they go low-budget and use recorded animal noises offstage?"

Rawlings stared at him a few seconds. "At the Shubert? They had real animals, of course."

Cliff contemplated the doctor for a long beat.

The doctor put both hands flat on his desk, preparatory to rising to his feet. "If you don't have any more questions—"

"Only one, really: What were you doing at Maria's house that night?"

"Dunbar—"

"There aren't any animals in *Zoo Story*."

Rawlings withdrew his hands from the desk. His tanned forehead became shiny.

"Care to talk about it?" said Cliff.

"About what? I just had a lapse of memory."

"Did you hallucinate instead? You thought you saw lions and tigers up there and now you realize you didn't?"

Rawlings had no answer.

"Come on, Rawlings, confession is good for the soul."

"If I had anything to confess, I sure as hell wouldn't do it for an unfrocked English teacher. Go screw yourself."

"I'll need to check on actual curtain times, but let's see:

That society photographer almost loused up your plans. Awkward, wasn't it? You were planning to dash over and get back as fast as possible. So, it would take about three or four minutes to escort Gwyneth into the theater, five or six minutes to retrieve your car from the underground garage, fifteen or twenty to get to Huntington Palisades—I'd guess you entered Maria's house somewhere between nine and nine-fifteen, maybe nine-twenty—"

Rawlings shot to his feet. "Out!"

Cliff rose. "Okay. You'll be hearing again from Lieutenant Puterbaugh, of course, but you'll have time to tidy up your alibi. Better make it good."

18

"WE COULDN'T HAVE picked a prettier day to drive to Santa Barbara," said Cliff. "Look at that ocean."

They had passed through Camarillo, Oxnard, Ventura, through green fields and citrus groves and roads lined on both sides with arching eucalyptus. On the far side of Ventura they came out to the ocean. The Pacific sparkled and shimmered— millions of silver dollars, newly minted, twinkling on the blue water. The horizon was a darker blue line, drawn with a ruler.

"Where are we staying in Santa Barbara?" said Mona.

"San Ysidro Ranch."

"Is it really a ranch?"

"Not now, but it was once. I think you'll like it. Laurence Olivier and Vivien Leigh were married there."

"I love it already. How did you know about it?"

"Lionel Atterbury recommended it."

Mona bit her lower lip. "Do you think he's as innocent as he lets on?"

"I don't know. Nearly everybody in this case seems to have had axes to grind, irons in the fire, and aces up their sleeve, including Lionel. And look at Doctor Rawlings."

"You look at him," said Mona. "You ought to get down on your knees and thank God you're not that handsome."

"Oh, I do! Nightly."

Masses of trees and greenery on both sides of the highway let them know they had arrived. Santa Barbara is a jewel, with its lemon groves overlooking a curving blue bay, its clear air, its clean streets sloping down from the hills to meet the sea. Students at Santa Barbara City College, up on a hillside, can sit in the grass and enjoy their lunch while looking at a national park: the Channel Islands of Santa Cruz, Santa Rosa, and San Miguel. State Street, the principal shopping street, is shady with trees in large cement planters that overflow with begonias and impatiens. The Porsche proceeded up State Street and turned right onto De la Guerra. They found Underwood's Art, Jewelry & Gifts and went in.

Their first impression of the place was of light and space, glass and china. Customers wandered among tables and along counters, occasionally picking up a piece of Baccarat, Steuben, or Waterford glass, Lenox china, Ginori earthenware.

They saw Lionel Atterbury at the jewelry counter in the back, showing necklaces to a woman in a beige knit suit. He nodded to them. They moved on toward the doorway leading into the adjoining gallery. A pretty young woman with shiny, shoulder-length brown hair and large brown eyes like those of a deer stood in the doorway. She was thin in her ecru silk blouse and tabasco skirt, and her complexion was very fair for someone who lived so near to sun and sand.

"If I can help you at all," she said as they passed, "just let me know."

They thanked her and strolled around the gallery, where they saw evidence of a clever mind at work—surely Lionel's. The paintings on the walls were superb, done by artists who were becoming known but were not yet famous: Dubic, the Haitian primitivist; Pescina, the young impressionist of Mexico; his older countryman Juan Ramírez García, who painted aquarelles on canvas. Good prices, good investments.

When Lionel joined them, they saw he was only marginally better groomed than the last time they saw him. He wore a light brown tweed jacket, a white shirt cut full at the waist to accommodate his small pot belly, and dark brown wool slacks that the pot belly pushed down on and wrinkled. His black hair was combed straight back, and his thick lower lip gave him a perpetual pout.

"What do you think of the place?" he said. "Not exactly

Atterbury's, is it? But come into my office where we can talk."

He led them back through a door at the side of the jewelry counter, and down a short carpeted hall to his office. He poured coffee for them from a Silex on a hotplate.

"I think your store is beautiful!" said Mona.

"It isn't my store."

"You know what I mean."

"Sure. I've done my best with it."

"They were lucky to get an Atterbury to run it," said Cliff.

"Think so? I almost didn't get this job. Underwood took a lot of convincing. He couldn't decide whether to throw me out because I was overqualified or throw me out because I was a boozer. He was so confused he ended up giving me a chance, and now people think he's a mercantile wizard."

"Does he give you credit?"

"Not much. He's starting to believe his publicity. I hope you two are bringing good news. Anything new about the will?"

Both Cliff and Mona looked at him oddly.

"The will?" said Cliff. "You're not interested in the murder?"

"Not primarily."

"And yet," said Mona, rather acidly, "you offer a Suzanne Valadon drawing if we catch the murderer?"

"Connie sort of tricked me into that."

"I'd give up on the will if I were you, Lionel. It looks less and less as if another will exists."

"Why? The way Aunt Maria talked—"

"I know. And apparently she did intend to revise her will, but Sidney Colfax has admitted he was dragging his feet. Not only that, she had Rosetta Stone watching her like a hawk, in cahoots with Doctor Rawlings. And at first, even Socorro Contreras was spying on her for Gwyneth, until Socorro got the picture of what was going on and gave Maria her full loyalty. That's quite a gang Maria had circling around."

147

"She could have done her own will in her own handwriting. It would have been legal."

"In theory, sure. In actuality, doubtful, with people watching her all the time. And from what Doctor Gates told me about myasthenia gravis, Maria would have been so exhausted at the end of the day—and in the night—that she couldn't possibly have composed a will. She could barely lift a teacup in the evening, and I'm not exaggerating."

"Then why are you here? You could have written all that on a postcard."

"We're back to the murder, Lionel."

Lionel glared at him.

"Everybody's still a suspect, you know," Cliff added.

"You're a slow learner, aren't you? It's in the police files. I was here in Santa Barbara all evening."

"So you said. Now we need proof."

"Who's 'we?' "

"Mona and I and the law."

"I don't have to tell you anything. And anyway I'm innocent till I'm proven guilty, and don't hold your breath for that."

"That's rather an odd thing to say at this juncture, but you're right. However, Lieutenant Puterbaugh can make life miserable for you. He can force you to drop everything and come down to West L.A. for interrogation; tip off the newspapers; reporters and cameramen show up; news photos show 'Atterbury Scion' entering the jailhouse for questioning. I'm not threatening, mind you."

"The hell you're not."

"No, I'm describing reality, which you, Atterbury, seem to have one hell of a time accepting. God, you're a denier! But if you don't want to talk, fine. I'll let Puterbaugh know your decision. Come on, Mona."

He stood up.

"Well, shit! If you'll pardon my French, Mona."

"In French it's *merde*."

"What exactly is it you want?" continued Lionel.

"It will help a lot if you can nail down your alibi and thus eliminate a suspect."

Lionel picked up a ballpoint pen and clicked the button in and out. "Let's make a bargain. I'll tell you the truth, but I want to protect innocent people, of which, by God, I am one. So here are my conditions: Number one, my wife Beryl—who is visiting in Cornwall at the moment—never hears of this. Number two, you can mention facts but no names to Puterbaugh. I wouldn't try that on a cop, but you seem like a decent guy. What do you say, Dunbar?"

"Sounds okay to me. How about you, Mona?"

"Okay, with one proviso: If we ever end up in a courtroom witness chair, we don't perjure ourselves."

"Agreed," said Lionel, rising. "One second."

He went up the hall and motioned to the young woman in the tabasco skirt. She followed him back to the office, walking stiff-legged, her eyes big as Bambi's.

"Alwyn, tell these people where I was the night my Aunt Maria was murdered."

"Why, how would I know a thing like that, Mr. Atterbury?"

"No, it's okay, Alwyn. Go ahead and tell them. And I mean the absolute and literal truth. Don't be afraid. Beryl will never know, and I'll certainly never mention it to Mr. Underwood. Your job is perfectly safe—and so is your reputation."

Alwyn's face turned a uniform strawberry color, and she looked down at her shoes.

"He spent the night in my apartment on Milpas Street," she said hurriedly. Then her head snapped up, and she added, "It only happened that once. I want you to know that!"

"Don't be embarrassed," said Mona. "We've all done the same thing."

Alwyn gave her a small, grateful smile.

"Thanks, Alwyn," said Lionel. "I think you can go now."

Alwyn hurried out.

"Do you believe her?" asked Lionel.

Cliff laughed. "No question about it. Lionel, you most certainly did not kill your Aunt Maria!"

"I often wanted to, the damned old chickabiddy. Yeah, yeah, I know your sister was crazy about her, but your sister didn't have to beg her for money, and she didn't have to pass a moral examination every few months. And yes, I'm referring to the booze . . . and the publicity. At least Aunt Maria was broadminded enough not to look down on my wife because she was a Las Vegas showgirl, I'll give her credit for that. But as for my father, Maria thought he was not only a genius but some kind of allegorical figure with a banner across his chest that said 'Perfection.'"

"That isn't the way I heard it. My impression is she thought your father and your mother were disasters as parents."

"She distorted things. It wasn't their fault their children screwed up. We did it to ourselves."

Cliff shrugged his shoulders. "I won't argue the point. I'll leave that to your various psychiatrists. But getting back to the murder, do you have any suggestions about what we might do next?"

"You've been talking to everybody, I suppose? Colfax and Rawlings and the rest?"

"Oh, yes."

"Then, I don't know. But the store seems to be at the center of the case. Why don't you go back there and look over the books and records?"

"For what purpose?"

"Oh, to see what shape the store's in, for instance. Look at liquidity. The cash flow. Was Grant bankrupting the joint—which I think probable—and got desperate? How about the loan ledger? Is Grant snagging all the best stuff for himself, and salting it away? Has Gwyneth had her fingers in the pie? Is Colfax pulling fast ones? Now that the gold mine up at Quartz Hill is back in operation, is it making any money? If it is, are the profits getting onto the store's balance sheet? That sort of thing."

"Lionel, I'm not a CPA. And I can't just go in there and audit the books."

"Give it a try. You'd be surprised how much you can learn."

Cliff was feeling positively chirpy as they drove up into the hills toward San Ysidro Ranch. Drumming his fingers on the steering wheel, he said, "That narrowed the field, didn't it?"

Mona felt less chirpy about their interview with Lionel. "You had a happy childhood, didn't you, sweetheart?"

"I'd say so. What made you ask?"

"Your assuring Lionel he's obviously innocent."

"You don't agree?"

"Maybe. Maybe not. But it impresses me how ready you are to put your trust in people, with your record of being shot, knifed, threatened, and jumped on. Mind you, I love you for it, but it bowls me over that you're Pollyanna and I'm the cynic."

"You're saying I'm a lousy judge of character?"

"Maybe hasty is all. The girl Alwyn could be just a good actress, you know. And it bothers me that Lionel always wants to get off the subject of the murder as fast as possible and talk about—dum, dum dum dum, DUM!—The Case of the Missing Will."

"You're right. I admit it. Wishful thinking, I suppose. It's so inconvenient having a suspect way up in Santa Barbara, I just want to write him off." He heaved a sigh.

"Forget it and put your hand back on my knee."

19

"I ALREADY KNOW he's nice," said Alison.

"But of course it's his paintings that are important," said Cliff. "I know how busy you are, and I wouldn't drag you down here if I didn't think he was good. But I'd say Rollie has lucked out. He's burning to be a charterboat skipper, not an artist."

"So the way this crazy world works," said Alison, "he's probably ten times as talented as the average person who's burning to be an artist and ought to be skippering a boat."

They arrived at Rollie's place. Alison and Mona smiled at the sight of the bumper sticker on Rollie's Subaru.

"Who in hell is Huitznahua-whoever?" said Alison.

"Not hell—heaven," said Cliff. "A minor Aztec deity."

He was about to knock on Rollie's door, but once more stayed his hand when he heard a guitar inside break out into a series of D and A7 chords, and a familiar voice with a bit of a chortle in it launched into "The Dying Cowboy." At the beginning of the chorus came a line never heard on the streets of Laredo:

"I see by your outfit that you are incontinent—"

whereupon the song broke off because the singer had doubled up with laughter at his own joke.

Alison was delighted. "I don't care what Rollie may have done or not done, I love that man!"

"So do I!" said Mona. "I wish he'd continue!"

152

But it was not to be. The Sweet Singer of Paradise Cove had shot his wad. Cliff knocked on the door.

Rollie appeared at the door still smiling, and his smile broadened when he saw his trio of guests. "Hi, Cliff!" said he. "And, hey, are these two gorgeous flowers for me? But you're Alison Stephens, aren't you? I remember you now. And you must be Mona Dunbar. Come in. Let me pour you a cheap libation!"

As Rollie opened four bottles of Dos Equis, Alison and Mona looked over his bachelor quarters, with particular attention to the watercolors.

"Is there any more to that song you were singing?" asked Mona.

Rollie looked sheepish. "Nope. I quit after that one line. Didn't want to spoil it by going any further. But if you liked that, you ought to get a kick out of this verse of 'Red River Valley.' It's the real thing, too; I didn't make this up." Strumming his guitar, he sang plaintively:

"From this valley they say you are going.
If you do, can your darling go, too?
Would you leave her behind unprotected
When she's loved no other but you?"

They all laughed, and Alison said with a smile, "You do get a charge out of life, don't you?"

"I do, indeed."

"You have talent, too. These watercolors aren't jokes, and they aren't just pretty-pretty. They're full of feeling. Your love for the ocean and boats and fish simply billows out of the frame . . . and in this one, so does your fear of the power of moving water."

"Not fear. Call it respect."

"You also know the craft. Who taught you to paint?"

"Aunt Maria, when I was a kid. She painted herself, you

know. She was great. She showed me how to mix colors and all that, and told me a little bit about composition and high and low horizons and so on, but she never told me what to paint and she never knocked what I did paint."

"A good teacher, in short."

"The best. She didn't ruin my faith in her by praising everything I did, either. If I showed her something crummy, she'd just say, 'It's all right, but you've done better.' I miss that old girl. Got any ideas yet on who did her in?"

"Inklings. But we'll get back to that. Let's stick with your painting."

"What about it?"

"I'd like to carry your stuff."

"You're kidding! In your gallery? You're not just being nice?"

"I'm a businesswoman."

"You're an artist."

"I'm both. And I don't have room on my walls for just being nice. You're very good, and there couldn't be a better market for your stuff than Malibu—except Marina Del Rey, maybe."

"What do you think you can get for these?"

"A minimum of two hundred and fifty—in Malibu if you charge any less than that, they suspect the quality. My commission is fifty percent, by the way."

"So, for those eight paintings, it's possible I could get a thousand clams?"

"Assuming they catch on. And here's a suggestion: Paint some twice that size and they'll go for five hundred—at least after we get your name established."

"Listen, this is exciting as hell! It'll sure help toward my getting that boat in Kona. However, I've got a couple of caveats and whereases you may not like."

"Try me."

"Most important of all, even if it would help promote my stuff: not one word about all the Atterbury jazz. Not even whispered behind your hand to a promising customer. Okay?"

"Agreed."

"Second . . . Oh, just a general comment. Don't expect me to act like an artist—however it is they're supposed to act—or get caught up in the artistic swirl. I'm a fisherman and I'm going to stay one. Painting's great, but it'll always be a sideline, and I'll paint only when I feel like it. Right now, mind you, I feel like it a lot because I want that money. But if I ever had to choose between art and fish, the fish would win, fins down. Do I make myself clear?"

"Gotcha. And here's a fishy handshake to clinch the deal."

Alison smiled and held out her small right hand. Rollie smiled and took it in his big work-roughened one. He didn't let go, and he looked down with pleasure. "Your hand feels good!"

"So does yours," said Alison.

"If you two sex maniacs will break it up," said Cliff, "we have other matters to discuss."

"Buzz off, Cliff," said Alison. "We're artists."

"He's right, though," said Rollie. "We need another round of Dos Equis. Or let's make it Carta Blanca this time."

"Nice Spanish accent you have there," said Mona.

"*Seguro que sí, Rubia.*" Rollie plied his bottle-opener again. "And what are these other matters, Doctor Dunbar?"

"We need a big favor from you. Would you run interference for us on a visit to Atterbury's store?"

"The store? My God, I haven't set foot in that place for years! What do you need me for?"

"To take a look at the books and get an idea of how the store's doing, clear the way for me to examine the loan ledger, show me the ropes in general. What do you say?"

"Sounds like fun! Especially because it'll really bug Grant when I come barging in."

20

"ROLLIE!" CRIED A voice in the china department. "Can that be you?"

A black-haired woman with olive skin and brown eyes rose from behind a counter with a length of violet silk in her hand.

"Hi, Dina. Dina Balsamo, folks." He introduced Mona and Alison and Cliff.

"How's the fish business going, Rollie?"

"Swimmingly."

Dina laughed, showing perfect white teeth. "It's been too long. Come see us more often and brighten our days."

"Only fair, Dina. You've brightened mine."

"That's a beautiful piece of silk," said Cliff. "What are you going to do with it?"

"Display some crystal stemware on it."

"You ought to make it into a dress," said Mona.

"Might be nice at that," said Dina. She draped it over one bare shoulder. The electrifying result would have caused a stampede on the Via Veneto.

"Superb!" exclaimed Alison. "You simply must steal that silk! With your coloring, you'll be gorgeous in it!"

"And when you return, Rollie," added Dina, "bring this perceptive lady with you!"

Something Dina saw behind them made her face cloud over. She put a thumbnail behind her teeth and flipped it, in an old Italian gesture. ". . . And have her go into Round Two with Princess Prissy!"

They turned and saw Molly Teague striding through the

store with her nose in the air, looking imperious. Molly wore an artist's smock over her black faille skirt.

Alison blushed. "You mean you've heard about what happened between me and her?"

"The whole store has heard. You're the local heroine!"

"We need to talk to her," said Cliff.

"About the murder?" said Dina. "I hope she did it, and I hope she's caught."

"Do I detect animosity?"

"You'd think she owns the place. And the rumor is, that's what she has in mind."

"Rollie," said Cliff, "why don't you and Alison go on ahead, and we'll catch up with you."

"Okay. See you up there."

Cliff and Mona followed after Molly, who had mounted two steps into a front show window, where she was completing another autumn display.

" 'Season of mists and mellow fruitfulness,' " said Cliff.

Molly looked up with a pleased smile that quickly turned quizzical and then dark.

"You're Dunbar, aren't you—the Karate Kid's brother."

"Can we talk to you? Ask a few questions?"

Molly chewed her lip. "Front sidewalk."

They followed her out. "I don't have to talk to you, you know that," she said, turning to face them and thrusting her hands into the pockets of her smock.

"That's right, but it's amazing the number of people that think I'm more charming than the police, and more fun. Lieutenant Puterbaugh's very good at his job, but there's no getting away from it, people around town keep saying, 'Puterbaugh's an ogre. Opt for Dunbar.' "

Molly regarded him steadily. "Mind cutting the bullshit?"

"But that's part of my charm."

"The hell you say. How about you?" she said, turning to Mona. "Do you know what the questions are? If so, you ask 'em."

"Glad to, Molly, but geez, I'm sort of a bullshit artist myself. I married him, and it turned out to be catching."

One corner of Molly's mouth twitched with amusement. "Look, I'm busy, so let me fill in the blanks. You're checking up on Grant's alibi and mine, right? I have witnesses to verify I was at home that night, okay?"

"Home being your apartment on Harold Way, above Sunset in the Hollywood Hills. It's all in the record."

"Grant dropped by that evening for a drink and a chat about some floor plans I drew up, and then he left to go practice with his group. The Town Musicians of Bremen, they call themselves. Unfortunately, I'm the only witness that can verify he was at my place, but that's the way it is."

"What time did he arrive at your place?"

"If it's all in the record, how come you have to ask?"

"We don't have the record with us."

"Something like eight-twenty, eight-thirty."

"Are you sure of the time?"

"Hell, no. Who times that sort of thing? Sure, if I'd known he was going to be a murder suspect, I'd have taken a Polaroid shot of him sitting in front of a clock and a calendar, holding up the front page of that day's *Beverly Hills Tattler*."

"I know," said Mona, with a winning smile. "I'm just trying to be the eagle-eyed sleuth. Your times are plausible. I do remember from the record that you worked a little late that evening and left for home at about eight. Two or three people verified that."

"So what else?"

"Did Grant Atterbury attend that auction where they sold off props and stuff from old TV shows?"

"What are you talking about?"

"The way he zips around town, I thought he must have bought the Batmobile. Or did you buy it yourself?"

Molly turned to Cliff. "Would you mind translating Goldilocks's riddle for me?"

"Sure. She means you two must drive like a bat out of hell.

158

Unless the traffic is really light, twenty minutes is pretty fast from here to the Hollywood Hills. And if Grant got to your place at eight-twenty—let alone eight-thirty—I imagine he'd have to leave the motor running in the Batmobile, dash into your place, chug-a-lug a drink, talk fast about the floor plans, give you a peck on the cheek, hop in the Batmobile, and drive like Bobby Unser to join his group at Sixth and California at nine-ten or nine-fifteen or even nine-twenty way out in Santa Monica."

Molly tensed her right arm. "Are you calling me a liar?"

Cliff turned to Mona. "Are we, Mona?"

Mona backed up a step or two. "Yes." She thrust an arm out and added hurriedly, "Listen—I don't know karate but I'm a physical therapist!"

Molly glared at her and breathed heavily.

Cliff took a step forward to intervene. "Come on, Molly, where were you two that night? Your story just won't cut it. The night of the murder, Gwyneth Atterbury had dinner with Doctor Rawlings and then they went to a play. So Grant gave the cook the night off and scrounged a snack for himself. What he was doing from six until nine is anybody's guess, but he had plenty of time to whack Auntie in the head and mosey over to band practice."

"Thus killing the goose that laid the golden egg."

"There can be other motives for murder."

"Such as arranging for Lionel to take over the store so he can finish it off for good this time. Turn it into a liquor store, probably. Then we'd all be freed, like Rollie, right?"

"Talk sense, Molly. Grant wouldn't have to kill Maria to give Lionel the store."

"I'm going to make a statement, and then I wash my hands of this business. Of all the people I know, Grant is the most underrated and the most misunderstood. Some people say it was a fluke, and unfair at that, his taking over the store instead of Lionel. But who else could have, with Lionel refusing to lay off the Flit? Consuelo? Ha! Rollie? Double ha. Grant had no choice. I wouldn't have blamed him, though, if he had schemed his way to the throne. His self-esteem was in terrible shape. Lionel was groomed for the presidency, so the old man couldn't care less when Grant majored in music at Stanford.

"For a while, marrying Gwyneth helped Grant—it won him the envy of every man in town. It did *not* help when Gwyneth turned out to be hot as the hinges of hell with other men, and cold as a fish with him. Know what would really make him happy . . . and make me happy? If he didn't have a nickel. Then he could join some group with his clarinet and try to come unstuck from the so-called Atterbury mystique."

Molly thrust out a pink lower lip and blew a lock of black hair away from an Irish-blue eye. "And that's all she wrote."

"I still have a few questions," said Cliff.

"I'm out of answers. Grant hasn't done anything, so forget it. And if he were guilty . . . yes, I'd lie. I'd cover up like crazy for him. Ciao!"

With a swirl of her smock, she turned and went back through the brass-and-glass doors.

"Well, Goldilocks, what do you deduce from that?"

"She knows more than she's telling," said Mona.

They rejoined Alison and Rollie at Helen Turin's desk outside Grant Atterbury's office. It obviously had made Miss Turin's day to see Rollie again. "Barge right in," she said. "It's a family reunion."

Inside, they saw what she meant. Consuelo was there, fitting an English cigarette into a foot-long carved-ivory holder.

"Hello, kiddies," she said. "Nice to see you again. And, good heavens, do my eyes deceive me or is that Don Rolando, *el famoso pescador de* Paradise Cove? *Qué tal, Manito?* And where did you get that shirt? I want one."

Rollie was wearing his Mexican guayabera shirt with the embroidered butterflies.

"*Qué tal, Chamaca?* Got it in Ensenada. You'd look good in one."

"I'll appreciate it," said Grant, leaning forward in his

swivel chair, "if neither one of you ever shows up in the store again wearing those things."

"Gotcha," said Rollie. "I'll wear a Harrow school tie with it next time."

Connie rose from her chair. "Kiddies, I've got to run, but take a tip and forget it if you're here to ask any favors. The Reluctant Dragon isn't in the mood."

Grant's left nostril lifted. "Why don't you go treat yourself to a good high colonic, Connie?"

"See what I mean? Well, tinkerty-tonk." She adjusted her mink jacket and stalked out.

"You will never believe what that dumb sister of mine wanted," said Grant. "She wanted me to send her to Europe as European buyer for Atterbury's—at a lush salary, of course."

"Not a bad idea," said Rollie. "It's shocking she wants to work, of course, but she ought to be pretty good at it. She's got good taste, and she speaks Spanish, French, and Italian."

"And what are you here for?"

"I'd like to look at the books. Second quarter balance sheet and profit-and-loss statement ought to be enough."

"Why the interest? I thought you voted yourself out of the family."

"Favor for my detective friends here."

"What if I say no?"

"I'm a stockholder, remember? Two shares, preferred."

"So?"

Rollie administered a vigorous scratching to his curly head. "California law says a stockholder is entitled to look at the company books. If you say no, I report you to the Department of Corporations in Sacramento and they do terrible things to you, and hence to the illustrious name of Atterbury."

Grant gazed at Rollie in disgust; Rollie gazed back benignly and picked a flake of skin off his sunburned nose.

"All right, Roland. If you think you can recall your high

161

school bookkeeping, go see Per Quanstrom in Accounting. I can save you some trouble, though, by telling you in advance that I've increased sales thirty percent in the last five years."

"While inflation has gone up fifty. Losing money, are you?"

"Get out of here."

Rollie grinned and went out. Grant watched him go, and then turned to Alison, Cliff, and Mona with a pleasant expression. "It's sad but true," he said, "that I always feel better instantly when people in my family go away."

"We've noticed that," said Cliff, also smiling. "By the way, we ran into Molly Teague a while ago. She tells us you dropped in and had a drink with her the night of the murder."

Grant hesitated for a moment or two before answering, "Yes, I did. What time did she say I was there?"

"Around eight-twenty, eight-thirty," said Cliff and instantly cursed himself for his stupidity, knowing he should have waited to hear what Grant would say.

"That's about right, I suppose," said Grant, frowning. "Made me a little late for rehearsal. I hope you didn't have a run-in with Molly," he said with a short laugh, looking at Alison. "Especially in the china department."

"Cliff and Mona talked to her. I haven't seen her at all."

"Did you people want something, or did you just come along with Rollie?"

"I'd like to look at the loan ledger, if I may," said Cliff.

Grant swiveled his chair to the left and pulled a thick and battered business ledger with triangular red-leather corners from a two-shelf bookcase. He handed the ledger to Cliff and said, "How's that for service? You'll see there's a lot of history in that book. Also, since you must be primarily interested in Aunt Maria, you'll find a list on the last page of all the items she had out on the loan ledger. I thought it would save trouble to list them all together neatly instead of making her old page in the ledger even more unreadable than it had become."

"You wrote in these entries yourself?"

162

"I did. Sidney Colfax thought it would be wise to call in all these things and start with a clean sheet, and I agreed with him. They're sellable assets of the store, after all, and this way we keep everybody honest. Why don't you take the ledger out onto the floor; there's good lighting and sofas near the restrooms. If you'd like coffee, I'll have my secretary bring it to you."

They found a leather sofa and a coffee table in a quiet corner. Cliff sat between Alison and Mona and opened the ledger on the table.

"The red carpet again," said Cliff. "Taken a fancy to us, hasn't he?"

They entertained themselves for a few minutes by perusing the early entries in the ledger, dating back to 1905, 1910, many of them inscribed in beautiful copperplate handwriting, tracking objets d'art and articles of furniture as they circulated back and forth between the store and members of the family.

For instance, there was an Emmaline Atterbury, a great-aunt, it would seem, who took out and returned at one time or another between the years 1907 and 1915: "1 Aubusson tapestry; 1 Gobelin tapestry; 1 Louis XVI escritoire; 1 Sarouk runner 2'3" × 19'5"; 1 Chinese rug 15'6" × 23'7", blue and cream, bat-and-lantern design in border"; and assorted tables, glassware, and Tiffany lamps.

Maria Atterbury, it appeared, never withdrew articles of furniture; instead, she used the store as a sort of lending library of art, taking out paintings, statuary, and the like and returning them in five or six months. She did this to such a point that she had filled up an entire page, which was dog-eared and smudged. An irregular fragment about an inch long had also been torn from the margin at some point in the past.

Grant had devoted part of a new page to the list of items returned to the store in September from Maria's house. The list was not long:

163

Utrillo, "Jour de Pluie, Place du Tertre," oil
Boinay, "Lake in the Bois de Boulogne," oil
Ivory jui, T'ang Dynasty
Rose jade jui, Manchu dynasty
White jade Kwan Yin, modern, 11" tall
Jade koi (fish), pigeon's-blood-on-snow, late Ming dynasty, approx. 15$\frac{1}{2}$"
Celadon bowls (2), crackle glaze, 11$\frac{1}{2}$ in. dia., Chien Lung period (18th cent.)
Juan Ramírez García (Mexico), "Dia de Plaza," water-color on canvas, 35 $\times$ 45 centimeters
Rufino Tamayo (Mexico), "Wild Dog," lithograph, signed and with notation in English, also in Tamayo's hand, "Printer's proof to Lloyd Boggs"
Ebony screen, 4 sections w/4 panels ea. of spinach jade, Chien Lung period
J. Dubic (Haiti), "Renommé Devant," primitive oil, 24" $\times$ 36"
Head of Bodhisattva, Cambodian, 9$\frac{1}{2}$" tall on 5" teak-wood base.

Alison remembered that the Kwan Yin and the jade koi were among the items that the "burglar" had thrown onto the pile of items in the middle of Maria's bedroom. It still seemed a stupid thing to do.

She and Cliff checked back to Maria's old ledger page and found the koi, the Kwan Yin, and one of the jui—whatever those were—listed together next to the tear in the margin. Only the wording was slightly different. The fish was simply called a fish back in 1939. "Koi" became a popular term in postwar years under Japanese influence. It was listed as "Jade fish, pigeon's-blood-on-snow, Ming dynasty (?), 15$\frac{1}{2}$ inches long."

"Obviously the same fish and Kwan Yin," said Cliff. "Wouldn't you agree, Alison?"

"Oh, yes, no doubt about it."

Several similar items had been retrieved from Lionel Atterbury, plus one large rug: a replica of an antique Chinese rug, burnt orange and light blue, that was in the Metropolitan Museum, hand-woven in Hong Kong by special order of Atterbury père. Only four items had been retrieved from Consuelo, presumably because she was always on the move, flitting from Paris to Pontresina, to Mexico City, Zihuatanejo, San Miguel de Allende, Papeete, London, Costa del Sol, and Beverly Hills. Nothing at all had ever been signed out to Rollie Atterbury Freed.

"Well, there it is," said Cliff. "Either of you see anything out of the ordinary?"

"Not me," said Alison.

"I see one thing that's a little odd," said Mona, "but I suppose it doesn't amount to anything: All through this ledger, things are itemized by quantity—one this, one that, three of those, one set of these, one pair of such and such. But Grant has listed Maria's stuff merely as 'Kwan Yin, jui, fish, screen,' and so on. He does say 'Celadon bowls (two),' but aside from that, the only numbers he uses for quantities are those panels in the four-section screen, and that's just a description."

"What do you make of it?" asked Cliff.

"Nothing."

Rollie Freed, in turn, reported that he made nothing out of examining the books beyond what he already surmised. "You can't really tell much from a balance sheet anyway," he said, when he rejoined them. "So what you do is read the auditors' comments first. And when I read between the auditors' lines, the message I get is this: Five or six more years of Grant's management and this place has had it. He'll have to cash out, but that won't be so bad because he and Lionel and Connie will come into a nifty hunk of money. They just won't be able to impress anybody with the Atterbury name anymore. The end of a great mercantile dynasty. Sniff, sniff. Ah, well, it's been fun making my final appearance in here, and the main purpose anyway was to gain entrée for you people. I'm going back to my fish now."

After Rollie took off, Cliff said, "Listen, if you two don't mind, I'd like to drop in at Waldenbooks to buy a book on the Atterburys that Rollie told me about."

Waldenbooks was in the Beverly Wilshire Hotel building just down the street from Atterbury's. When they walked in, they were mildly surprised to see Consuelo leaning on one of the counters, talking easily with another woman.

"Monday, then," said Consuelo. "And I'm sure it'll be a boundless joy, but to be on the safe side I'd better lay in a supply of Red Cross shoes and Supp-Hose. . . . Ah! Here are the Three Musketeers again, back safe and sound from battling the evil Duke of Burgundy!"

Consuelo introduced them to the manager, Mrs. DeWeese, a poised and amiable black-haired woman with nearly jet-black eyes. Alison later speculated that the two women hit it off because they were virtually twins, although Consuelo had the edge with her lush Spanish beauty.

"Guess what," said Consuelo. "You are looking at the nation's latest entry into the labor force!"

"You've gotten a job?" said Mona.

"Here, thanks to this charming lady. We think I should make a great success, partly because I will force my entire entourage of friends to give us their exclusive business or it's no more freeloading on the *pâté de foie gras avec cornichons.* Tomorrow I'll buy myself a Betty Boop lunch pail and apply for a Social Security card."

"I congratulate you," said Cliff. "However, aren't you going to cause shock and amazement among your friends?"

"You bet your bassoon I am. The *pièce de résistance* is that it will scandalize Grant to have his sister working just down the street. Well, the nerd wanted me to get a job, so his dream has come true."

Cliff grinned. "Want to warm up on me as your first customer? I came in to buy a copy of *East Meets West: The Atterbury Story*."

"That chestnut! It should be shelved under Fantasy and Science Fiction, but I've seen it over there under Business. Oh, well, at least half the truths in the book are half-truths, so your money isn't entirely wasted. Here we are. The Atterbury Story, or How to Make Chicanery Respectable. You'll have to take it over to Mrs. DeWeese; I'd be happy to ring it up myself just for the practice, but I don't know how. Besides, cash registers don't ring anymore, do they? They go 'boop boop' instead. So Monday I'll learn to boop up purchases. Did you find out anything worthwhile from beloved brother Grant?"

"Not that I know of."

"I didn't think you would. You'd learn more holding a conch shell against your ear. At least you'd find out what the wild waves are saying."

"Maybe I'll learn something from the book."

"No, you won't; but there's lots of pretty pictures."

21

ALISON AND ROLLIE were having coffee and laughing together when Cliff and Mona walked into the gallery. Alison was radiant again in her bright red Don Manuel Osorio Manrique de Zuñiga outfit. Her eyes sparkled, presumably in amusement at something Rollie had just said, but her gaze was so riveted on him as to suggest there was something more to it than that. The implication was not lost on either Cliff or Mona.

"Hitting it off okay, are you?" Cliff observed with a knowing smile.

A roseate blush appeared on Alison's cheeks. "We just finished hanging five of his paintings," she said, "and I predict Rollie will be able to buy his Bartram next spring, but tell them about the crabs at Atterbury's, Rollie!"

"I was telling Alison," Rollie said, "about the time during Lionel's brief presidency at the store when crabs suddenly infested the executive washroom. It was scandalous. Right there in Beverly Hills, the entire executive staff had crabs. One day when Lionel was busy as hell at his desk, old Per Quanstrom tiptoed in. Did you meet him? Guy about sixty-four with a gray mustache and Vandyke? Extremely proper and dignified. Wears garters. He hesitated and said in a low voice, 'Lionel, what's the best way to get rid of crabs?' Lionel thought he was referring to the washroom. He looked up from his papers and said, 'Well, I understand a blowtorch is pretty effective.' Quanstrom's eyes bulged out, and he turned around and ran out of the office."

The four of them rocked with laughter.

"How about some coffee with a little Kahlua?" said Alison. "That's what we're having." She busied herself getting out cups and saucers. Behind her, in a corner, stood a wooden easel with two or three squares of drawing paper pinned to it. She was preparing to resume with Maria's portrait. Mona went over to look.

"Are those your original rough sketches?" she asked.

"Yes. I had those at home when she was murdered."

"This one is that jade fish."

"Right. And you've no idea how hard it was to get exactly that shade of pigeon's-blood-on-snow."

Mona frowned. "But this isn't the same fish—not the one Grant showed us in the store!"

"But it has to be!"

"No! The one in your sketch is curving in the opposite way! Cliff, do you have the police file?"

"In the car."

"Get it!"

Cliff returned with the folder and took out the glossy police print of the chaotic pile in Maria's bedroom. In the middle of it lay the jade fish, curving, undoubtedly, in an arc opposite to the one in Alison's sketch.

Alison smacked her forehead. "Good grief! Remember when Puterbaugh showed us that photo that had been printed backward? And then he showed us the same photo printed the right way, and I still thought something was wrong? Well, that was it. Everything else was all right, but the fish was backward!"

"Aha! So there was a pair of these things!" said Cliff. "You never saw the other one, Ali?"

She shook her head.

"How about you, Rollie?"

"No, the only one I ever saw was that one on her mantelpiece."

"All right, so the question is, where's the other one?"

"There's also another question," said Rollie. "What differ-

169

ence does one fish more or less make? And I ask that as a professional," he added with a grin.

Cliff mused. "Let's see. It means the murderer tossed the wrong fish onto the pile. So now the question is, did he or she know the difference, or had Maria changed fish for some reason?"

"Maybe I'm just being stubborn," said Rollie, "but I still say what difference does it make?"

"Hell, I don't know," said Cliff. "But we're hard up for clues, and this must have some connection with the murder."

"Can we even prove there was another fish?" said Mona. "Alison's sketch might not persuade other people."

"The answer is yes," said Cliff. "I'm going to go see our pal Grant once more."

22

"YOU ARE CERTAINLY persistent, Doctor Dunbar, but at the risk of sounding inhospitable, you're on the verge of turning into an extremely tiresome person."

"My friends tell me the same thing. They accuse me of imitating Bulldog Drummond. Badly."

"For the life of me, I don't see why you can't leave matters up to the police. I'm willing to humor you this time, but from now on I cannot have you running into this office and interrupting business every time you've found a strange button in the ice cream. You will henceforth phone and make an appointment with Miss Turin. Agreed?"

"Agreed."

"Now, what makes you think there was another jade fish? And by the way, I hope you're right, because they'd be extremely valuable as a pair."

"I dropped into Waldenbooks when we left you the other day. Consuelo sold me a copy of *East Meets West: The Atterbury Story.*"

Grant leaned back in his swivel chair and looked down his nose. "I'm going to try to get her fired. And so?"

"Take a look at the photographs on pages twenty-six and twenty-seven—the customs documents for a shipment of goods your father bought from a Chinese merchant in nineteen thirty-seven."

Cliff held the book out to him. Grant disdained to take it. "I hardly need you to educate me about the family history."

" 'One pair jade carp, pigeon's-blood-on-snow,' it says. So where's the other one, Grant?"

"Perhaps it was sold long ago, and it's Mister Atterbury to you, Doctor Dunbar."

"Would you mind checking your records, Mister Atterbury?"

"Yes, I would. You may go soak your head, Doctor Dunbar."

Cliff smiled. "Would you at least check the loan ledger, Mister Atterbury?"

"With pleasure." Grant spun in his chair and plucked the ledger out of his bookcase. "But haven't you already gone through it, Doctor Dunbar?"

"Yes, I have, Mister Atterbury, and I discovered an oddity. You have checked one jade koi back in, from Maria's house. But on Maria's previous page, recording her original withdrawal, a piece is torn out of the margin. I suspect the entry originally read, 'One pair jade fish' or whatever, but now it just says 'jade fish.' "

"Maybe that's all it said in the first place. 'Fish' can be either singular or plural."

"Yes, but how about the fact that the word 'jade' isn't capitalized, the way the first word of all the other entries are?"

"Beats me, Doctor Dunbar. Let me take a look."

Grant turned to the original ledger for Maria and examined it closely. Then he looked at the photo in *East Meets West.* "Fascinating. All right, Doctor Dunbar, I concede I probably owe you an apology. But where has all this gotten us? What comes next?"

"I'd like to find that fish."

"So would I. In fact, bring me that fish and I'll give you a two-thousand-dollar reward. Anything else on your mind?"

"Not at the moment."

"In that case." Grant flicked a switch on his intercom. A muffled burst of laughter came through the door. "Helen, after you've regained control of yourself, would you please show Doctor Dunbar out?"

172

Miss Turin opened the door, her eyes full of mirth and a broad grin on her face. Cliff followed her out and she closed the door.

Cliff smiled at her. "Was that you laughing out here?"

"Under the Ancien Régime," she said, "that is, during the reigns of Maria Atterbury and Lionel Atterbury, I didn't have to be so damn dignified. But ever since the Lost Dauphin took over . . . Oh, well, maybe I'd better stop reading this book before it gets me fired."

"What's the book?"

"A hard-boiled murder mystery from the thirties. I hit a line that cracked me up." She picked up the book. "It says— it says . . ." Her voice quavered. " 'The roscoe yammered from across the room.' " She bent over gasping, stifling her laughter. At length she straightened up and poked a corner of her handkerchief under her glasses to wipe away a tear.

"I wish something would yammer in this case," said Cliff, grinning. "You've seen a lot of the people who are involved. Got any suggestions?"

"Sure. As it says in this book, *cherchez la femme.*"

"That isn't much help. I've already found four of them."

23

Two DAYS LATER on Wednesday, Cliff found himself a bachelor again for the evening. Mona had gone to an orientation seminar at UCLA for people thinking about applying for medical school. The seminar was slated for 7:00 to 10:00 P.M., and she planned to go out for coffee afterward with her friend Clara, a fellow physical therapist who was also interested in becoming a doctor. Mona warned him that she might not be back until midnight.

At loose ends, Cliff prowled the house trying to think of what he wanted to do. He looked guiltily at his copy of Barbara Tuchman's *A Distant Mirror,* which he hadn't read yet, although it dealt with the fourteenth century, on which he was supposedly an expert; he simply did not feel intellectual. He considered television, but then he didn't feel mentally retarded, either.

He decided to go visit Alison. After phoning to make sure she was at home, he hopped into his Porsche.

He smelled the familiar scents of the chaparral as he drove up Topanga Canyon: the heavy medicinal odors of laurel leaf sumac, black sage, and white sage, like a combination of cough medicine and Vick's Vapo-Rub; the sweet licorice of fennel; the peppery smell of the sycamores growing along Topanga Creek. He drove up the steep winding curves and through the cluster of stores in the little village on the flat. Mounting the still steeper ascent of Entrada Drive, he caught a startled coyote in his headlights.

Cliff had given up trying to persuade Alison to move out of her small house perched on a hillside in Topanga, where terrifying fires roar over the hills every few years and burn off the chaparral, followed by mudslides that sometimes close the canyon road for a week or more in the rainy season.

"Look, I love it up here," Alison always said. "Here I am, right next to the city, but it's quiet, it's green, and the air's better. It really is the country. And where else in Los Angeles can you see, in a single month, horned owls, red-tailed hawks, coyotes, foxes, woodpeckers, raccoons, quail, rattlesnakes, and deer?"

"And arsonists."

"An occasional fire is good for the place. The Indians used to burn it off on purpose."

This evening if was Alison's turn to nag Cliff. "You better watch it, Big Bruvver. Mona's a hard-working realist. If she starts practicing medicine while you're still lolling around the house listening to Mexican music and eating bananas, I don't care how much she loves you, she isn't going to like it. But never mind that, I've got great news about the portrait. Guess who else is coming this evening—Sidney Colfax Roman Numeral Three."

"Colfax! Why?"

"He himself is bringing the portrait over."

"But this isn't Monday."

"He says he persuaded Grant to let go of it. I just hope he's careful. The paint isn't anywhere near dry yet."

They heard a car pull up in the driveway, and in a few moments the doorbell rang.

Colfax followed Alison into the living room, carrying the portrait in a cardboard container and uttering greetings and expressions of concern.

"Oh, I'm sure it's all right," Ali assured him. She slid the portrait out of the cardboard and propped it on her easel. "Yes, it's fine. I really thank you. What can I fix you to drink?"

"Whatever you two are having."

"We're having something called a boccie-ball. It's merely a

suit-yourself mixture of Amaretto, orange juice, and a bit of soda, but I think you'll like it."

"It sounds delightful. It'll take me back to the Italian hill towns."

Cliff looked at him with interest. This was a born-again Colfax. The lawyer was wearing a navy blue blazer, tan slacks, and a polo shirt with an alligator on it. But the big change was in his face. Lines of stress had disappeared from his cheeks, and the crow's-feet had smoothed around his eyes. His personality seemed to have smoothed out, too. Gone was the man's smug sarcasm.

"I'm impressed," said Alison, "having an important attorney making like United Parcel."

"It's a privilege and a pleasure," said Colfax. "And this boccie-ball has indeed taken me right back to San Gimignano. I'll remember the recipe. As for the delivery, it's the least I can do. I'm indebted to both of you—especially to you, Doctor Dunbar—for restoring me to sanity."

"Don't overdo it. My motives weren't benevolent."

"The effects were. But let's drop this embarrassing subject. I'd like to do you a small favor. I don't know if it will help you solve Maria Atterbury's case, but let me tell you about a small matter."

They waited. Colfax looked down in his glass. "Mind you, I'm being deliberately cryptic and terse because I don't want to get myself disbarred, but let me say this: As the attorney drawing up Maria's will, supposedly according to her wishes, I purposely moved with a speed more like that of Stepin Fetchit than of Mary Decker." He looked squarely at Cliff and repeated, "Purposely. This means that Lionel Atterbury at least had the right idea."

Colfax finished his drink and rose to his feet. "And with that, I will bid you an affectionate *buona sera* and God bless."

As Alison showed him out and thanked him, she added, "Thelma's pretty lucky after all."

"So am I."

When they heard him drive off, they went over to Alison's easel to examine the portrait.

"What's that white stuff on her chest?"

"It's going to be Mechlin lace, if you'll give me a chance to finish. Maria's red-velvet dress had white lace over the collar and a patch of it on her pocket. My problem is how to suggest delicate lace using the slap-it-on impasto technique. I think I'll get right at it. But how about you? Want another boccie-ball?"

"No, I'd better be going myself."

24

GRINDING BACK DOWN the curves of Entrada Drive in velvet blackness, Cliff suddenly felt that either Colfax or Alison had said something of great significance—some fact or phrase or perhaps even a mere word. Mexican music? Impasto? Mechlin lace? Red velvet?

Just as the possible, although truly far-out, answer came to him and he pounded his fist on the steering wheel in the thrill of discovery, his motor conked out. He put his excitement on hold and pulled over onto the shoulder, annoyed.

He tried the starter. It turned over briskly, but the motor wouldn't catch. The gas gauge registered half full. There was a 76 gas station in the village, not far down the road, but he wasn't sure it had a mechanic, so he didn't want to risk either walking or trying to coast down. He could walk back to Ali's house and call the auto club, but it would be a long upward climb in street shoes. He decided to check under the hood to make sure it wasn't some dumb problem he could correct using a dime or his thumb and forefinger.

He raised the hood and was about to turn and get a flashlight out of his glove compartment when a car pulled up behind him. The driver hopped out, a beefy fellow wearing black jeans and a denim shirt embroidered with red and yellow flowers.

"Car trouble?" he called out in a cheery voice.

"Yes, the motor just cut out on me. The starter's okay and I've got plenty of gas."

"Sounds like a fuel pump or a fuel line. I'll take a look. I'm a mechanic."

"Now, there's a stroke of luck."

The man shone his own flashlight onto the motor. "Yep, I see your trouble already. There's a little tiny C-clamp squeezin' down on your flexible fuel line. That oughtn't to be there, should it?"

The man looked at him with a foxlike grin. Cliff's gut froze.

"But my partner back there's got a tool that'll solve everything."

A gaunt man stood beside the other car. He wore a red plaid shirt and khaki pants. His narrow face was scored with deep vertical grooves, and his hand held a Colt .45 pistol.

"Course, I got me one of 'em, too."

When Cliff looked back at the mechanic, he had moved off six feet or so and was pointing an identical pistol at Cliff.

"Okay, Doc, just move to the back of our car there."

Cliff looked at the two of them and his heart sank. Unlike two knife-wielding punks he had once clobbered in a Westwood parking lot, these two thugs were professionals. It also looked as if they had had army training. They stood close enough so they couldn't miss, but far enough away so that he might as well forget karate or judo. Running was out of the question. A .45 slug would make an entry hole in his back the size of a golf ball and an exit hole in his chest that would take a basketball. Sadly, he moved to the rear of the car, a 1964 Ford Galaxy that needed a paint job so badly he couldn't see what its true color was.

Gaunt opened the trunk while Beefy covered Cliff.

"Get in," said Beefy.

Reluctantly, Cliff crawled in. Gaunt slammed his pistol into the side of Cliff's head and shut the trunk lid.

Cliff fell over stunned, but he didn't quite pass out. For long minutes, though, he was disoriented, like someone who has wakened from a bad dream but doesn't know at first where he is or whether what his eyes are seeing is dream or reality. Wherever he was, it was dark, it stank, and people talked in muffled voices.

It also bounced, and that shook him into realizing where he was—locked in the trunk of a car with exhaust fumes coming up through the floorboards. He came close to vomiting from terror, the stink, and the splitting pain in his head, but forced himself back into control just in time, as the acid heartburn of vomit rose to his throat. Crawling around in his puke could only deepen his misery.

"But why take the chance?" said a voice. "We could've iced him back there and been done with it."

"Don't be an asshole, Artie. Use your head."

"What the fuck you think I'm usin', my left tit?"

"Risk is what you'd be takin', asshole. What if—it won't happen, I'm just sayin' what if—what if the cops stopped us for some goddamn reason like failing to signal for a right turn and got suspicious and said open the trunk. You want to explain what a stiff is doin' back there?"

No answer.

"Rather go to the slammer for murder instead of kidnapping or maybe just assault?"

Silence.

"Okay, then!"

Cliff was overwhelmed with sadness and bitter self-reproach. So this was to be the end. This was the penalty for his smugness and arrogance. Oh, he was so much smarter than the police! He was the hotshot amateur private eye with his name in all the papers for upsetting a gubernatorial election. He saw Mona's face distorted with agony and tears. The promise of a lifetime of happiness with her was gone. He couldn't tell her one last time how much he loved her.

His handkerchief over his nose helped a little to filter out the exhaust fumes. His head throbbed.

"Did you remember to take that C-clamp off?"

"I got it. They'll never figure out why he stopped there."

Muffled laughter.

My God, a Camel would taste good right now! One last Camel. The attorney general has determined that murder-

180

solving is hazardous to your health. Alison . . . would she take a close look at that portrait?

"Wanna tell me now where we're takin' him?"

"Deer Canyon, up past Zuma Beach. According to our meal ticket, one of those antherpology professors from UCLA dug up some Indian stuff and then filled the holes up again. Two, three hundred years old. About a quarter mile off the highway. We reopen a hole, stick him in, and he's good for two hundred more years."

"I won't mind doin' a little diggin' for ten grand."

"Five. We split fifty-fifty."

The Ford was probably on the Coast Highway now. Salt air and a fishy smell mingled with the exhaust fumes. . . . Death, and worse—the fear of death. He had come close, so close, in Vietnam. Sergeant Phil Fixico's black face had looked so beautiful when he had dragged Cliff, bleeding, out of that jungle stream! The fear of death. *Timor mortis.* What irony! Five hundred years ago, the best-known poem by his direct lineal ancestor William Dunbar, the Scot, was about the fear of death, and the man meant it, too. Every stanza ended with an outcry of how that fear disturbed him:

I that in heill wes and gladnes
Am trublit now with greit seiknes
And feblit with infirmite:
Timor mortis conturbat me.

Conturbat the hell out of me too, William. *Deus in adiutorium meum intende.* But supposedly, God helps those who help themselves. . . . Hey! My mind must be ticking over okay if I can still quote that opening stanza.

Cliff groped about in the trunk, but his hand encountered no Kalashnikov rifle or Luger pistol that had been conveniently overlooked. Instead, fate presented him with a single-socket lug wrench and an old umbrella. But that's all any of us heroes need, right? Clint Eastwood or Bruce Lee would erupt from the trunk swinging the lug wrench and flatten Beefy and Gaunt; and Errol Flynn or Richard Chamberlain would leap out yelling "En garde!" and run 'em through with the umbrella. In real life, he would soon be looking at the black death-holes in the barrels of two .45-caliber pistols from a distance of eight feet or so.

No, his only hope was that the police actually would stop Beefy for some traffic violation, but Beefy was being careful not to speed, and there would be no right turns at all until he turned off the highway at Deer Canyon.

But what if the car had some mechanical defect? What if it poured out blue clouds of exhaust? Or what if it had no license plate? Or no taillights?

Now, there was an idea. Those old Ford Galaxys had big round taillights. Cliff squeezed himself over to the right wall of the trunk, braced himself, put his foot against the taillight assembly, and pushed with gradually mounting pressure.

Wires broke. Screws loosened.

"Hellzat?"

"What? I didn't hear nothin'."

He did it again. This time the whole assembly pushed out to the rear, rusty chrome, red reflector and all. The thugs up front didn't react. A shaft of fresh air washed in.

Cliff scrambled to his knees and peered out the hole left by the vanished taillight. He recognized motels and houses on the ocean side of the highway in Malibu.

At one point, although he couldn't see it, he was pretty sure they were passing the Malibu sheriff's substation on the inland side. God willing, maybe a car from there or from the highway patrol would come after Beefy. But it didn't, of course. When you need a policeman, thought Cliff, he's dunking a free doughnut at Burger King.

Through the hole, he saw the lights of Malibu pier. A couple of minutes later he knew they had passed Alison's gallery, then the turnoff into Malibu Canyon. Beyond Malibu the highway rose steeply. As the car climbed the hill, he could look back and see more and more of the lights garlanding the curving coastline that circled Santa Monica Bay and ended far down in Palos Verdes. The cliché was true: They did indeed twinkle like jewels at the edge of the water.

It was incredibly beautiful—so much so that tears filled Cliff's eyes. He closed them and rested his head on his forearm, remembering that recurring line in *Shogun*, "Life is so beautiful, Anjin-san, and so sad."

Forlorn, he looked out the hole again. Perhaps he should try somehow to signal one of the cars that occasionally passed by. Or perhaps he should shout at the two thugs and try to buy them off. But no, that would be useless. He wondered who had hired them. Whoever it was obviously believed Cliff was dangerously close to ferreting out him or her.

Beyond the summit of the hill, the road began a long gradual descent toward Paradise Cove and Zuma Beach. His remaining fragment of life had now dwindled to minutes. If salvation were to come, it would have to come fast.

Was it wishful thinking, or did he see a wide rectangular object on the roof of the car behind him? He squinted his eyes, but he could not be sure, until the highway leveled off at the beach and an overhead light somewhere revealed that the car back there belonged to the highway patrol. Cliff guessed that the officer or officers in it were tracking the Ford Galaxy, trying to decide whether to bother citing the driver for having only one taillight.

Cliff's heart bounded with hope. He seized the umbrella, thrust it out the hole as far as he could reach, and pressed the button on the handle. The umbrella flew open, and in a matter of seconds Cliff saw, filtering through the thin black fabric of the umbrella, the blurred splotch of a shining red light. It was more beautiful than a Waikiki sunset.

"Aw-aw, now we're in for it!" said the voice of Gaunt.

"Cool it, asshole! Can't be anything important. Just ack natural!"

The two cars pulled over onto the shoulder of the highway.

Cliff dropped the umbrella. He saw the driver of the police car get out carrying a shotgun. Another car door slammed. The officer must have had a partner, who approached Beefy's car on the passenger side.

"What's up, officer?" Cliff heard Beefy say in a polite voice. "Ain't done anything wrong, have we?"

"Maybe not," said the officer, with a short laugh, "but you sure must have thought you were breaking the sound barrier."

"Huh? I don't getcha."

"Well, you had to pop out your drag chute to come to a stop. Just like a B-52 bomber."

"What the hell are you talking about?"

The officer then uttered words more poetic than anything to be found in the *Norton Anthology*.

"Get out of the car and open your trunk."

25

BY THE TIME he had answered all the questions put to him by the highway patrol officers, had accompanied them to the Malibu jail where they dropped off Beefy and Gaunt, had been chauffeured back to his car in Topanga, and had driven home, Cliff was giddy with mingled exhaustion and elation at being alive. He was also amazed that it was only 11:15. One can certainly pack a lot of living into three or four hours.

Tears again came to his eyes when he turned off Sunset into the driveway of his one-story Spanish dream house near UCLA. God, or the President of the Universe, or whoever that intellect was out there, had evidently decided to grant him a lifetime with Mona after all—and he resolved to take no more chances on blowing it. Humbly, he conceded that the Ph.D. after his name was insidious. It lured him into thinking he was brainier than he actually was. Or maybe he was brainy in certain ways, but no doubt about it: Mona had better common sense.

He dragged himself into the house, feeling an overwhelming need to pamper himself, to take things in, to replenish himself. A bath was certainly called for. The filth from Beefy's trunk was ground into his skin.

He went to the refrigerator, took out a bottle of Chardonnay and poured himself a full Baccarat glassful. He was glad that the wine was chilled far colder than was proper. Then he plucked a paperback murder mystery out of a bookcase and went into the bathroom. He drew a tubful of hot water, positioned the little inflatable bathtub pillow that Mona had bought, took off his clothes, set the wine on the edge of the tub, and eased himself in.

"Ohhhhhh, boy oh boy!"

Not since Vietnam had a bath felt so good to him. He took a good mouthful of wine, "chewed" it like a connoisseur, settled his head against the pillow, and took up the murder mystery.

"Hair of the dog," he said to himself, grinning.

Had he ever been psychoanalyzed or had he even been a little more mentally alert, he also would have grasped the significance of the book he had chosen. It was an old paperback edition of *Trent's Last Case,* by E. C. Bentley, with the edges of the pages dyed red. He turned to Chapter One.

"Between what matters and what seems to matter," he read, "how should the world we know judge wisely?"

Now, that's what I call an opening sentence. Makes you think. Cliff snuggled down in the water a bit more, took another sip of Chardonnay, noting, as he often did, that it was the same color as Mona's hair, and read on.

Five minutes later it took stubbornness to read on, because his eyes were starting to swim; but he was feeling so deliciously good that he wanted to prolong the experience. Wouldn't hurt, of course, to close the eyes for a minute or so, to rest them. A good idea, in fact. . . . And while his eyes were resting, his right hand, also needing a rest, sank under the water with the book. . . .

Mona came into the bathroom twenty minutes later. When she saw Cliff lying unconscious in red-stained water, his mouth open and a large reddish-purple bruise on the side of his face, she screamed.

A scream in the bathroom is impressive—as impressive as taking a full swing at a golfball in the bathroom.

Cliff leaped up, grabbing for his rifle and helmet to fight off the Cong attack, slipped, and fell back into the tub, cracking the back of his head when he hit.

A dead body leaping into the air is also impressive in the

bathroom or anywhere else. Startled, Mona jumped back, skidded on a chenille bathmat, fell, and cracked her head on the toilet seat.

"Goddamn you, Clifford Dunbar!" she roared. "What the goddamn hell have you been doing?"

Cliff's mouth fell open in awe at hearing her use language that was so totally out of character. He peered at her over the edge of his bunker.

"Answer me, you bastard!" she yelled, tears of rage in her eyes.

He closed his mouth and swallowed, his mind too addled to come up with anything reasonable. He grinned weakly and said, "When the cat's away, the mice will play."

That did it. Mona rose up like some leather-winged demon out of Moussorgsky's *Night on Bald Mountain*. Berserk, she threw everything at him that she could get her hands on: a bar of Neutrogena soap, the soap dish, a plastic bottle of Princess Marcella Borghese shampoo, a jar of Nutribel Nourishing Hydrating Emulsion by Lancôme, a plastic bottle of Progrès Texturizing Moisture Lotion for the Body, also by Lancôme, two terrycloth guest towels, a glass bottle of Aramis after-shave, an emery board, dental floss, a box of Kleenex—and finally, herself. She hurled herself into his arms, sobbing, kissing him on the cheeks, ears, and neck.

The second nag being well under way, Cliff, now comfortable in a tan flannel bathrobe, decided it was high time they broke out that bottle of champagne he had bought to celebrate the first nag. He took it from the refrigerator, procured two tapered Swedish crystal flutes, worked the cork out, and poured.

"L'chayim."

"To life," Mona agreed.

They touched glasses.

"And since we're celebrating life, sweetheart," Mona continued, "I'm going to hold you to your promise. From now on, you will do nothing in connection with this case—you will talk to nobody—unless Lieutenant Puterbaugh is with you, all right?"

"Agreed."

"And once it's over, no more Fearless Fosdick . . . okay?"

"You may rest easy. Already, the whisper is going round the chancelleries: Clifford has had sufficient. Besides, the killer is really after me now, because he or she thinks I'm ready to finger him or her. Please note the absence of male chauvinism."

"And are you ready to?"

"I know I'm getting close, but nothing like as close as I'm going to stick to Puterbaugh. But what about your seminar this evening? How'd it go?"

"I'm excited. I have an excellent chance to get into med school . . . partly because I'm a woman. And sports medicine is a terrific specialty for Southern California. And what about you? Have you thought about going back into teaching?"

"Nope. I'm going to return to poetry, and I think I'll also be a writing consultant. The whole country seems to be inundated with words that mix technology with illiteracy in one gooey glob. I see a desperate need for clear explanations of all sorts of things: laws, insurance policies, computer manuals, pension plans. There's a lot of money to be made just by talking plain. But have you any idea what time it's getting to be?"

Mona looked at her watch. "It's—"

"Don't tell me. I'm going to go collapse and hope I won't be too stiff to get up in the morning."

"You'd better stay in bed tomorrow."

"Can't. Got to see Ali about that portrait. And if my hunch is right, I'll have to get hold of Puterbaugh in a hurry."

188

26

THE SCENTS OF coffee and frying bacon and toasting toast filled the kitchen. Clear September sunshine came through the open windows. In the distance, thousands of leaves on tall eucalyptus trees shimmered green and silver in the autumn wind. On a day like this, the flyfishing would be superb at Hot Creek. Reluctantly, Cliff picked up the phone and punched Alison's number.

"Ali? Hey, remember what you were telling me about painting lace on that portrait? Okay, I want you to try something. Take your palette knife—oh, thanks. No, not you, that was Mona serving breakfast."

Cliff went on with what he wanted her to do.

"Yes, I'll hold on," he said. He sipped his coffee and munched on toast until Alison came back to the phone.

"Aha! I thought so! Okay, Ali, leave it exactly as it is and I'll phone both Colfax and Puterbaugh. We'll all meet at your house. Oh, by the way, it doesn't amount to anything, but I've got sort of a bruise on my cheekbone. Tell you about it when I get there."

"Sort of a bruise," Mona murmured to herself.

"Well, Fosdick!" said Lieutenant Puterbaugh upon entering Alison's living room in Topanga and viewing Cliff's bruise, which now resembled half of a putrefying hamburger patty. "Peered over one transom too many, did you?"

"Yeah. I'm surprised detectives aren't required to wear plastic helmets, like motorcyclists."

"It may come to that. And what's this big discovery of yours?"

"I don't know exactly yet, which is why I called both you and Colfax. But let me explain a few things first. I think we've all been rather obtuse—possibly starting with Socorro Contreras, but she's got the excuse of a language difference. Remember what she said were Maria Atterbury's last words?"

"Yes. Maria said to look in her pocket . . . which we did."

"But Maria said it in Spanish. Mona and I went to San Miguel de Allende to check out exactly what she said. Something nobody had ever bothered doing. And her exact words really were, *'Dile que mire en la bolsa.'* Literally, that means, 'Tell him or her to look in the pocket.' The question is: What pocket? What him or her? She didn't mean the police or she would have said *'Diles'*—plural. Besides, the police would look in the pocket of her dressing gown as a matter of course. So she meant some particular person and some other pocket."

"Good Lord!" Sidney Colfax exclaimed. "I think I see!"

"I think you do. When you returned the portrait to Alison last night, she said something about the problem of rendering lace in the impasto technique on Maria's collar and pocket. It finally penetrated my thick head that the 'her' is Alison and the pocket is the one in the portrait. Okay, Ali."

Alison inserted a palette knife at the corner of the pocket of Maria's red-velvet dress in the portrait. She lifted the corner and then, with thumb and forefinger, pulled out from underneath the thick red paint, still wet, a thin, plastic Baggie containing a folded paper.

"Notice the smudges of red paint on Ali's thumb and finger? You'll remember the same thing happened to Maria."

Alison carefully pried open the mouth of the Baggie and, with a pair of tweezers, extracted the folded paper. It appeared to be a rice-paper flyleaf torn out of a Bible. She handed it to the lieutenant, who unfolded it and handed it to Colfax, after a quick glance. "This is in your bailiwick, Colfax."

190

Colfax put on his bifocals and began to read.

" 'Last will and testament.' Good Lord!" he exclaimed, looking up. "Grant Atterbury suspected that Maria was contemplating something like this, and he actually got to wondering if the portrait had anything to do with it."

"So!" said Alison. "He must be the one who pulled those staples out of the canvas!' "

"Yes, but keep in mind he did that as an afterthought, long after the murder."

Lieutenant Puterbaugh ran his hand over his head, polishing his bald pate. "Why don't you go on reading," he said, "and leave the detective work to me?"

Colfax resumed. "It's dated August nineteen, the day she was murdered; and she says 'Evening.' " He squinted. "The handwriting is really tiny. Anyway: 'Last will and testament. Obviously, I am unsound of body, but nothing is wrong with my mind unless I am suffering from a paranoid fantasy—but if I am, I can destroy this tomorrow or the next day and no harm done.

" 'I am surrounded by untrustworthy people. Today I was seized by the overwhelming conviction that my life is actually—and immediately—in danger. Ergo, this will. Tomorrow I will get a new doctor and a new lawyer—' "

Colfax stopped, cleared his throat, and looked up sheepishly. " '—If I could, I would also acquire a new set of relatives. I drugged Rosetta Stone's tea with my own sleeping pills to get her out of the way so I could write this. For the same reason, I returned to the five Prostigmin originally prescribed by Dr. Gates instead of Dr. Rawlings's monstrous overdose of Mestinon, which can be correct for some patients but left me far worse off, not better.

" 'But to the point. I won't pretend to precise legal language. I want all the provisions of my previous will now in the hands of Sidney Colfax to remain as they are, with the following additions and exceptions: I leave five thousand dollars to Socorro Contreras. I have already instructed S. Colfax in that regard, but he may be dragging his feet on that, as he has been on everything else.' "

The lawyer did not look up this time. If he had done so, he would have seen small smiles on four faces.

" 'I leave five thousand dollars to Alison Stephens over and above the five hundred I have already given her. She's wonderful, she's trustworthy, and I love her. I bequeath one hundred thousand dollars to the California Chapter of the Myasthenia Gravis Foundation, Inc. I bequeath the Atterburys' ancestral Malibu property to the State of California on condition that it be made into a state park. If the state declines to do so, the land is to be sold and the proceeds divided equally among Grant, Lionel, and Consuelo Atterbury. I implore my nephew Roland Atterbury, now known as Rollie Freed, if he loves his old Auntie, to please, please, accept the hundred thousand dollars I hereby bequeath to him so that he can buy his boat—on condition that he name it *Maria*.

" 'It is time to repair, insofar as I can, the damage wrought by the disastrous child-raising practices of my brother Lewis and his wife, which have promoted enmity among the three children, driven Lionel to drink, and virtually required Consuelo to become a useless drone. I bequeath fifty-eight percent of the stock in Atterbury's, Inc. to Lionel Atterbury so that he can resume his rightful position as an effective president. I bequeath twenty-one percent each to Grant and Consuelo Atterbury. All of them will thereby be rich by most people's standards. I wish them all happiness. I affectionately urge them to join hands as loving brothers and sister. If they decline to do so and don't like these arrangements, well, to employ an expression I have often heard Rollie use, tough titty.' "

They all laughed. Colfax squinted and held the paper closer to his eyes. "The handwriting is really starting to deteriorate and straggle," he said. "Let's see: 'I am nearing exhaustion. It is no treat to be myasthenic. I am amazed I was able to write all this. Rawlings is either incompetent or shallow or malevo-

192

lent. I want Dr. Gates again. I must hide this now. I bear hatred toward no one. To friends and foes alike: *Que dios ponga Ustedes en buen camino.* Maria de Castillo Atterbury.' "

There was a long silence. Mona's eyes shimmered, while twin tears rolled down Alison's cheeks. The three men were solemn.

"Is it legally sound?" said Puterbaugh. "Hold up in court?"

"Oh, yes. Holograph wills are legal. I don't think there'll be a problem unless Grant wants to contest it—which would be silly."

"What does that last part in Spanish mean?" Mona asked.

"Roughly," said Cliff, " 'May God set your feet on a prosperous road.' "

"Quite a woman, wasn't she?" observed Puterbaugh. "Colfax, I'll take the will and make photocopies and return it to you so you can file it with the County Clerk. In the meantime, I'm asking all of you to keep its existence under your hats for the time being—and I'm talking to you in particular, Colfax."

"I understand, and you can put your mind at rest."

"Well, Fosdick," said Puterbaugh, "Maria seems to have solved quite a few family problems, but we still don't know who killed her."

"I'm getting some pretty good ideas on that," said Cliff. "And, if you'll come with me tonight on a project I've got in mind, I think we can come a lot closer."

27

CLIFF HANDLED THE tiller of the rented motor-skiff as he and Lieutenant Puterbaugh took off from Santa Monica Pier and headed up the coast. The gibbous moon looked cold in the sky, and the spray from the bow was icy.

"I'm not convinced," said Puterbaugh. "We could've just gone straight out there in the daytime. Or if we had to do it at night, we could've checked out a police launch and been there in twenty minutes."

"I know, I know. But we don't want to get our suspects all stirred up if we don't have to."

"Sometimes it's a good idea to stir up the hornets' nest."

"You're right," said Cliff, "and I appreciate your going along with this as a personal favor. My sister really likes the guy, so it would be embarrassing if I got caught doing this and he turned out to be completely clean."

Puterbaugh grumbled. "And why Santa Monica Pier? Why not Malibu, which is a hell of a lot closer?"

"That's the reason. He has to be known to everybody around Malibu Pier."

Puterbaugh wrapped his down-filled stadium coat closer to his body and hunched down on his seat, looking much like a fluffed-out bird on a wintry branch.

Paradise Cove is fifteen statute miles on a straight line from Santa Monica Pier, the course being like a bowstring and the beach curving like a bow. Had the night been a little warmer, it could have been a pleasant ride, coasting along the beach, looking at the lights mounting the hills above the Coast Highway. It looked something like the Amalfi coast in Italy.

194

When they arrived at Paradise Cove, Cliff cut the motor and took up the oars so they could approach in dead silence. At the far west-by-south extremity of the cove, just off Point Dume, he turned on a small flashlight and, after a short search, found the orange marker-buoy he was looking for.

"This should be it, Lieutenant. Care to do the honors?"

Puterbaugh began hauling in the buoy and its attached line, hand over hand. It was a tedious job that went on and on.

"Jesus, Dunbar, how deep is it here?"

"Only twenty fathoms."

"Gosh, I was afraid it might be over a hundred feet."

"Do I detect sarcasm?"

"I'd rather be bowling."

Finally, the end of the line appeared at the surface, attached to what looked like a wooden crate. It was a lobster trap, but no lobster was inside it. Instead, there was a fish—a gorgeous pigeon's-blood-on-snow jade fish, still swirling after some unseen tidbit above its head.

"I'll be a son of a bitch!" said Puterbaugh.

A glaring white light suddenly illuminated the scene.

"Hold it right there!" said a voice in tones of steel.

They looked up at the shadowy silhouette of a man holding a two-foot flashlight in one hand and a shotgun in the other.

Lieutenant Puterbaugh slowly moved his right hand inside his stadium coat up toward his shoulder holster and his 9mm Beretta.

"No, no, Lieutenant, it's Rollie. It's us, Rollie! Cliff Dunbar and Lieutenant Puterbaugh!"

"Well, I'll be go-to-hell!" said Rollie. He turned off his flashlight, put down the shotgun, and rowed closer.

"How did you manage to sneak up on us without our hearing you?" Cliff asked.

"Ever heard of muffled oars? I've had to do this before with poachers. . . . Well, I see my little secret is out."

"Let's go back to your place and talk about it," said Puterbaugh. "I can hardly wait to hear the alibi you'll cook up between here and the landing. You go first."

Both Rollie and Cliff fired up their outboard motors with a roar and headed back toward the landing at the foot of Paradise Cove Pier, Rollie leading the way—and Puterbaugh watching him from close behind, with the Beretta ready between his knees.

As far as Puterbaugh was concerned, Rollie made up for his sins by plying them with mugs of hot Jamaican coffee.

"I may as well tell you the straight truth," said Rollie.

"Think so?" said Puterbaugh. "Well, we do live in an age of innovation."

"It isn't anything so bad. Gwyneth showed up here one day with that fish and wanted me to keep it for her or hide it somewhere."

"Why?"

"She said she heard through the grapevine—no doubt meaning Colfax—that Aunt Maria was considering changing her will in favor of Lionel and just might leave Grant next to penniless. Also, she hadn't been getting along very well with Grant. Also, who knows what the future might bring? So she wanted a nest egg. So she lifted this jade fish out of Maria's house and nobody missed it, so who's hurt? If she's ever hard up she can probably get thirty or forty thousand for it; otherwise, she just loves the piece and would like to keep it for herself."

"And you believed all that?"

"Sure. Look, let's face it: We all know Gwyneth will never make Phi Beta Kappa. She's got that unbelievable body, but you know what she is underneath? The scared, totally insecure little daughter of an Orange County mosquito control officer. A few times when she's been at loose ends and wanted to get away from all that Atterbury jazz, she's come down here and I've taken her fishing. Meanwhile, she thought she'd better grab everything she could, while she could."

196

"Did that include you?" said Cliff.

Rollie looked back at him steadily. "Yeah, briefly. Not that I'm proud of it."

"I'm not condemning you."

"You guys, I'd still rather be bowling," said Puterbaugh. "The point is, Freed, that you went along with her story."

"Sure. What she did made as much sense as a lot of things I've seen people do. What the hell. Swiping the fish was silly, but why make a federal case out of it?"

"Because Dunbar and I think it was the murder weapon."

If it's possible to be staggered sitting down, Rollie was staggered. It was hard to read his expression, but excruciating embarrassment seemed to predominate.

"What makes you think so?"

"The wound on the back of Maria's head. It reminded the coroner of the Morse code 'V', or the opening of Beethoven's Fifth: da da da, dum. He thought the weapon would resemble something like a kid's toy baseball bat with some nails driven in it. I think it'll turn out that the ridge along the fish's back, and the spines of the dorsal fin, will neatly fit that description."

"Okay, but maybe it was the other fish—the one you found in the mess on her bedroom floor."

"Nope. No blood, no hair on that one."

"Maybe the killer washed it off."

"And then put it neatly back on the heap? Nope. Whoever it was was in a hurry—and had to beat it fast when he heard somebody at the door." He stood up. "Let's go, Dunbar. And Rollie: If you want to help us nail your aunt's killer, keep all this under your hat. Don't talk to anybody; if you do, I can arrange all sorts of annoying trouble for you."

"Sure. Mum's the word. Cliff, I haven't had a chance to ask you about that bruise on your face."

"I'll tell you all about it later. Matter of fact, I've got some news for you too, but I suppose it can wait."

"Give me a hint?"

"It has to do with live fish."

"That's enough, Dunbar," said Puterbaugh. "Let's go, Rollie. You're giving me a ride back to Santa Monica."

"I am? Oh, okay."

"What about me?" protested Cliff.

"Bon voyage."

28

LIEUTENANT PUTERBAUGH JOINED Cliff and Mona at their house on Sunset Boulevard for coffee and rolls the next morning.

"I've got to hand it to you, Fosdick," he said, buttering a bear-claw. "You've just about wrapped up this case. That hunch of yours about the jade fish in the lobster trap—well, to repeat: You've obviously got a good head for detective work. Sure you don't want to go for the license?"

"No. I thought Vietnam was a bummer, but going bye-bye in the trunk of Beefy's car won the buckskin medallion. No more for me."

"Made you carsick, did it?"

"There were some other parts I didn't like either."

"More coffee, Lieutenant?" said Mona.

"No, thanks. I said we'd be there around ten."

"Gwyneth will be alone, won't she?" said Mona.

"So she said, and I certainly hope so. It'll be a lot better if we can talk to her without Grant around."

"Isn't he at the store?" said Cliff.

"Probably. Miss Turin told me he's expected in."

"Too bad we couldn't have done this yesterday," said Puterbaugh, as they made for the door. "Grant Atterbury was gone all day, visiting that gold mine up at Quartz Hill."

"Gold mine! Wait a minute!" Mona exclaimed. "Holy smoke! I just remembered something from my pharmacology course. This is far out, but let's see if I can get hold of Doctor Gates."

She ran to the phone. Cliff and Puterbaugh exchanged baffled looks.

"Doctor Gates? This is Mona Dunbar. Right. Listen, do you by any chance have any amyl nitrate in your black bag? You do? Can we have some—a perle or two? . . . What? Oh, right, I guess I do mean amyl nitrite. No, there's no emergency yet, but it could turn into one. Swell, we'll be by."

"What was that all about?" said Puterbaugh.

"Tell you on the way. Let's hurry."

At Doctor Gates's house the lieutenant made two quick phone calls, one to Gwyneth to say they'd be a little late and one to Atterbury's in Beverly Hills. Grant still hadn't arrived, but Miss Turin said he had called in to say he was at Switzer Litho and might or might not make it in by lunch time.

At ten-thirty Cliff turned off Lexington Road and onto Grant Atterbury's brick-paved drive. Mona and Puterbaugh looked at the surroundings with admiration. "Did all right for herself, didn't she?" said Puterbaugh.

"She took what she wanted and paid for it," said Cliff.

Gwyneth seemed more watchful than frightened when she let them in and escorted them down the hall. Today she was wearing a white Gibson-Girl blouse with puffed sleeves and a blue skirt, with the result that she looked less like a sexpot and more like Matisse's model for "La Blouse Roumaine."

She went behind the bar immediately, as if it were a fortress, and inquired, "Anyone for a drink?"

They declined. She darted a defiant look at them. "Well, have a seat and excuse me if I indulge myself with a Ramos fizz."

She switched her blender on. It roared angrily for a few seconds. She poured the frothy drink into a glass and seated herself.

"And to what," she said, "do I owe the honor, et cetera, et cetera?" She had obviously gathered her wits and looked all set for a session of nimble fencing.

Mona and Cliff watched with interest to see what Puterbaugh's strategy would be. Neither of them was prepared when the lieutenant went straight for the jugular.

"I want to nail down which one of you killed Maria Atterbury: Was it you or Grant?"

Gwyneth sucked froth back into her windpipe and went into a violent coughing fit. She jumped up and hurried behind the bar for a glass of water—which she took her time drinking—and blew her runny nose in a Kleenex.

When she returned she stood by the table with her hands on her hips. "Have you gone completely cuckoo?"

"We found the fish, Gwyneth."

"Fish? Fish? What fish?"

"The one in Rollie's lobster trap."

Gwyneth stared at him, eyes wide, clearly trying to select the best reaction and coming up with nothing better than a stall.

"What is this? I've gone fishing with Rollie, but certainly not for lobster."

"How do you describe that fish, Dunbar?"

"The loan ledger calls it a jade koi, pigeon's-blood-on-snow, Ming Dynasty, fifteen and a half inches long. Also, it's one of a pair."

Gwyneth bit her lower lip.

"All right, I give up. I took it. So what? Are you going to arrest me for petty larceny?"

"Nope," said Puterbaugh. "Wouldn't be petty anyway. I'm told that either one of those fish would be worth about forty thousand dollars. Where did you take it from?"

"Maria's sewing room—that little room at the east end of her house, just off the living room. Maria hadn't used that room in years, and nobody paid any attention to that fish. All it did was collect dust."

"It ended up collecting gray hair and blood."

"What?"

"It's the weapon that killed her."

"My God! What makes you think that?"

"Did you swipe it before or after the murder?"

"Why, after, of course. You mean the killer washed it off and put it back in the sewing room?"

"If, and only if, that's where you got it. So you went through the house and just lifted it, did you?"

"It's beautiful and I wanted it for myself and I knew Grant would never let me have it because he'd want to put it with the other one and sell them as a pair to make a profit for the damn store. And besides, I wanted something to remember Maria by."

A long pause ensued, during which Puterbaugh gazed at her steadily, she alternately gazed at him and into her fizz, and Cliff and Mona watched both of them.

Gwyneth gave in first. "If a jade fish killed her, why not the other one?"

"It curves the wrong way, Mrs. Atterbury. Whoever did it was right-handed, held the fish by the tail, and hit Maria in the back of the head."

"And Grant is right-handed, is that it? Well, so am I and so are you and the two Dunbars here, and so are Sidney Colfax and Craig Rawlings. For all I know, so is Socorro Contreras."

"Yes, she is," said Cliff.

Gwyneth turned to him with an air of relief. "You're intelligent, Cliff. Can't you talk some sense into this man? Grant is no murderer, and obviously I can't be either if I was at the theater that evening."

"I know, but you can see the problem, Mrs. Atterbury. Theoretically, at least, you could have gone to Maria's house with Doctor Rawlings that evening."

"Do you think I did?"

"No, actually."

"Do you think Craig killed her?"

"Nope. I think he planned to, but somebody beat him to it."

" 'Somebody' being Grant?"

"Yes."

"And meanwhile, why do you two giant brains think Craig would leave a play and go out there planning to bash her head in?"

"We think something tremendously urgent must have come up, so he had to act fast."

Gwyneth uttered a scornful laugh. "So Craig is the killer after all, not Grant."

"No, but let's get back to that problem I mentioned. The fish is the problem. No jury would believe that nonsense about your wanting something to remember Maria by, and then giving it to Rollie to hide for you when you could have hidden it in a hundred other places. And then there's the difficulty that it was the murder weapon."

"Well, I didn't know that. In fact, I still don't know it." She looked scornfully at the two men. "Talk about fishing expeditions! You two have no proof at all of anything you've said or you'd have arrested me by now. I certainly didn't kill Maria. And if Grant did, do you think I'd stick my neck out to cover for him?"

"Oh, yes," said Cliff.

"Why? Because I adore him with a flaming purple passion?"

"No, because if he killed Maria he couldn't inherit a nickel, he'd go to prison, and you'd have to start all over again back at mosquito control."

Gwyneth glared at him, her nostrils flaring.

"Tell you what, Mrs. Atterbury," said the lieutenant. "Why don't we let Dunbar give you his reconstruction of events and you be the judge of what to do or say afterwards. Okay?"

"I'm all ears." Gwyneth lit another cigarette and picked a shred of tobacco off her tongue. "But keep it short. I've got a luncheon date at the Polo Lounge."

"Gladly," said Cliff. "Two elements underlie all this. Number one: Everybody wished Maria would hurry up and die.

My guess is that your friend Doctor Rawlings wasn't averse to facilitating the happy outcome, shall we say?"

"Suddenly Craig is the murderer again?"

"No. But a couple of lines in a poem called 'The Latest Decalogue' fit him neatly:

'Thou shalt not kill; but need'st not strive
Officiously to keep alive.' "

"And what the hell do you think he hoped to gain from killing his own patient?"

"Quite a prize: you. Plus a pile of money when you divorced Grant. And moving right along, element number two: Lionel was afraid Maria wouldn't change her will in his favor. You and Grant and Rawlings and Colfax were afraid she would. You learned from Colfax that she planned to change it, and you persuaded the poor fool to keep stalling, hoping she'd die and wishing Rawlings would get a move on."

"So now Sidney is a co-killer or whatever?"

"Sure. And to anticipate your next question: Colfax, too, hoped to win the grand prize—you, plus the Malibu property. So now we arrive at the night of the murder."

"This ought to be good."

"Some event that evening got everybody's wind up."

"Don't tell me you don't know what it was!"

"No, I don't know exactly. Maybe it was something Colfax found out, or something Maria said. Anyway, it was enough to get Rawlings to page himself at the Shubert Theater and whiz off to Maria's house for a purpose I'll leave to your imagination."

Gwyneth darted a cigarette ash in the general direction of an alabaster ashtray.

"When he got there and got a good look at the shambles in Maria's bedroom," Cliff went on, "he must have been scared spitless—and also relieved. He got out of there fast and rushed back to the Shubert to give you the good news."

"If you're so damn sure Grant killed Maria, why aren't you talking to him instead of me?"

"It was a toss-up, but we talked to you first because you had the fish."

"Want to tell us exactly how you did get it?" Puterbaugh asked.

"You figure it out. You'll have to leave now. I've got to get ready to go out."

Cliff looked to Puterbaugh, who nodded. They got up.

"There's no point in protecting Grant anymore, Gwyneth," said Cliff. "Maria did indeed change her will, and we've found it. Grant is no longer head of the Atterbury store."

"I don't believe you!"

"Phone Colfax after we've gone. And let me remind you again that Grant can't inherit a dime if he killed her. . . . Well, thanks for your hospitality."

Gwyneth blew her nose, and followed them down the hall.

As if struck by an afterthought, Mona turned and said, "Oh, Gwyneth. If you sniff or snort any cocaine today . . ."

"I do not snort cocaine! I merely have one of those summer colds."

"Let's put it this way, then: If anybody in the house does happen to have any nose candy lying around—maybe the maid or the houseboy—they should be especially careful today."

"We don't have addicts working here, either."

"Your husband visited the gold mine up at Quartz Hill yesterday."

Gwyneth rolled her eyes heavenward.

"They use cyanide salts," Mona went on, "to separate gold from crushed ore or paydirt."

Alert eyes descended and settled on Mona.

"The salts are white, but they're sensitive to light; so if anybody's cocaine happens to look a little darker today . . . it might be smart to give it a miss."

As Gwyneth absorbed this information, Cliff spoke again.

"Also, Gwyneth, you might keep in mind that if Grant did kill Maria, you're the only person in the world who can prove it. Ticklish spot to be in, isn't it? Well, toodle-oo."

"Have a nice day," said Lieutenant Puterbaugh. He closed the door quietly behind them.

They had no more than settled themselves in Cliff's Porsche when the front door flew open and Gwyneth rushed out, her mouth open, terror in her eyes.

"I'll tell you! I'll tell you!"

They followed her inside once more. Gwyneth clawed her hair, breathing heavily.

"Maria phoned here that night—told Grant she changed her will! Said to tell other people."

"Did he?" Puterbaugh asked.

"He told me and I told Doctor Rawlings. And he phoned Sidney Colfax. Grant nearly went crazy—told her not to do anything hasty until he and Sidney talked to her the next day."

"And I suppose," said Puterbaugh, "Doctor Rawlings left the Shubert just to go reason with her?"

Gwyneth wrung her hands.

"That doesn't matter now! Grant actually went to his schnickelfritz band practice, but when I got home that night and walked into the bedroom, he was wrapping the jade fish in a white plastic bag from the cleaners."

"What did he say?"

"Nothing. He just stood there and stared at me, and I stared at him and the fish. The fish had blood on it. And a tuft of gray hair was caught in the spines on its back. All of a sudden Grant went to pieces, sobbing and saying over and over he didn't mean to kill her, but she kept jeering at him. He wanted to see the will she wrote. She wouldn't show it to him. She said she hid it where he'd never think of looking. He forced her to open her safe. The will wasn't there. She laughed at him, and he went sort of berserk. He grabbed that fish off

206

her mantelpiece and hit her in the head with it. Then he ransacked the bedroom. He searched Maria's pockets, looked under her mattress, under the rug, behind pictures, in her books, under tables, inside lamps—everywhere. He threw stuff in a pile in the middle of the room. He took money out of the safe to make it look like a burglary. He tore Rollie's signature off a promissory note to throw suspicion on him. He looked through Alison Stephens's paintbox. Then he realized his fingerprints were on that fish, so he ran and got the other one and threw it on the pile and kept the bloody one. He never heard Socorro Contreras unlocking the front door. He just thought he'd probably never be noticed if he slipped out the bathroom door into the garden. And he was right. He slipped out and drove off to Santa Monica."

Gwyneth seized a Plymouth gin bottle, poured a dollop into a glass full of ice cubes, agitated it, and took a great gulp.

"Why did he give you the fish—and why did you take it?" Cliff asked. "How come he didn't just wash it off, take it to the store, and put it back in the treasure room?"

"He was afraid somebody at the store would see him with it, or the police would somehow prove it was the murder weapon—but, God, that's making him sound reasonable. He was in a panic! He was shaking! He begged me to take it . . . get rid of it for him . . . destroy it or deep-six it in the ocean."

With a wan smile, Puterbaugh said, "Is that how you got the idea of recruiting Rollie and feeding him a cock-and-bull story?"

"It wasn't cock-and-bull. I knew Grant couldn't inherit if he got caught, but at least I'd have a nest egg."

She looked down into her glass and then suddenly lifted her head. Tears welled in her eyes. "Now I won't even have that!"

A long silence followed. Gwyneth began to weep softly. Mona rose and put an arm around her.

A thud in the next room jarred the floor and they heard the crash of breaking glass. Cliff and Puterbaugh jumped to their feet and hurried to a door in a corner beyond the bar. It was locked. Puterbaugh broke it open with one kick of his size fifteen shoe, and the four of them rushed in.

Grant Atterbury lay on his back, his chest heaving.

"Is it a heart attack?" said Cliff.

"Oh, my God!" exclaimed Gwyneth. "He snorted the cyanide himself! He's been listening all this time! He's killing himself! Do something!"

Mona snatched up her purse from the glass-topped table and rushed back to kneel beside Grant. She grabbed a handful of amyl nitrite perles from her purse and laid them on the carpet.

Foam gathered around Grant's mouth and his breathing slowed almost to a stop. His face began to turn red. The almond-like smell of cyanide hung on the air.

Mona broke one of the thin-glass perles just under Grant's nostrils. A large wet spot darkened his crotch. His sphincter control had gone.

Not at all sure she was doing the right thing, Mona broke another perle and let its contents drop into Grant's mouth. She then stood up.

"Lieutenant!" she ordered. "Get going with mouth-to-mouth resuscitation!"

Looking none too eager, Puterbaugh knelt beside Grant and went to work. He was good at it, however. Grant's chest rose and fell a full inch with each inflation.

After a half minute or so, Mona broke another perle under Grant's nose; his breathing was faint and feeble, but the treatment was working. Puterbaugh resumed, pinching the nostrils shut while he blew into Grant's mouth. At the end of the next minute, Grant was breathing more deeply. Mona crushed another perle.

Puterbaugh bent over, ready to resume, but Mona stopped him. "He'll make it on his own now."

In a short while, Grant had recovered. However, he was still overwhelmingly weak and dizzy. He could have been taken for a myasthenic. They undressed him and carried him to a bed. Gwyneth remained at his side.

Out by the bar Puterbaugh said, "That little episode totally ruined one of my minor pleasures in life."

"What?"

"Peanuts," he replied. "Atterbury had been eating peanuts."

"What do you think will happen to him?" said Mona.

"I'd guess five years for manslaughter," said Puterbaugh.

29

LIEUTENANT PUTERBAUGH'S GUESS was right on the button. Grant Atterbury could have been nailed for second degree murder, but plea bargaining reduced the charge to voluntary manslaughter (which Puterbaugh scornfully reduced further to "man's laughter"). But because he was also guilty of soliciting a homicide—Cliff's, at the hands of Beefy and Gaunt—the terms of Grant's sentence were such that he was slated to serve out a full five years on a minimum-security prison farm in northern California.

To his great surprise, he found it pleasant to work outdoors pruning grapevines and, when the weather warmed up, planting corn, squash, and artichokes. Better yet, with all the free time he had for practicing his clarinet, he rose from fifth rate as a jazz musician to third rate, which, as Molly Teague pointed out, is very good indeed when you stop to think of it. However, he would always see blood on his hands when he played.

Everyone else's life changed, too, mostly for the better. Lieutenant Puterbaugh caught the man who had killed a young couple with a two-by-four under the Santa Monica Pier.

Alison's October exhibition of portraits by Southern California artists was a smashing success, the center of attraction being the portrait of Maria in which she had hidden her will. Alison got her money, sold all of Rollie Freed's watercolors, married him, and moved to Kailua-Kona on the Big Island of Hawaii, where they put painting aside while they got the *Maria* ready for the summer marlin tournament.

Lionel's wife, Beryl, returned from Mousehole (pronounced "Muzzle") near Penzance, and she and Lionel took over both Atterbury's and the house on Lexington Road.

Consuelo made the strange discovery that work can be not only joyful but also fulfilling. Back in Paris, she opened her own polyglot Left Bank bookshop on the rue de la Huchette, cater-corner from the mouth of the rue du Chat Qui Peche.

Doctor Craig Rawlings's practice throve on his lurid publicity. He became the rage of the social season, so busy with rich and beautiful women coming to him for injections—of one sort or another—that Rosetta Stone gave up on him and went to work for another doctor. He in turn dropped Gwyneth. Gwyneth, in turn, instead of returning to mosquito control in Orange County, went off to Gstaad, Diavolezza, St. Moritz, and Cortina d'Ampezzo with a wealthy oilman who couldn't believe his good fortune in landing such a prize.

In January, Mona was awarded her Master's degree in physical therapy and was notified of her admission to UCLA medical school, starting in September. Cliff began writing a suite of poems and a police-procedural mystery novel.

Meanwhile, during that first winter following Maria's death, nature, as if contemptuous of the piddling changes that humans are capable of, went to work on the California coast. For starters, fires roared down out of the Santa Monica Mountains, driving deer, field mice, coyotes, and rabbits before them. One fire leaped the Pacific Coast Highway and burned all the way down into Paradise Cove.

Then, once the protecting grass and chaparral were burned to ash, torrential rains tore at hillsides and closed canyon roads with mud and boulders.

Storms at sea generated giant waves and tides that battered piers up and down the California coast for days on end until, almost in unison, they began to break apart. More than a fourth of Santa Monica Pier collapsed into the bay, taking the

Coast Guard station with it and piling shattered wood high on the beaches.

Six hundred feet of Paradise Cove Pier broke off, leaving a stubby two hundred feet. The skiff rental business was ruined, and the sole commercial fisherman who had planned to take Rollie Freed's place changed his mind and went to Oxnard instead. With no customers in the Cove, the local bait boat followed him.

In the relentless cold rain, one dark-blue day, the saturated ground under Maria Atterbury's house began to move. In the facade of the house a fissure appeared, extending from the roof, in a zigzag direction, to the base. This fissure rapidly widened and, in a series of loud cracks like bolts of lightning, the concrete foundation broke, timbers snapped, and the seaward half of the house, including Maria's bedroom, tumbled down the slope, followed by a cascade of mud and cobblestones that closed the Pacific Coast Highway to all traffic for days.

On a balmy night in late April, with the scent of star jasmine and mock-orange blossoms floating through the open windows, Cliff and Mona sat facing each other across a small table, tying trout flies.

"I was on the Coast Highway today," said Cliff. "They've torn down the rest of Maria's house. It's gone."

"Oh, dear. I'm glad Alison's portrait is hanging in the store. A woman like Maria should never be forgotten."

She tied a neat pair of wood-duck wings on her Light Cahill and glanced up at Cliff. "Why are you looking at me like that—sort of sappy?"

"Because I love you. It's sort of premature, since you've only just been admitted to med school, but how would you like to play doctor with me?"

"Fine, if you'll show me how."

"Come with me."

If you have enjoyed this book and would like to receive details of other Walker mystery titles, please write to:

Mystery Editor
Walker and Company
720 Fifth Avenue
New York, NY 10019